Covenant with Hell

Books by Priscilla Royal

Wine of Violence
Tyrant of the Mind
Sorrow Without End
Justice for the Damned
Forsaken Soul
Chambers of Death
Valley of Dry Bones
A Killing Season
The Sanctity of Hate
Covenant with Hell

Covenant with Hell

A Medieval Mystery

Priscilla Royal

Poisoned Pen Press

Copyright © 2013 by Priscilla Royal

First Edition 2013

10 9 8 7 6 5 4 3 2 1

Library of Congress Catalog Card Number: 2013933216

ISBN: 9781464201936   Hardcover
       9781464201950   Trade Paperback

Poisoned Pen Press
6962 E. First Ave., Ste. 103
Scottsdale, AZ 85251
www.poisonedpenpress.com
info@poisonedpenpress.com

Printed in the United States of America

In memory of Edmund M. Kaufman, a man of wit and grace, who gave so many of us a place to be heard.

Acknowledgments

Christine and Peter Goodhugh, Henie Lentz, Dianne Levy, Sharon Kay Penman, Barbara Peters (Poisoned Pen Bookstore in Scottsdale AZ), Robert Rosenwald and all the staff of Poisoned Pen Press, Marianne and Sharon Silva, Lyn and Michael Speakman, the staff of the University Press Bookstore (Berkeley CA).

We have made a covenant with death, and with hell are we at agreement; when the overflowing scourge shall pass through, it shall not come unto us: for we have made lies our refuge, and under falsehood have we hid ourselves.

Isaiah 28:15
(King James Version)

Chapter One

He stood in the shadows, watching men enter and leave the inn. It was a respectable place, one he knew well, and close by the holy shrines of Walsingham, but the promising warmth of the hearth fire and boisterous voices of men did not gladden his heart. Leaning back against the rough wall of some merchant's house, he squeezed his eyes shut against the light from the inn that assailed him with rude persistence.

How often had he sworn that he would cease this work and return fully to the vocation he claimed? But he knew he would not and mocked himself for holding on to such a delusion so long.

The rewards were high, and he took them willingly enough, but the extra coin meant little to him. He put most of it into a damaged pot and buried it in the garden near the privy. This choice of hiding place was deliberate. Every time he added to the hoard, he dug within the stench of his own excrement. That was a small penance, very small, for what he did.

So he did not accept these undertakings for coin, a jewel, or even praise. His masters were grateful when he succeeded, as they prayed he would, but his efforts would never be praised by all men. Some would laud him and others denounce. He chose to set aside such debates. On the day of his death, he would care about the fine definitions of good and evil because eternity mattered. Until that hour, he believed these grave questions were best left to saints and popes.

In truth, his reasons were out of the ordinary. He took on these tasks because he could live in the shadows for awhile. Others longed for the sun, reaching out for the warmth and praising the bright hours as belonging to God. For him, day was a time of falsehood when his speech became the model of trickery, his body the temple of deception, and everything he did a practiced lie. Only in obscurity could he be honest, even if that truth was an evil thing. Only in the velvet embrace of darkness could he find comfort and peace.

A man walked past, then hesitated and turned to look at him. He shook his head.

The man went on his way.

He watched until the figure disappeared into the black maw of narrow streets.

It was not yet time to allow himself that indulgence, a sin he would confess when God reached out for his soul but not before, a transgression most would say was worse than the one he committed for coin.

A priest always forgave him for all crimes required to satisfy his masters' will, but that priest was chosen to do it. Thus his penance was light, and absolution granted with a smile. God might not be so kind when he faced final judgment on crimes regretted only out of fear.

With effort, he willed himself to step away from the wall.

The moment had come to face the light.

Clenching his teeth, he strode toward the inn.

Chapter Two

Trying not to fidget, Sister Roysia pressed her back against the sharp stone wall of the audience chamber wall. Impatience lingered despite the rock stabbing through her habit. This meeting had lasted since the midday meal. Would Prioress Ursell never bring it to an end?

Outside, the ashen daylight of early spring was swiftly retreating before night's determined assault. This was the Lenten season, and gloom was appropriate. It inspired penitential ardor in the hearts of those who would soon arrive in great numbers to visit the shrines of Walsingham during the favorite pilgrimage season of Easter week. Now was the time to order the badges the crowds would long to buy, making this lengthy discussion necessary.

Although Sister Roysia knew this, she wished it had been otherwise. She usually did not mind standing here for long hours. As the prioress' chosen attendant, she overheard much that amused, now and then thrilled, and occasionally proved useful to her. The moment she folded her hands and lowered her pale eyes, she faded into the gray walls, and visitors forgot the presence of the preternaturally thin nun with a wan face. They would start confiding in Prioress Ursell of Ryehill Priory whatever transgressions had brought them to this holy site, the latest news, or other matters hidden in their hearts, some of which might give even the Devil momentary pause.

And so, had it been any other day, Sister Roysia would not have regretted the time lost to prayer or other duties. But this discussion was strictly a matter of business. The negotiations between her prioress and Master Larcher, craftsman of pilgrimage badges, were always wearisome. Today's had become interminable.

The relics for which this pilgrimage site was famous were the responsibility of the Augustinian canons of Walsingham Priory, but the nuns of Ryehill Priory had been given the privilege of selling badges to support themselves and Father Vincent, the priest assigned to them. This trafficking was managed by Prioress Ursell, a task for which she was well-suited.

Perhaps too well-suited, Sister Roysia thought, as she kept her eyes focused on the stone floor to prevent anyone from reading her thoughts. Her prioress had the reputation, both within and outside this priory, for being firm in her principles. When it came to acquiring coin, her resolve hardened into indestructibility.

As sharp-witted as she was sharp-featured, the prioress could match wits with any merchant. Few men were as resolute as she when it came to paying the least for the best quality badges and other tokens eagerly sought by penitents.

The objects sold by the priory all came from the local shop of Master Larcher, a man skilled in their design but especially the quantity of production. Since he was also the only craftsman in Walsingham so talented, Ryehill Priory was fortunate to engage him. The quality of badges from Canterbury might be better, but even that popular site could not match the volume or the variety made by Larcher of Walsingham.

Each time the merchant and the prioress met to negotiate the purchases, the craftsman arrived determined to win the better deal. Inevitably, Prioress Ursell ground him into a coarse powder like seeds with a pestle. Their disputes were brutal. Had this priory not been dedicated to God, Sister Roysia might have concluded that the negotiations were taking place in Hell itself.

There was a loud rustling amongst the assembled group. With restrained hope, the nun glanced up through her eyelashes.

The men were rising.

Prioress Ursell remained seated in her oaken chair.

Father Vincent stood beside her, a bone-thin cleric with yellowish skin and glittering blue eyes. Most people would not recognize that twitching of his lips as a smile, but Sister Roysia did.

She had nothing in common with him, a man she disliked, but suspected that they shared relief that these negotiations were finally concluded. The priest would be eager to return to his altar, where he could resume prayer in front of the small relic he had obtained and obsessively count the number of pilgrims who joined him. At his insistence, the relic had been acquired for the priory's main chapel, but few came to worship Father Vincent's beloved acquisition.

Sister Roysia's greatest reason for gratitude was different from his but equally compelling. Increasingly nervous as well as impatient, she began to sweat. She must speak with Master Larcher, yet was fearful about doing so. In the past, she had been able to plan for their occasional meetings. This time, she could not. But considering what she must tell him, perhaps it did not matter. She would not have to see him again.

Master Larcher bowed to Prioress Ursell. A rotund man of ruddy complexion, the craftsman enjoyed great esteem in the town for his skills. He was equally well known for his love of red wine, fine cuts of red meat, and the red tresses of his favorite leman. Fortunately, his clever business tricks kept his pale-haired wife content with fine garments and the occasional jewel. Only with this prioress did he lose the bargain game.

Many would tell him that his soul was the richer for the defeat, Sister Roysia thought, but the worldly profit from the volume of sold badges was quite satisfactory. He forfeited little except pride when Prioress Ursell bested him, yet his expression seemed unusually glum today. That troubled Sister Roysia. Something besides this deal must have soured for him.

"I shall deliver the requested badges in the number, time, and quality requested," the merchant said, properly confirming what had been agreed upon.

"The design will include a clear image of the Virgin, separated from the Archangel Gabriel by a potted lily, and all this shall be set within the top story of the Holy House." The prioress' voice was strong despite the hours of discussion.

"I have sworn it earlier and shall promise it again," Larcher replied, weariness evident in his voice.

"And also vow not to forget the smaller badges showing a lock of hair, depicting the strands from the Virgin's head which we keep in our own chapel." Father Vincent's voice rasped, but he always suffered from catarrh between autumn and spring.

These badges were a new addition to the usual order. Sister Roysia suspected the priest had begged for them, hoping that the sales would bring more income to the struggling convent at Ryehill.

Larcher shot him an annoyed look and grunted.

Prioress Ursell's face cracked into an unaccustomed smile. "We have settled on the price as well."

Master Larcher nodded with a restrained sigh.

Prioress Ursell beckoned to Father Vincent, who bent down so she might speak more privately with him.

The craftsman looked at Sister Roysia and quickly raised a questioning eyebrow.

Catching his signal, she raised her head, abruptly nodded, and lowered her gaze before either prioress or priest noticed the interchange.

Larcher's face had now grown pale, and beads of sweat glistened on his forehead. Shivering with unease over the cause, the nun wondered if he guessed what she must tell him and feared it. Courage was a virtue she had long suspected he lacked. Against her better judgment, she chanced another glance at him, praying she conveyed reassurance.

Prioress Ursell caught her look and rose, her eyes sparkling with fury.

Ashen-faced, Master Larcher now faced the leader of Ryehill Priory. His lips were visibly trembling.

"We have finished here, but I shall expect prompt delivery," Prioress Ursell snapped. "Timeliness is essential with the anticipated arrival of the king. Many more will visit Walsingham, longing to cheer him on in his endeavors against the barbarous Welsh and hoping to emulate his admirable piety. Purchase of a badge from us will have even greater worth to our eager pilgrims. They may wish more than one. You must return to your workshop immediately, Master Larcher."

Master Larcher mumbled something inaudible.

Father Vincent eyed him, and then bent to whisper something to the prioress.

Ursell nodded and again focused on the craftsman. "It is also crucial that you speed completion of that pewter medal of your best quality for the prioress of Tyndal." Ursell's mouth pursed as if she had just tasted something foul. "I promised her a gift. Without it, she might delay the completion of her pilgrimage vow."

The craftsman nodded and wiped his glistening forehead.

Perhaps his reaction has nothing to do with me, Sister Roysia thought. She had not listened to the discussion over badges. Prioress Ursell might have said something that troubled him.

"King Edward counts her brother as one of his favored men. Were the king to enter the town while Prioress Eleanor was still here," the prioress continued, "her presence would surely distract him, leaving him less time to appreciate the glory of our own shrine and new relic." Her mouth twisted into a mockery of a smile. "Your share of the sales profits was increased on the assumption that our earthly king would favor us with gifts as well as Walsingham Priory. Let that inspire you to swiftly craft the piece for the prioress from Tyndal."

Father Vincent nodded with enthusiasm.

Although this discussion of ridding Ryehill of a bothersome guest had seemed to calm Prioress Ursell's anger, Sister Roysia grew more anxious for the priest and Master Larcher to depart. The merchant was so pale she did fear he was ill.

Prioress Ursell shattered the nun's musing with a brusque command.

Rushing to the chamber door as ordered, Sister Roysia opened it and stepped modestly to one side.

Father Vincent was the first to depart. As was his habit, he drew his robes closer around him to avoid any contact with the nun as he passed by.

When the merchant approached, he stopped and gave her a feeble smile. "The bells did not ring for Compline last night," he said, chewing his lower lip.

Sister Roysia took in a deep breath, then replied with the planned response. "I thought they had, Master Larcher, but I will most certainly make sure they are rung tonight."

"Perhaps I slept through them." He bowed again to the prioress and strode out. "I shall carefully listen for them," he murmured, passing by the nun. The words faintly echoed as he sped down the long hall.

Trembling with relief that she had conveyed her message, Sister Roysia dutifully shut the door and turned to ask her prioress what further tasks she might have for her.

Prioress Ursell glared at her with white-hot rage.

Staggering back as if slapped, Sister Roysia put a hand to her throat and suppressed a cry of fear.

"I noted what passed between you and the merchant." Prioress Ursell's sharp gaze stung like a dagger point. "Had he been troubled by the bells not ringing, he ought to have addressed his concern to Father Vincent or to me. He had no reason to speak to you at all."

Instinctively, the nun wrapped her arms around herself.

"Or did his words convey a special meaning, significant only to you both?"

"Absolutely not, my lady!"

"It is not the first time he has had some communication with you. I am not a fool, Sister."

"I do not grasp your meaning." The nun shook her head, hoping to suggest complete innocence. "I remember nothing improper said or done in the past by Master Larcher. As for today, I was surprised by his pallor. Did you not see how ill he looked? If I responded inappropriately to what he said, my reply came from relief that he seemed well and not possessed of a fever."

She was babbling and tried to calm herself. "His humors must have been…" Seeing the naked contempt in her prioress' face, she knew she had failed to deceive.

"Do not speak further, Sister, for your mouth only spews Satan's lies. You are as shameless as the whore of Babylon." Prioress Ursell's eyes narrowed like those of a cat about to pounce on a rodent. "Leave my chambers, and take the stench of evil with you, but do not think this incident will be forgotten." An executioner facing a traitor on the scaffold could not have looked grimmer. "The punishment for the sin you have committed shall be a harsh one."

Sister Roysia fled from the room.

Chapter Three

Spring in East Anglia was a troubling time, in particular for the poor who had barely survived the dark season. Daylight hours held the promise of a warming earth, but long nights retained winter's icy cold. For a girl on the threshold of womanhood, with neither parents nor kin, survival thus far would be thought a miracle. To believe she had any hope of living much longer went beyond all reason.

Gracia huddled into a small space between two houses to escape the wind. Like a wary animal, she peered down the dark road leading to the major shrines. Her eyes half shut against the biting wind, she took her time before concluding she was safe.

She longed to eat.

Earlier today, she had been fortunate. A red-haired monk walking to the chapel had discovered her. When he learned she was hungry, he had begged a portion of bread and even a mouthful of fish and cheese from the nearby inn. Were it not for pilgrims, she would starve. Since they were strangers, many living in Walsingham distrusted those who came to see the shrines, but she survived on the mercy of these penitents, their souls tender with the pain of sin and fearful of how greatly they had offended God.

She was also lucky that the monk had given her the food before Father Vincent caught her near the chapel. If the priest had seen her, he would have chased her off, hurling rocks and screaming that she was Satan's creature who polluted God's shrines.

Not long ago, he had caught her in his chapel as a merchant was swyving her. The man swore she had enchanted him, and, when he promised a donation to the priest's shrine, the priest's eyes grew blind to the fact that a bone-thin child had little protection against a man who was three times her weight. Father Vincent would deny that the gift affected his judgment, but Gracia knew better. When her parents died, she lost the privilege of innocence.

On reflection, she knew she would have been wiser had she swallowed her anger and claimed demonic possession when he accused her of being the instrument of the Devil. Making an enemy of a man who owned the means to offer charity was ill-advised, and she had few ways of keeping herself alive. Had she been a boy with no kin she might have joined others who formed packs like dogs, stealing what they could use or sell. Girls, whatever their age, were left to whore.

Gracia had been determined to do otherwise. After the death of her parents, she had learned to become as efficient as a feral cat. With keen senses and clever wits, unusual in one so young, she had survived.

She had also been lucky.

Glancing around again, the girl still saw no threat and concluded she might allow herself the distraction of eating. She lowered her head and began to gnaw carefully and slowly at the monk's gift. Hunger demanded she gorge herself. Her wits advised her to save some for the morrow. One meal was never a promise of another.

The bread was fresher than she usually ate, containing no mold or bugs and still soft enough for her loose teeth and tender gums. The cheese was pale but pungent. The fish was filled with bones. She tore the latter into tiny bits and sucked on them, spitting out sharp fragments before swallowing.

This was a king's feast.

Gracia again paused to peer about, her eyes searching for any hint of danger in the narrow street overhung with looming buildings. Nothing alarmed her, so she went back to her meal, reflecting on a tale she had overheard.

If it were true that King Edward was coming here to worship the relics at Walsingham Priory, might she not hope to enjoy a tiny bit of a king's bounty?

Being short and thin, she was able to slip around adults or between their legs. They would be distracted as they cheered the king's entry into Walsingham. If she crept close enough when his minions tossed coins, she might snatch one or even two.

That was a dream, and fancy was a luxury only full bellies could afford, but she decided she was not foolish to expect to reap some benefit.

As soon as word spread about King Edward's visit, additional pilgrims would travel to this famous religious site. Shrines drew those who longed for God's grace, but kings lured men who hoped for an earthly lord's favor. Between the crowds who came for God and those who came for the king, there would be more people to toss her scraps, bits too small to interest a dog but enough, perhaps, to keep her alive a while longer. Extra coin might even get her through another winter…

She froze.

There had been movement in the shadows down the road.

Pulling the rag of a hood over her head to keep the pallor of her face from betraying her in the darker shadows, she pressed the food to her chest and listened.

Footsteps echoed in the silence of the streets.

They came closer, slowed, and stopped.

Too close, Gracia thought, and shivered in terror. She had been a fool to let hunger overrule caution and eat without first finding a better place to hide. A howl of dread filled her throat, but she swallowed it. Any sound from her might bring a beating, another rape, or even prove fatal.

She bit her lip. If God were kind, she would remain unnoticed in the gloom. If He were not, rape was surely more likely than death. She reminded herself that she had survived abuse once. She could endure it again. Those were brave words, but her trembling belied her belief in them.

The footsteps began again, slower but increasingly distant. The girl peeked out through a hole in her hood.

That shadow belonged to a man, she decided, but he was not the one who had made her bleed. She would never forget his stoutness. This shape owned a leaner form.

Holding her breath, she waited until the man's shadow slipped past the inn and merged into the deeper darkness beyond.

Then she rose from her corner, looked down the road in both directions, and escaped toward the Augustinian priory.

The wind muted all sound of her flight.

Chapter Four

Thomas lay on his back and stared at the indistinct outlines where two dark beams braced the ceiling of his small chamber.

He shifted onto his side.

The stone floor was hard, and his thin straw mattress scratched his face. Although he could ignore those annoyances, sleep's mockery he could not. For once it was not his familiar attack of melancholia that kept him awake. The unbalanced humor, from which he suffered tonight, was choler.

With a sigh, he surrendered to the futility of trying to sleep and sat up. After rubbing grit from his aching eyes, he glanced behind him and saw that the narrow bed in which Father Vincent should be sleeping was vacant. Above the priest's bed a large wooden cross hung on the wall, a vague shape made clearer by weak candlelight that flickered through the partially open door. The priest must have gone into the chapel to pray, he thought.

"As well he ought," he muttered in a low tone that betrayed dislike for his host. But it was not the priest's evident displeasure at having to share his tiny room that drew Thomas' ire. It was the man's lack of compassion.

Earlier in the day, Thomas had noticed a skeletal child in the street sitting against a urine-stained wall. Although he had seen other beggar children, this girl had caught his particular attention.

Her clothing possessed more holes than cloth, and she stank of the filth she slept in. When she opened her mouth, her breath was foul from rotted teeth. But there was something about her eyes that drew him to her. From one angle, they were ice blue, from another a warm gray. In either case, they revealed an intelligence rarely seen in one so young and worn by hunger.

"Have you eaten?" he had asked. The answer was obvious, but he wanted to hear her voice and hoped to gain her trust.

She had tilted her head to look up at him, and then murmured a reply. There was no guile in her expression, only a straightforward longing for bread.

And so he had gone to the inn to ask for scraps, failing to mention the exact mouth to be fed. If the innkeeper thought the food was for a monk, the man might choose a greater charity. Taking the offering, Thomas bowed his thanks and left to pass the still warm nourishment on to the child.

As he feared, she had snatched the food and fled. What he did not foresee was her whispered word of gratitude as she rushed by, a courtesy unusual amongst small beggars who rarely lived as long as she.

Like a burr, the troubling image of this girl buried itself into his heart, and Thomas decided to mention her to Father Vincent, priest of Ryehill Priory and guardian of a minor relic some distance from those of Walsingham Priory. Surely, the monk said, a warm corner in which to sleep and regular food from the nuns' kitchen could be provided the unfortunate child.

Father Vincent's face had become apoplectic at the very mention of the tiny beggar. "An imp from Hell," he shouted, pointing a trembling finger at his feet. "You have fed Satan's whore who dares to use the name *Gracia*! Is it not blasphemy for a demon to call itself *Grace*?"

"Nay, Father, a child, not a woman. This one is a little girl."

"I caught her some weeks ago with a merchant. She had dragged him into this chapel to sate her unnatural lust." Father Vincent shook like the last leaf clinging to a barren tree. "Into this sacred place! She dared—"

"Weeks ago? You are confused about the beggar I mean. This one bears no signs of a woman's body. She cannot be the whore of which you speak."

Father Vincent's nostrils flared with contempt. "You are sadly ignorant of the Evil One's cleverness, Brother. After I had found them coupling like dogs, the merchant wept in contrition and confessed the Devil's dark hand had covered his eyes and blinded him. He swore he did not know what he was doing until I awoke him from the terrible enchantment. This man is generous to the shrine and well-respected here. I have good cause to believe that he had been put under a spell by an imp in Eve's form."

Thomas was horrified, but the priest had not finished.

"She, on the other hand, claimed she had committed no willful sin and was innocent of any wrong. When I later caught her in the street, she showed no remorse for the sacrilege she had committed. Instead, she swore it was the good merchant who forced himself upon her. Nor has she come to me since for confession and penance."

"And why did you not believe her? She is a tiny thing and starving. The merchant, you say, is a grown man and surely well-fed. Which was more likely to force the other to sin?"

Holding his hands out as if they were balances, Father Vincent nodded at his right hand. "Here we have a man of proven charity who grieves over his crime." Then he indicated his left. "There we have a whore who blames another for her wickedness." Raising the left hand to suggest the proper answer, he glared at Thomas like a master with a dull pupil. "Her brazen refusal to confess her guilt in the wickedness proves she is Satan's creature. As the merchant claimed, she bewitched him."

Thomas squeezed his eyes shut. "Perhaps she was telling the truth," he replied through clenched teeth. In prison, he had felt no culpability when his jailor raped him, and he had been a grown man. Surely a child must bear no blame at all.

Father Vincent stared at the monk in disbelief. "An honest Christian confesses his transgressions. The Devil's handmaid denies all sin. Surely you see the difference."

At that moment, the only thing Thomas could see was blind rage. He did not understand how this priest could casually dismiss the terror this girl must have felt, but he saw no point in arguing further. Before he forgot his vocation and struck the priest, he willed himself to deliver a curt nod, and escaped into the street.

Once there, he looked for the child, but she had disappeared. With sorrow, he realized that he could do too little for her. He was both a stranger and a visitor to this place. When tears slipped down his cheeks, he did nothing to stop them.

Hours later, the anger had still not diminished, and it was the sparks of renewed fury that chased away all hope of sleep. There was no help for his misery except to walk until exhaustion forced him into uneasy dreams. At least, Thomas thought, the priest was not in his bed. He was not sure he could remain courteous if the man were to awaken and speak to him.

The monk adjusted his robes, then walked through the opened door into the empty chapel, his soft footsteps disturbing the profound stillness of night.

A few cresset lamps flickered in niches along the stone walls, causing shadows to dance with eerie grace.

The whoosh of wings rippled through the silence. Thomas looked up. Some flying thing had been disturbed in its resting spot near the roof.

As he approached the altar, he paused and knelt to pay homage to the small box containing a few hairs from the Virgin's head.

He was surprised that Father Vincent was not here either, since he was known to revere this relic he had worked so hard to obtain, but Thomas remained grateful that he need not meet the man. Muttering his complaints to God about the priest, Thomas had little doubt He might share this outrage. Whatever quarrels he had with God, the monk never doubted that He expected compassion from the creatures He had made in His image.

Rising, Thomas looked around in the uneven light but still failed to see the priest anywhere. Perhaps Vincent wished to avoid him as much as he did the priest. *If I were charitable,* Thomas thought, *I would conclude that the priest suffers remorse over what he said about the beggar child and cannot bear to face me after his cruel words.*

His mind insisted the supposition was possible. His heart dismissed it.

Thomas walked toward the chapel door and emerged onto the road. Taking a deep breath, he tried to calm himself. The chill night air did begin to soothe him.

He would be wiser to set aside this anger, he decided, and devote his wits to bringing succor to this girl. As he watched his breath grow white in the darkness, he acknowledged that fury was as useless as it was consuming. "Let God deal with Father Vincent," he muttered and leaned back against the chapel wall.

For a pilgrimage route that attracted many faithful from abroad as well as England, this road grew surprisingly quiet once the sun had set. Noise came from the nearby inn, but the massive stone priory lay between this chapel and the inn, dulling the sound. The major shrines of Walsingham were also located at the other end of this road. Pilgrims, so burdened by sins that they must seek powerful relics after dark, would walk away from Ryehill Priory and the chapel attended by Father Vincent, leaving this part of the road empty.

The night air nips like the taste of a tart apple, Thomas thought, and then chuckled at that image coming to him so quickly. When he had first arrived at Tyndal, he disparaged the coastal reek of fish and other earthy smells. His upbringing had been in towns, castles, and with soldiers. Swords and battlements came to mind sooner than fruit, but rural things were now his life. That was a good change, he thought.

Stretching, he felt a little peace slipping into him.

A woman's scream shattered his newborn calm.

It seemed to come from the other side of the priory, near the bell tower. Thomas ran in that direction, fearing the woman had been attacked by a band of ruffians or drunken men from the inn.

The street between chapel and priory was narrow, as was the one that led to its bell tower. The darkness was almost palpable, and the houses were so close that only two men might walk side by side. But he met no one on the way.

When he reached the base of the bell tower, he spun around, seeking a glimpse of a fleeing shadow and listening for running footsteps. He saw nothing. The only sounds, apart from the inn's muted joy, came from water dripping out of the mouth of a stone gargoyle high above him and the sigh of an intermittent breeze.

Then he noticed something on the ground.

He knelt and reached out. His hand touched warm flesh. As his eyes grew used to this gloom, Thomas knew he had found what he feared most. He bent closer.

It was the body of a woman.

He checked for breath but felt none. Quickly, he searched for wounds. Her skull was soft, likely shattered, and her neck was certainly broken. If he could do nothing to aid a living woman, he could at least give ease to her soul, and he whispered God's mercy into her ear.

Suddenly, he felt the hair on his neck prickle. He looked up, thinking he had heard a sound.

Near the far corner of the priory, the inn's light outlined the edge of an extended shadow, and he thought he saw movement. "Father Vincent!" he shouted. But there was no reply and no further suggestion that a mortal stood there.

"I was mistaken," he whispered to the corpse. His eyes, now more accustomed to the darkness, focused on the body. It was a young woman, and, if Thomas was not mistaken, she was the nun who had announced their arrival to Prioress Ursell. He looked straight up. From her injuries and the position of the body, he guessed she had fallen from the priory bell tower. Was this death an accident, a self-killing, or…

It was not his place to question and he began to rise, but something caught his eye and he slid back onto his knees. Reaching out, he tugged at an item clutched in the woman's hand. It was a piece of cloth, soft and finely woven. Bending closer, he decided the color must be brown or black. A brighter or light shade would have been clearer in this darkness. Feeling it, he noted that the edges were uneven, torn as if the dead woman had grasped something in a futile attempt to save herself from falling. That suggested another person might have been with her in the tower, yet he heard no second voice crying out in dismay.

He tucked the cloth back into the corpse's fist and placed her hand under her body to keep the item safe. Then he left to seek help. As sad as it was, this death and its cause were not his responsibility. Someone else must look at the evidence and decide what had occurred.

Thomas hurried toward the priory entrance with the news. Rounding the corner of the building, he collided with Father Vincent. Before the priest could express outrage at the unintentional assault, the monk told him he had found the body of a woman, one he feared was a nun, under the bell tower.

The man gasped. "Go back to the chapel and pray for the creature's soul, Brother Thomas," he said. "I will alert Prioress Ursell. This tragedy is our grief." Then he spun around and ran back the way he had come.

Thomas watched the priest disappear into the priory. If he had seen someone in the shadows, might it have been Father Vincent?

He shook his head. He had called out his name, when a shadow seemed to move, but no one had replied. As much as he disliked the man, Thomas was sure the priest had more important tasks than to lurk in the darkness near the inn. A more logical explanation for Father Vincent's absence from his bed and chapel was an errand of mercy somewhere nearby or in the priory itself.

Thomas walked back along the narrow street to wait by the dead woman until the priory could retrieve her corpse. Although Father Vincent had told him to go back to the chapel, he thought it cruel to let her hovering soul fear her body had been abandoned to foraging animals in the night. He could pray beside her corpse just as well as if he knelt in front of the altar.

Rain had begun to fall. The drops felt sharp as ice against his face. If God were grieving, Thomas thought, surely His tears would feel like this. As deep fatigue seeped through him, he knew sleep would come once he returned to his bed.

It was a prospect he did not welcome. Too many troubling things had happened this day. Any dreams would slay all hope of rest.

Chapter Five

"My lady."

Prioress Eleanor struggled to remain within that sweet embrace of sleep. She was about to hear something important, an answer she desperately needed to learn.

"Please, my lady, awaken!"

Why did this rude and annoying voice not cease? She opened her mouth to protest, but no sound came forth.

A hand gently shook her shoulder.

Her dream fled like a stag before a hunter and with it all hope for the peace of revelation.

Feeling a bitter cold, she reached for her blanket, but the covering she grasped was thin and rough. When she sought the comforting softness of her orange cat, he was missing from his usual spot on her bed.

All was not as it should be. The chill was now joined by ill-defined foreboding. Apprehension dragged her with merciless persistence toward raw consciousness.

"You must awaken." The voice spoke close to her ear, its sound both familiar and troubling.

Eleanor opened her eyes.

The gray light revealed bare stone walls. The beloved tapestry that hung in front of her bed was missing; the air was heavy with damp. Taking a deep breath, she winced at the pervasive reek of unwashed bodies. Had she drifted into a cruel nightmare? This was not her chamber at Tyndal Priory. She rubbed her fingers to bring back feeling.

"You must rise."

The woman kneeling next to her looked more like a wraith in the dull light than anything earthbound, but Eleanor recognized her as mortal. She was a fellow pilgrim, a merchant's widow called Mistress Emelyne, who shared this room and their straw pallet. As part of her penance, Eleanor had rejected the offer of chambers suited to her rank and instead asked to stay in the quarters assigned to women of lower status. In this moment, that choice felt very austere indeed.

"Is it time again for prayer?" The prioress was sure she had just fallen asleep, but perhaps the journey from Tyndal had wearied her more than she realized. Or else this damp cold had sapped her strength. What weak faith I own, she thought, if these minor discomforts are greater than I can bear.

"It is not, my lady." The woman nervously wrung her hands together and bowed her head. "Prioress Ursell has summoned you."

Eleanor blinked in confusion. What cause had Ryehill's prioress to ask for her at such a strange hour? Had a dire tragedy struck Tyndal? Her sub-prioress would never beg her to come back for anything less.

She struggled to rise, but every part of her ached. When she finally stood, she bit her lip but could not prevent a small cry of pain. The soles of her feet felt as if they had been beaten raw. What a fool she had been.

Insisting on this thin straw mat laid over a stone floor might have been acceptable as atonement for her sins, but walking bare-footed along the pilgrim's road for that last mile had been imprudent. Penitential humility often masked pride. Now she feared she had fallen victim to the vice. In any case, she was too soft a creature to have removed her shoes and walked that far over the rutted, stone-littered road. Meant as a singular act of piety, she had only confirmed her foolishness.

Reaching out to brace herself against the wall, she implored God to forgive her for the luxuries she allowed herself in her own priory. And if this absolution was not too much to ask, she also begged Him to accept her pain as atonement.

Now she grimly attempted to ignore her tender feet. The effort was more than she could manage, and tears rolled down her cheeks.

The widow braced Eleanor's elbow to help her stay upright. "Shall I bring some shoes for you, my lady? I own a soft pair that might fit." Glancing down at her own feet, she added, "We are much the same size."

The offer was kind, but the prioress did not welcome the charity. Gritting her teeth, she brusquely refused the offer, then the woman's assistance in walking, and stubbornly limped toward the chest provided by the nuns for those pilgrims who had worldly possessions to store.

As she reached the chest, she bent over and braced her hands against it for support. "Pride," she muttered. "Pride is sin." A hand lightly grasped her shoulder. Annoyed, the prioress looked around, sharp words ready to punish such impertinence.

"Forgive me, my lady, but I anticipated your wishes and found the ones you had brought." The merchant's widow pointed to a pair of shoes on the ground. "I do have others that might be softer. Yours are sturdy, meant for mud or snow."

Eleanor closed her eyes in defeat, murmured gratitude, and sat down on the chest. One of her feet had left a bloody mark on the floor.

The merchant's widow knelt and wrapped the wounded foot in a white cloth before easing on the shoes.

Eleanor looked around. The only other person in the room was another pilgrim who lay snoring in the far corner, her child clutched in her arms. Other straw beds were empty. No one stood waiting, and the chamber door was shut. "Did Prioress Ursell send a messenger, Mistress Emelyne?"

"She sent one of her nuns, but I told her to wait outside while I awakened you. I feared a strange voice would alarm you, and mine is familiar from our travels together."

"You were kind to think of that." The prioress struggled to rise, then reluctantly accepted the widow's proffered hand until she was able to stand without support.

She was not unappreciative of the woman's thoughtfulness, nor had she taken for granted the compassion the widow had shown by helping her on with the shoes. But Eleanor had had more than she wished of the woman's companionship on the road from Tyndal. As ungrateful as it seemed to her now, she still found the widow's company annoying.

I am just out of sorts, Eleanor decided on swift reflection, and taking my ill humor out on a good woman. Wincing with the pain from her abused feet, the prioress forced a grimace into a stiff smile. "Now, Mistress Emelyne, if you will call the nun to me?"

Nodding, the widow walked to the door. As she swung it open, the ill-fitting wooden slats creaked ominously on rusting hinges. Peering around the corner, Mistress Emelyne waved at a hidden figure in the hall.

The hollow cheeks of the young woman who entered were paler than the weak light would explain. When she saw the prioress of Tyndal, she bowed with courtesy. "Prioress Ursell requests your presence in her chambers, my lady," she stammered. "Your monk waits there as well."

"Brother Thomas?" Eleanor willed herself to walk with stiff-legged dignity toward the nun. "Has disturbing news come from Tyndal?"

The nun's eyes glistened with restrained tears. "Nay, my lady, but he has discovered a corpse lying beneath our bell tower. We fear it is one of our sisters."

Eleanor glanced upward with dismay. She had come on this pilgrimage as penance for her sins, to seek answers for troubling questions, and find peace in the worship of the holy relics. Why, she now asked God, could He not send that grim reaper of souls to accompany another for a change? Death's fondness for involving her in his more violent acts was always wearisome, but she had long tolerated it as part of her service to God. On this one journey, however, she begged for a respite from the vile creature.

Her silent protest ceased when she saw tears flowing from the nun's deep-set eyes. "I grieve to hear this news," she said, "and pray that God sends comfort to the hearts of all in this community."

Murmuring gratitude, the messenger swiftly brushed her hands over her face.

With no further hesitation, Eleanor followed the mournful sister to meet with Prioress Ursell and hear what Brother Thomas had discovered. Whatever dismay she felt over this interruption in her pilgrimage, she was still God's servant and would follow Him no matter where He led her. And, she reminded herself, I owe Him joy in the performance of my duty, not resentment.

As she carefully walked along the narrow hall, she concluded that the dead nun must have been well-loved to cause such grief in this sister. Shamed by her pettiness, Eleanor acknowledged that this sorrow was of far greater import than any minor complaint she might have about enjoying an undisturbed pilgrimage.

Chapter Six

Thomas disliked Prioress Ursell almost as much as he did Father Vincent. Although he tried to hide the evidence of his disdain, he had gotten no sleep, his temper was short, and his willingness to remain polite was growing feeble.

The woman was tall for her gender, he noted, and as long in the face as a horse. Had she chosen marriage as her duty, men would have called her plain as a kindness and ill-cast if they had no cause for courtesy. But she had entered the religious life, and thus such criticism was muted. This prioress should be granted all respect appropriate to her rank, he thought, but horses owned more grace.

Thomas knew he was being petty but could not quite repent this failing. When some claimed that God could only create beauty, and thus it was the Devil who crafted unsightly things, Thomas reminded them that Satan himself had been a splendid creature. Like all men, he responded to beauty, but even in the days before he took vows, he thought it cruel to mock uncomely women. Today he had lost the battle to remain charitable. Prioress Ursell had deeply offended him.

A knock at the door disrupted his thoughts. He was grateful.

A nun escorted Prioress Eleanor into the chambers, bowed to the leader of Ryehill Priory, and left without a sound.

Prioress Eleanor, hands folded and eyes lowered, stood quite still in front of the seated Prioress Ursell.

Nearby, a hearth fire snapped, then bravely flared, but gave forth only a little warmth.

The silence grew oppressive, and Brother Thomas became impatient. The leader of Ryehill Priory had yet to offer his prioress a chair, a rank discourtesy. There was no reason why Prioress Ursell should treat a woman, her equal in worldly rank and surely her superior in God's service, like a wayward nun called to confront her sins and be rebuked. He knew it was not his place to express outrage, but his self-control was rapidly weakening.

"Please sit," the prioress of Ryehill said at last, her tone as icy as the air. She pointed to a stool in a corner.

Thomas looked around.

The maid servant had been dismissed, and the nun by the door did not move. Father Vincent stared at the crucifix on the wall as if in deep conversation with God.

Furious at the insult, the monk started to walk to the stool, intending to bring it to his prioress.

"I prefer to stand," Tyndal's leader replied.

Thomas stepped back. The firmness in her voice delighted him for the quiet rebuke it suggested, but he grew concerned when he saw her tensed jaw and narrowed eyes. Some might conclude she was angry, but he knew better. His prioress was in pain, and he knew the cause.

On the day of their arrival, and against his counsel, she had dismounted from her donkey, removed her shoes, and walked the last sacred mile into Walsingham. Seeing a prioress of high birth humble herself so, several of her fellow travelers emulated her, a gesture that proved quite agonizing to some. His prioress had suffered most.

Her choice of penance was admirable, but he feared the results. Sister Anne had not accompanied them, and, by the time they reached Ryehill's entrance, he had seen blood on one of her feet. He hoped this priory had healers more skilled in their arts than Prioress Ursell was in courtesy.

"Your monk has disrupted the peace of this priory by bringing us very disagreeable news," the prioress of Ryehill said, glancing at him with open disapproval.

Thomas bit his tongue at the implied rebuke. Surely that dead nun would have chosen not to suffer a cruel death, and he knew he would have preferred not to have found her broken body. Neither of them had wanted this tragedy to happen. Of the three, he concluded that this priory had suffered the least.

Ursell cleared her throat. "He has said—"

"I would hear Brother Thomas speak for himself."

Ursell's eyes narrowed.

Eleanor's gray eyes took on the hue of storm clouds.

"As you will, but all speculation is unwarranted. I insist he keep to the facts of what he found. Those are grievous enough."

Prioress Eleanor raised an eyebrow, then gave her monk permission to speak.

"As Father Vincent's guest, I sleep in his chambers attached to the chapel next door to this priory."

The priest turned away from his contemplation of the wall and scowled at the monk. "The Shrine of the Virgin's Lock. Call it by its proper name, Brother."

Thomas bowed with intended courtesy but suspected his eyes betrayed a contrary attitude.

Father Vincent swiftly renewed his contemplation of the crucifix.

"While it was still dark, I awoke and, unable to fall back asleep, walked outside."

The priest muttered. His words may have been inaudible, but his pursed lips made his censure plain.

Thomas felt anger spark. Did this man find all mortals worthy of frequent rebuke, or just him? His mouth suddenly dry with indignation, he longed for wine or ale to moisten his throat but suspected a man could beg for succor in this room and Death would arrive faster than charity.

Calming himself, he continued. "The street was quiet, empty of men, and the only light came from the nearby inn. A moment later, I heard a woman's scream from the direction of the priory bell tower. Fearing she had been attacked, I rushed down the road, hoping to prevent a theft being committed or other great injury."

Father Vincent inclined his head to Prioress Ursell. "A questionable act for a tonsured man. Had he come upon armed thieves, he could not have committed violence against them. His vocation prohibits it." His eyes narrowed with scorn. "But surely he meant well, and so I conclude his dubious act was less blameworthy than ill-considered."

This priest is insufferable with his endless, critical commentary, Thomas thought. I should have learned to expect that, but now the man is daring to suggest in public that I have acted with impropriety.

He inhaled sharply and turned to Prioress Eleanor to plead his case. No one but his own prioress had the right to reproach him or decide if his behavior was unseemly.

She shook her head, her look soft with understanding.

That soothed him, and he was able to swallow his angry retort and keep a wiser counsel. To retain his calm, he vowed himself to silence until she, and only she, gave him permission to speak further.

Prioress Ursell waved impatiently at him to go on.

Pointedly, he looked to Eleanor.

She allowed him to continue.

"When I reached the base of the tower, I found a woman's body. From her simple dress, I feared she was a nun, and then I recognized her as the one who welcomed us here. The injuries and position of the corpse suggested she must have fallen from the bell tower, although I reflected on whether she might also have…"

"That will be conjecture enough, Brother. I forbid more."

"Indeed?" Eleanor's eyes widened in mild surprise.

Prioress Ursell stiffened as if some novice had dared to speak without permission.

A lesser woman might have quailed. Eleanor smiled, her expression changing into one of patient expectation.

"To be brief," Ryehill's prioress said, "your monk found Father Vincent close at hand. Our priest alerted me to the tragedy. The body now lies in our chapel. I have seen the corpse and identified the nun as Sister Roysia. That is all there is to this tale. It was a dreadful accident."

Eleanor looked over at her monk.

His sideways glance conveyed his disagreement.

"If that is all," Eleanor said, her expression growing less amiable, "I do not understand why I was told that that our cooperation was so necessary that I must be brought here at such an early hour."

From the tower outside, the priory bell rang for the early Office.

Ursell murmured something, then fell silent and turned her attention to the several tapestries covering the walls of her audience chamber. As if seeing them for the first time, her study took some time.

Thomas noted the embroidery was ill-crafted, but was not surprised that they pleased this insensitive woman. He glanced at his prioress.

Eleanor's eyes were half closed like a cat in deceptive sleep.

"As the leader of a priory yourself," Ursell finally said to the head of Tyndal, "you know how fragile our reputations are. Nuns are often suspected of committing sinful acts. If our priory were tainted with even a hint of ignominy, the faithful would shun us and take their coin elsewhere. I have nuns to feed and clothe, women devoted to prayer for souls in Purgatory. We are not richly endowed and have suffered a decrease in donations of late. We survive on the sale of pilgrimage badges and the hope that penitents will leave gifts when they visit the small shrine in the chapel across the way. I cannot afford scandal."

Eleanor expressed sympathy.

Despite this woman's disagreeable manner and troubling arrogance, Thomas conceded that Prioress Ursell was right. The concern she expressed for the welfare of her nuns was frank enough to be sincere. Were any to find cause to suspect that this nun's death might be self-murder, for instance, the entire priory would be blamed.

"I would therefore ask that you forgo any idle speculation on what might have happened here. After observing the body, I have concluded that our dear sister lost her footing and fell over the edge. There is absolutely no reason to believe otherwise." Ursell motioned to Father Vincent. "Do you not remember? Only yesterday, someone complained that our bell had not rung for Compline."

He blinked as if confused, then nodded with enthusiasm.

She looked back at Eleanor. "Sister Roysia overheard the criticism. I am certain she was in the bell tower to make sure the bell-ringer had not fallen victim again to self-indulgent sleep. Her death is unfortunate, but nothing other than an accident should be concluded from the facts."

Thomas wanted to ask whether the bell-ringer had been in the tower when the accident occurred, but he knew he would be rebuked rather than given a satisfactory answer.

"We are disinclined to chatter," Eleanor replied in an even tone. "Surely you did not mean to suggest otherwise."

The monk noticed that Prioress Ursell's lips now began to tremble. Perhaps she had just recalled that Prioress Eleanor's eldest brother stood high in the king's favor? Offending such a woman would not be prudent if Ursell cared about the future prosperity of Ryehill Priory. Thomas suppressed a smile. His prioress was gaining the edge in this unpleasant encounter.

"Of course, I did not," Ursell replied, her speech hoarse with emotion. "I merely ask that you not speak of this sad event when others are near enough to hear."

Eleanor shook her head as if amazed that the prioress had even given voice to such a peculiar request. "Is that all?" The words may have been spoken as a question, but there was no doubt that the prioress of Tyndal had just concluded this audience.

Ursell opened her mouth as if to say more, then seemed to reconsider and simply murmured assent.

"Brother Thomas and I shall go to the chapel next door and dedicate our time to praying for Sister Roysia's soul."

The priest spun around and stared. "That is most compassionate, my lady! Your charity on behalf of our dear sister is commendable, but do not further delay your journey back to

Tyndal. Your own flock must long for your prompt return. Spend the little time you have left here contemplating the glory of the great shrines." He cleared his throat. "Our Shrine of the Virgin's Lock is, of course, worthy of your favor."

Thomas was surprised that Father Vincent had finally torn himself away from his profound reflection, not to criticize but to express an ardent concern for the needs of those in a distant priory. The anomaly was quite inexplicable.

"A few hours on our knees, pleading with God to treat her with mercy, is insignificant compared to the time she must suffer in Purgatory. As guests here, we believe it our unquestioned duty to do so. The act is such a small mercy." Eleanor smiled.

"Since she was not one of your nuns, you are very kind." Ursell looked at the priest, her eyes glittering with desperation. "Perhaps Father Vincent can guide you through the remaining hours of your intended penance to include this particular charity. Our sister's soul will benefit, and you need not remain here longer than you had wished."

"You speak of *hours*, Prioress Ursell. I thought to be here for several *days*."

"From the tales I have heard told, I am sure you do not own enough sins for such a long penance! Please confer with Father Vincent. He can advise you."

"Brother Thomas, and he alone, directs my penance," Eleanor replied, her smile turned frosty. With those words, she abruptly nodded to her fellow prioress and the priest, then glided with great dignity out of the audience chamber.

The nun near the door almost tripped as she rushed to open it in time for the prioress to depart.

Brother Thomas, hands tucked into his sleeves, swiftly followed.

Except for the hissing flames from the dying fire, Prioress Ursell of Ryehill Priory and Father Vincent were left with silence and an uneasy sense of defeat.

Chapter Seven

Father Vincent scurried down the road to the chapel where Prioress Eleanor and her monk had preceded him. Prayer would have been his chosen goal, but the reputation of both priory and shrine demanded he follow another.

In no particular order, he asked God to curse Sister Roysia for the sins that caused her death, Brother Thomas for finding her body, and Prioress Eleanor for betraying a most unwomanly determination to do as she alone willed. At least Ryehill's prioress remembered her place in creation often enough.

As he drew within sight of the inn, responsible for disturbing his sleep and prayer with unholy merriment, he stopped to catch his breath. The accursed place was quiet at the moment, and for that he thanked God. Revelers from the night before must be sleeping off their indulgence in rich food and strong wines, neither of which ought to be in the diet of any pilgrim. Recently, he had overheard two men comment on the innkeeper's Lenten fare, claiming it was delicious. If true, eating it must be a sin in these weeks dedicated to renunciation.

Much to Father Vincent's disgust, he suspected that some families actually came here less for true repentance than to escape the drudgery of their labor for a few days. Yet they did buy badges to prove their piety and thus fed the monks and nuns of Walsingham. And most did confess a few sins, perform a little penance, and contribute to his own sacred shrine.

A troubling question smote him, causing him to take in a sharp breath. Did God disdain gifts from the insufficiently repentant? Did He care about the source of the offering and the motive for giving it?

The priest bit at his knuckle.

Then came the flash of revelation, and he realized with relief that any gift given to God must be instantly cleansed of all foulness. He raised his hands to the skies in gratitude for this gift of understanding. He need not spurn coin for the Shrine of the Virgin's Lock just because it might have come from the fingers of those, foreign or local, who were wicked. His conscience grew easy about accepting all gifts for his holy site.

Walking on, he still cast a contemptuous look at the offending inn. As he did, his gaze fell upon a man watching him from the entrance.

Something about the figure caused the priest to stop. He looked familiar. Was this a pilgrim with whom he had previous dealings? He blinked, trying hard to remember.

The man began walking toward him, raising his hand in friendly greeting.

Father Vincent struggled to bring some name to mind. With a swift assessment of the man's finely made attire, he concluded he was an affluent merchant despite the modest lack of ornamentation in his dress. Surely he had spoken to this man before, but the priest could not recall either time or occasion. Unfortunately, it was too late to pretend he had not seen the merchant and avoid embarrassment by quickly passing on.

"What a fortunate meeting, Father Vincent!"

The priest was still struggling to find an excuse to escape when he saw the bright flash of a coin in the man's fingers. His impatience forgotten, Vincent smiled with benevolence on this supposed pilgrim and even prior acquaintance. With hope and discretion, he also opened his hand.

"I remember you well," the man said. "That I was given this opportunity to speak with you suggests that God has truly smiled on my pilgrimage here."

The priest bowed his head with expected modesty, and the coin was softly dropped into his moist palm.

The merchant knelt. "I beg a blessing."

The boon was quickly granted.

The merchant rose, his lips moving with the final words of some silent prayer.

Rubbing his fingers around the edges of the coin, the priest noted with delight that it was newly minted. Some pilgrims tried to pass off severely worn or even clipped ones of much reduced value. Suspecting that a blessing was not all this man wanted, Vincent waited to hear what was expected in exchange for the fine coin given.

But the merchant seemed more inclined to casual conversation as he took the priest by the elbow and suggested they walk on. "I am grateful to see Walsingham so peaceful during this visit. I have been here before when the crowds have been thick and the lines to get into the shrines very long."

"It is still the season of Lent. We pray that the weather will soon grow warm and more pilgrims will arrive," Father Vincent said, feeling relieved when the man ceased to direct him quite so firmly onward.

"During my early supper at the inn last night, I overheard mention of a visit from the king. As it was time for my prayers, I could not question the speaker further and thus remain ignorant of whether he has already been here or not. Have I missed him?"

"King Edward had not yet come to Walsingham," the priest said, "but we pray that he will honor all the shrines with his presence soon."

The man sighed. "Now I am truly perplexed. Shall I stay or must I leave? There will be so many who want to welcome our earthly lord. They and his attendants will demand comfortable lodgings." He shook his head. "My room is small, but the bed lacks fleas. Were I to stay, one of his men might toss me out of the chamber and claim it for himself." He laughed, a sound that lacked both mockery and cheerfulness. "What then should I do?"

Father Vincent again ran his finger over the clean edge of the coin and dared to hope there might be more of these if his reply was cleverly phrased. "I beg pardon, but my memory fails me on occasion. Your name, Master?"

"Durant, a merchant of fine wines." The man lowered his gaze as if discomfited by possessing such a worldly occupation.

"Of course! I do recall your other visits here." That was not true, but the name did sound familiar. "If you wish to stay longer, I could arrange plain but clean quarters so you need not fear if the king's men required your present room at the inn. King Edward himself will be given lodging at Walsingham Priory, but I can offer you my own chambers attached to the chapel next to Ryehill Priory. Perhaps this transformation had not yet taken place when you were last here, but that chapel has become the glorious Shrine of the Virgin's Lock. I have the honor of caring for it."

The Augustinian priory and Prior William would be obliged to find a spot for him to sleep if he had to give up his small room, Vincent thought, and this pilgrim seemed inclined to a generosity that should compensate him for that temporary discomfort. Staying at Walsingham Priory might also give him the opportunity to direct the attention of one of the king's courtiers, or even the king himself, to Ryehill's small shrine. Trying not to smile, the priest grew quite pleased with the merits of his idea.

Master Durant's expression blended gratitude with pleasure. "Your charity to this lowly pilgrim is admirable, Father, and God demands that such kindness not go unrewarded." He discreetly ran his hand over a bulging pouch near his waist.

The priest licked his damp lips and hoped this man did not habitually go into the streets with so much obvious wealth. Coins like the one he had just received were better given to God than some unholy thief. He opened his mouth to advise caution, but words failed to come forth. His eyes were fixed on that pouch.

The merchant rested a gentle hand on Father Vincent's shoulder. "Do you think the king might be visiting very soon?"

"We have not yet heard the precise date."

"But surely he would send a messenger so you could prepare the setting of this newest relic for a royal viewing. Although I have not yet visited the shrine of which you speak, I have heard others praise it. The king must have as well."

The priest's thin chest puffed with pride. "Our king is deeply attached to all the shrines here. He credits the Lady of Walsingham for saving his life."

"I believe I have heard that tale. Was he not playing chess when Our Lady inspired him to move just before a large stone fell from the roof?"

Vincent nodded. "It landed on the spot where he had been sitting, yet he was unhurt."

The merchant's expression grew soft with admiration. "Many say that his devotion to this place exceeds even that of his devout father," he murmured.

"You must be correct that he would want to seek our tiny but holy shrine." The priest looked meaningfully at the merchant. "Who would not long to worship strands of the Virgin's hair?"

The man smiled and put two fingers into that rounded purse. "And might you send word to me as soon as you know when our king will be entering Walsingham?" He nodded at the inn. "I shall remain there for the time being, as I have many sins and much penance to perform. When I know the date of the king's arrival, I shall arrange with you to lodge in the chambers of which you spoke. It would bring me joy to glimpse our king after visiting the shrines during this more peaceful time. And I shall not fail to offer a suitable gift to honor your own holy relic." He stretched his hand toward the priest.

Father Vincent swore to do as the merchant required, then closed his eyes and his hand. The man had given him *two* coins, so newly minted he could feel the details of the king's image on them. Fondling them, he savored this welcome gift.

But when he opened his eyes, the merchant had disappeared. The priest looked around, but there was no sign of him. Were he not holding these coins as proof, he might have wondered if he had imagined the conversation.

He tried to picture the man's face, but it had been of such common form that it was quite unremarkable. Now he feared he might not recognize him again.

He took in a deep breath and calmed himself. After all, he knew the man's name and where he was staying. That was sufficient to send a messenger as the man had asked.

Looking heavenward, Father Vincent smiled. All he need do is tell this merchant the date the king would enter Walsingham, endure a short time as a charity guest in the priory of the favored shrines, and find a way to urge King Edward to visit a new shrine near Ryehill Priory, acquired after the king's last visit.

Were God to smile with especial kindness on the little shrine, the priest was sure the coin from the wine merchant and any gift from the king would be enough to repay in full what he had secretly taken from alms due the priory to acquire that relic. For so great a blessing, he would cheerfully tolerate the itching from a flea-ridden straw bed.

Gripping the three coins he had already received, he hurried on to the chapel, praying that Prioress Eleanor and her troublesome monk were still there. If they had left, Prioress Ursell would be deeply angered over his failure to achieve what she required. And her fury could be awesome. Had he not seen her bow to the cross, an act no imp would perform, he might have wondered at the source of such hot rage when she was thwarted.

The merit in his delay was not anything he dared explain. The prioress knew nothing of what some might call *theft* from her coffers. Had he asked for the sum to buy the relic for the Shrine of the Virgin's Lock, she would have refused, citing the poverty of her nuns, but he was certain the holy object was worth a little less bread and ale for the religious. Women lacked a man's wisdom in these matters, and so he had gone ahead with his plan. He had told her the relic was a gift from a penitent, a tale that brought him respect and even awe from a prioress who occasionally failed to show the deference owed a man of his vocation.

He shrugged. After the relic was finally paid for by money from merchant and king, Prioress Ursell would conclude that he had increased income for Ryehill as offerings rose to what they had been before he had borrowed from them. In time, he was certain the relic would bring more pilgrims to the chapel and alms for the priory. When that occurred, and he was duly praised for acquiring the precious object, he would relish the acclamation but with eyes lowered. A show of humility was a virtue too often ignored by those less than pious. He sniffed with contempt.

As he rounded the corner of the inn, he saw the street child disappearing down a narrow street, and he clenched his fist in fury. Had he not been so delayed in his purpose, he would have chased after her, throwing rocks and casting forth imprecations.

Instead, he slipped inside the chapel and contented himself with asking God to send the vile creature the same fate suffered by the wicked Sister Roysia. Unlike the nun, whose vocation allowed her some mercy, he would make sure Gracia's corpse rotted in unsanctified ground.

Chapter Eight

Daylight struggled to enter the little chapel from one window placed high in the wall behind the altar. Where shafts of light struck the ground, the damp stones glistened, and the air was rife with the stench of must.

A few pilgrims wandered in, but they spent little time on their knees before the small box containing the Virgin's hair. Reverence was sincere but they quickly left, longing to see the sacred wells and the famous Holy House of the Annunciation, called England's Nazareth and maintained by the religious of Walsingham Priory, farther down the road.

Brother Thomas and Prioress Eleanor rose from where they had knelt. Seeking privacy, they walked to the inside columned walkway nearby, cupped their hands over their mouths, and bent their heads to muffle their voices lest someone overhear their words.

"Prioress Ursell wishes to conceal something about Sister Roysia's death, my lady."

"Perhaps she does, Brother, but there is no reason to believe this matter must be our concern."

Thomas looked around, then whispered, "More happened before your arrival that troubled me."

With evident reluctance, she permitted him to continue.

"When Father Vincent ordered me to return with him to the prioress' audience chamber, I assumed they wanted to hear what I had found and any conclusions I had formed. After making me wait, Prioress Ursell greeted me with a coldness to match the air in this chapel." He shivered. "What distressed me more was the lack of sorrow shown by either priest or prioress. Their eyes were as dry as a road in summer heat."

"Perhaps they did not wish to show their grief to a stranger."

He shook his head. "You heard what Prioress Ursell said about the tragedy. Sister Roysia's death was a possible cause for scandal, an annoyance. I have seen men banish tears of grief and grow pale with the effort. Prioress Ursell and Father Vincent had no need to hide what they did not feel."

Eleanor frowned as she considered his words. "They have reason to fear scandal. All religious houses do, and the prioress argued the concern well. Her duty lies in providing for her nuns, and I believe she cares deeply about that. "

Thomas concurred with her conclusion, then continued. "I confess that I did not tell them all I knew," he whispered.

She looked at him with surprise. "Why not? Prioress Ursell said that she did not welcome conjecture, but that would not prevent you from giving them all the facts."

"From the start, they treated me like an unwelcome guest and ignored the simplest charity of offering ale to ease the early morning chill. Soon after I began relaying my news, the prioress silenced me, called to her priest, and they spoke together in low voices as if I were not in their company."

"They did lack civility."

"Although Father Vincent failed to provide a guard for the body, when he went to alert the priory, I remained by the nun's corpse so that wild dogs would not despoil it. No one thanked me. Before you arrived, Prioress Ursell ordered me to say nothing about this matter, especially after my return to Tyndal. She felt obliged to remind me 'because all monks are like children and guilty of telling tales.' Forgive me, my lady, but I was angered."

"With cause." She frowned. "They greeted me with disrespect as well. Although pride is a sin, the expectation of courtesy is not. I do not understand why it should be so, Brother, but they seem to find our presence here unwelcome."

"When my temper cooled, I might have excused their rude-ness to a simple monk, but I could not tolerate their insult to you, a prioress worthy of the highest honor. That was unconscionable." He bowed.

Her face grew pink in the delicate light. "Their treatment of us both was unwarranted, yet to withhold information that was pertinent..."

"My failure to tell all was spiteful. That I admit, but with-holding a little would only have delayed the discovery of evidence they should have found. From their manner toward me, I concluded they did not want to hear what I had to say. Father Vincent asked only one question. He wanted to know if I had seen or heard anyone in the vicinity of the tower. When I suggested they examine the bell tower, lest there be more to this death than was immediately apparent, Father Vincent mocked me." His face flushed with anger. "He seems to delight in doing so, and I find that intolerable."

"Set aside your anger, Brother, and tell me the entire story, including all you omitted."

"I respected the dead nun's corpse but did seek the cause of her death. Her neck was broken and her head cracked open, both of which were consistent with the fall from the tower. But I doubted she was alone in the tower and was troubled that I did not hear another voice crying for help, although I had arrived shortly after she fell."

"Prioress Ursell said the nun in charge of ringing the bell had failed to do so on the previous night, and I understood that Sister Roysia was there to make sure the error was not repeated. Perhaps the bell-ringer had not yet arrived when Sister Roysia fell."

"If she feared the nun might sleep through the hour again, why did she not bring the bell-ringer with her?"

Eleanor agreed.

"I have not yet told you the one significant detail I did not tell them. It argues against the conclusion that Sister Roysia was the only one in the tower."

Eleanor raised an expectant eyebrow.

"Sister Roysia had something clutched in her hand, a piece of torn cloth. The weave was of good quality and the color dark. This is why I doubted she had been alone before she fell. That cloth must have come from a garment."

Frowning, Eleanor thought for a moment. "Prioress Ursell said she had seen the body and could only conclude that the death had been a tragic accident. Yet, as you said, the piece of cloth suggests other possible deductions. It was a detail she, or the nun who examined the body, ought to have noticed as well."

"Yet they said nothing about it. I am bothered by that."

"Even if the death was an accident, the torn cloth raises questions about why she fell. Assuming she and the bell-ringer were together, quarreled, or struggled, Sister Roysia might have lost her balance and fallen." Suddenly she froze and looked around as if she had heard something.

"Were that the case, and there was no wicked intent, the other person would have cried out in horror." Instinctively, he lowered his voice.

"I agree. And, if the nun was deliberately pushed, this is not a simple tragedy." The prioress paused. "I wonder if they questioned the bell-ringer."

"There was little time to have done so and examine the corpse before I arrived." He shrugged. "I did not ask. They would not have welcomed the question."

"I just remembered something else, Brother. The bells for the next Office rang while we were all in the prioress' chambers. If Sister Roysia was in the tower because she was afraid the nun would oversleep, she was there far too early for such a purpose. As I recall, the prior hour of prayer had occurred some time before."

"The earlier bell did ring long before I heard her cry out. The nun had no reason to remain there between the two Offices." Thomas looked up and watched a steady drip of water from the ceiling that was creating a growing puddle on the floor. The roof needed patching, he thought, a repair that never would have been left untended at Tyndal Priory. "Either they are lying or choosing to ignore the facts."

"I shall be honest, Brother. I fear they lie. Their observed lack of interest in the truth smells foul. Prioress Ursell was so fearful that we would discuss this between ourselves that I wondered why we should not." She looked up at him, eyes twinkling. "Her words were like the serpent in Eden offering the apple. I was tempted to disobey her, and here we stand, doing what they forbade us." Once again, she glanced into the shadows. "The real tragedy may not be the poor nun's death but what is being hidden behind it."

"Had it not been for the torn cloth she held, I might have concluded that Sister Roysia was alone, slipped, and fell to her death as they wish us to believe. The floor of the bell tower is probably as damp as the stones on which we knelt. But unless this is murder, the person with her would have cried out and run for help."

Eleanor gestured for him to stay where he was as she walked a short distance away, looked around, and returned. "I thought I saw someone in the shadows." She thought for a moment, then asked, "Are you certain that the piece of cloth was not lost when the corpse was moved?"

"I tucked it back into the nun's hand. When they wrapped the body and took it back to the priory, I did not see the cloth fall to the ground. I am certain they must have found it."

"They did not ask you about it?"

"No, and they do not know I found it."

"The more flawed part of my nature rejoices that you remained silent in the face of their discourtesy to you."

Thomas grinned.

"This death is their responsibility. If Sister Roysia died accidentally, there is no scandal, only grief. If she was killed, Prioress Ursell must investigate and determine what should be done to protect Ryehill as well as punish the murderer. But why distrust us so much? Had I been faced with a similar death at Tyndal, which was discovered by a religious, I would have been grateful for any information received, even if I begged for silence so I might resolve it myself. I do not understand why she and her priest asked no questions and behaved so strangely."

"Prioress Ursell has no reason to be wary of you. Your reputation for justice and compassion is well-known."

Eleanor bowed her head. "Perhaps she did not wish to trouble us. After all, I am here to do penance for my own sins, not to seek out the transgressions of others." She looked up at her monk. "We must leave the investigation into Sister Roysia's death with Ryehill Priory. Our efforts are no more welcome here than our presence."

Thomas stepped back in surprise. "Someone was in the tower with her, my lady. The torn cloth in her hand is proof." He fell silent. "Both Father Vincent and Prioress Ursell were unmoved by the death but were most concerned that it was I who found the body."

"Prioress Ursell has been quite clear. She does not want us involved in this death. We shall honor her wishes and continue with our original purpose of doing penance at the shrines." Eleanor looked up at the ceiling, then over to the altar, and sighed. "You long to draw us in where we are unwelcome. I understand why, for I share your concern about this death, but we ought to let this tragedy remain the responsibility of Ryehill Priory."

"As you will, my lady."

Eleanor looked up at him. "Brother, apart from your disappointment in my decision and anger at the discourtesy here, I believe you have more to say to me." Her voice was soft. "You may speak freely."

"God could have sent us here to perform another duty along with the worthy act of atonement." With hopeful eagerness, he looked down into his prioress' eyes.

"You are convinced of this?"

He nodded.

"Might your conclusion have less to do with the nun's death than the offenses against our pride?" She looked back at the altar. Her expression suggested she was struggling hard to hold fast to her longing to avoid an inquiry into murder. "Should we not make a singular effort, while on pilgrimage, to turn the other cheek when treated rudely? If you have no greater cause to disobey their request than that…"

"In truth," he replied, "Father Vincent has angered me so deeply that I am tempted to go against anything he wishes. He and I have quarreled over another matter, one in which he has ignored Our Lord's commandment that we practice charity."

Eleanor sighed. "Over what did you disagree?"

"It was about a child. She is a ragamuffin in tatters, very thin, who begs nearby. I asked that he find food and lodging for her. He refused and accused me of wanting to feed Satan's whore."

Her exclamation echoed throughout the chapel.

Thomas told her the story of Gracia's rape and Father Vincent's conclusion that she had bewitched the merchant into performing an unnatural act in a holy place.

"What age does this girl own? You call her *child*." Eleanor's whisper was like a hiss.

"And so she is, my lady. There is nothing womanly about her."

"Why does he withhold compassion?"

"Unlike the merchant, she refuses to admit wickedness or confess that she was under the influence of evil. To give her food and shelter, he said, is no better than offering comfort to the Devil."

She twisted her hands in fury. "And what shall you do in this matter?"

"I will continue to feed the child, my lady, and seek some other way of keeping her alive."

"If you had decided otherwise, I would have reproved you, Brother." Eleanor's expression suggested she had no doubt he would do as she hoped. "Father Vincent's lack of compassion shocks me. Another priest must be found who will gently guide her into more virtuous ways."

"These are cruel people here, my lady. They have insulted you and mistreated a starving child. The questionable circumstances of the nun's death are consistent with the endemic wickedness of this place. How can we not pursue the truth?"

"To begin with, Brother, I must reject vanity of birth and religious rank. I am a pilgrim here: a humbled, wicked, and lowly creature. Had this prioress a more kindly heart, she might have shown greater courtesy, but I am obliged to accept their rudeness as part of my penance."

He started to protest.

She raised a hand to silence him. "I am not finished. We both dislike those who lead Ryehill. I might forgive Prioress Ursell's rudeness to me, her implied insult to our priory, and, with difficulty, her treatment of you. What I cannot forgive is a priest's disdain for a hungry child."

He looked down at her with obvious relief. "Does that mean we may look further into the nun's death, my lady?"

"I am as troubled as you by what you found, but this death may yet prove to be nothing more than an accident or even self-murder. We are prejudiced against those in authority here. That may be our error."

"Other than feeding the child, you wish me to do nothing more against the commands of Father Vincent and Prioress Ursell?"

"If God wishes us to do more, He will make it impossible to do otherwise," she replied in a whisper. "Keep your eyes open, your ears as acute as always, and report to me if you discover anything of interest."

Thomas bowed and tried hard not to show his delight at her words.

"In the meantime, I am here to do penance, Brother." She motioned toward the door of the chapel. "Let us find the shrine where the vial containing the Virgin's milk is kept."

◇◇◇

After they had left the chapel, a skeletal figure slipped from the safety of a pillar's shadow. Father Vincent's heart still pounded from his near discovery by Prioress Eleanor. If she had walked only a few steps further…

He trembled so his knees knocked together.

Then he knelt for a brief prayer in front of his beloved Shrine of the Virgin's Lock. As soon as he was done, he raced from the chapel to the chambers of Prioress Ursell.

Chapter Nine

After visiting the one shrine, Eleanor chose to return to the priory gardens rather than continue on to other holy places for contemplation.

Restless, she paced along the paths, ignoring the decaying plants, blackened by winter frost, and the paucity of emerging green tendrils. The bleakness suited her mood. It was not the rudeness of the prioress here that gnawed at her. It was the dark image of a child condemned by Father Vincent as if she had no right to a decent meal or a gently cleansed soul.

Only with great effort could she swallow her anger over the cruelty to the little vagrant and not go in outrage to Prioress Ursell. This was not her priory, she kept reminding herself, but that argument failed to win her heart. Like Brother Thomas, she was determined to do something for the child. And despite her profound longing to concentrate on her penance here, the soul of the nun, whose suspicious death was being ignored, begged for justice with compelling urgency.

"My lady!"

Fearing another tragedy had occurred, Eleanor froze and looked over her shoulder with foreboding.

Mistress Emelyne stood just behind her, hands fluttering like uneasy birds hesitant to land. But her eyes sparkled with unmistakable eagerness.

The prioress tried hard to disguise her annoyance. She wanted to be alone and resolve her dilemmas. Looking down at her fingers, Eleanor decided she had too few on which to count her conflicting priorities.

"How fortunate that I have discovered you here!"

With forced benevolence, she flashed a smile at this pert widow and swallowed her impatience. Anyone on pilgrimage should not succumb to even the pettiest of transgressions, she reminded herself, and tried to cast aside this unseemly intolerance. The attempt was short-lived. Eleanor could feign only so much virtue without committing the greater sin of hypocrisy.

"I have heard such amazing tales!" The widow raised her hands as if awed by the immensity of what she had learned.

The prioress shut her eyes. On the brief journey here, this woman had tried to amuse her with innumerable stories of misdeeds, great and trifling, committed by the widow's neighbors in Norwich. Eleanor had often bitten her tongue, resisting the temptation to chastise Mistress Emelyne for bringing worldly matters on a pilgrimage intended to escape them.

Normally a decisive woman, she was therefore puzzled when she could not choose between ordering the woman to be silent or letting her talk. Concluding now that the former was based in arrogance, a sin she feared she owned, she once more chose the latter as a lesser evil.

"To what could you possibly refer?" She began to walk briskly down the path, hoping her clipped speech lacked the warmth of encouragement. With God's kindness, the widow might take the hint and leave her in peace.

Mistress Emelyne broke into a trot, just keeping pace by the prioress' side. "To the death of Sister Roysia," she puffed. "Have you not heard the news?"

Eleanor avoided the temptation to lie and had to agree that she knew. Why was God testing her with so many forms of sin?

The widow bent as close to her companion's ear as she could and murmured, "She was seeing her lover in the bell tower. Everyone knew she met him there."

Stopping abruptly, Eleanor stared at the woman in astonishment. This time, her reaction was genuine.

"Oh, I may be a stranger here, my lady, but my late husband always said that the wise must keep ears open for any news. One never knows when there may be value in it." Her expression grew suitably solemn. "Of course I would never spread this tale to others, but you are a woman devoted to God. Telling you can be no sin."

That was a new concept to Eleanor, but she did not want to discourage this important confidence. She was eager to hear what Mistress Emelyne had to say, yet still feared the woman would think she welcomed such stories. Deciding the widow was inclined to believe she welcomed them no matter what she did, the prioress told her conscience that any virtue in rejecting gossip had long been lost.

"Surely this is but idle tale-telling on the part of the unkind," the prioress said. Realizing her tone suggested censure, she quickly smiled to prove her interest in learning more.

"I heard it from several sources as I wandered through the shops today." Emelyne took a deep breath, girding herself for a longer exposition. "It grieved most that Sister Roysia had been bringing such shame to her priory." For a moment she hesitated, studying the prioress' face for any clue that she had taken offense. "From the way the story was told, I believed that the tellers were God-fearing and well-meaning folk."

"How could Prioress Ursell knowingly tolerate a nun in her flock to remain unchaste and unrepentant?" Eleanor returned the steady gaze.

"As I heard the story, she could do little about it."

Eleanor raised an eyebrow. This conversation was proving to be very interesting.

"The nun's lover may be Master Larcher, a man who contributes to the priory income by making pilgrimage badges sold by Ryehill. Without the income from his work, the priory would become impoverished beyond any hope of recovery." With a troubled expression, she lowered her voice and confessed, "I did buy one."

"*May be* is not proof of anything." Eleanor scowled. Prioress Ursell had the right to punish Sister Roysia's unchaste behavior, and the craftsman should fear Hell for coupling with a nun. If anything, Master Larcher ought to donate badges to the priory as penance for his terrible wickedness.

"Or," the widow continued as if the prioress had said nothing, "her lover is the priest, Father Vincent." She bowed her head. "The priest's name was spoken in a whisper, my lady, but both men were mentioned with equal certainty."

Eleanor stiffened, then calmed herself. When two rumors are of equal weight, the likelihood is that neither is accurate, she thought. Yet these stories proved that Prioress Ursell's fear of scandal had greater cause than she and Brother Thomas first thought. If there was a lover, this detail would also add strength to Brother Thomas' suspicion that Sister Roysia's death was not accidental and that someone was with the nun in the tower.

"You seem perplexed, my lady. Had you heard none of this, apart from the death?"

"I would not have heard that much if Brother Thomas had not found the nun's corpse under the bell tower. It was he who alerted Father Vincent, and the priest took the news to Prioress Ursell."

Mistress Emelyne's face glowed with delight.

Presumably he was happy at the prospect of being able to add a detail to the gossip already spreading, Eleanor thought. She regretted abetting the widow like this, but the information given would soon be learned by others anyway. Surely Prioress Ursell would have no justification for outrage at this confirmation of a harmless fact.

The widow's expression became solemn, and her lips lost all suggestion of worldly merriment. "But we are here for a higher purpose, are we not? And I should refrain from prattling on about mortal frailties."

Eleanor was surprised by the sudden change. Trying not to betray this, she nodded gravely. "We should."

The widow sighed and put a hand to her heart as if suffering profound remorse. "Will you join me in a walk to the healing wells on the great priory's grounds? Have you visited them already? If so, perhaps you would like to visit the chapel containing the knuckle bone of St. Peter?"

Eleanor admitted she had not seen either.

"If I could see the miraculous wells at your side, I would be honored." Mistress Emelyne motioned hopefully toward the door leading into the priory. "According to what I have heard from other pilgrims, the wells are noted for curing stomach ailments, an affliction from which I suffer, but drinking the chill water helps those suffering headaches as well. I wanted to buy a small container of the water to take back to Norwich."

Finding no good excuse to avoid this woman's company, Eleanor agreed. Perhaps a sip of the blessed water would cure her headaches. Sister Anne's feverfew remedy had helped for a long time, but the headaches were growing more virulent. Last summer they had caused her to see something that many called a vision. For her, the story had become a curse, not a blessing, and had been one reason for traveling here to the shrines of Our Lady of Walsingham.

"I've been told that the wells are perfectly round and always filled with pure water, even when the earth becomes dry," the widow said, her voice rising with fervor. "It was Our Lady of Walsingham who struck the ground and brought the water forth! Of course, nothing earthly could…"

But Eleanor had ceased listening. Following Mistress Emelyne out of the gardens, she prepared herself for the holy sites by reflecting on the goodness of the Queen of Heaven. Before all thoughts moved heavenward, however, Eleanor concluded she had been wise to suffer one more tale from the irritating widow. The information was important and must be passed on to Brother Thomas.

Chapter Ten

A light mist fell as Thomas trudged back to the chapel. After
he had accompanied his prioress to the shrine containing the
Virgin's milk and back to Ryehill, he sought Gracia but failed
to find her. Hoping she had found shelter from this weather,
he pulled the hood over his head and buried his hands in his
sleeves for warmth. The rain itself was soft and sweet, but the
chill air stung his flesh.

A man passed him in the road, then suddenly spun around
to face him, a surprised but delighted expression on his face.

Perplexed, the monk stopped and waited for the stranger to
speak.

"Are you Brother Thomas of Tyndal Priory?"

The monk did not remember having met him, although he
felt he should. A boyish charm belied the gray dusting in the
stranger's brown wavy locks. His hazel eyes glowed with comforting warmth on this cold day. But the man's features overall
were not memorable. Were he to walk by him later in the day,
Thomas wondered if he would recognize the man again, unless
he saw his eyes. Concluding he had forgotten a prior meeting,
something for which no blame was due, he opted for honesty.
"Do we know each other?"

"Nay, we do not," the man replied with a pleasant smile,
"but I know your reputation. I visited the hospital at Tyndal
Priory and stayed in the guest quarters there while my sick wife

sought treatment. Men know me as Durant of Norwich, a wine merchant in that town." The crisp air was turning his smooth cheeks a bright pink.

Despite the smile, Thomas thought he saw a hint of sadness in the man's eyes. "I grieve if we were unsuccessful in curing her," he said gently.

Master Durant blinked, then instantly brightened. "On the contrary! She returned home with renewed health and remains vigorous. Her cure is the reason for my current pilgrimage here. She wanted to accompany me, but when I am absent, our business only flourishes if she remains to tend it." He laughed with evident fondness. "I told her I would bring her a badge. Even if she is not by my side, her heart most assuredly journeyed with me."

"I am grateful that God was kind to you both. He has blessed Sister Anne, and those she has trained, with skill and knowledge. Being mortal, however, we cannot always prevail if God wishes a soul to come to judgment."

"God allows more to live within the walls of your hospital, Brother. Tyndal's reputation for healing has spread throughout the kingdom." Durant smiled. "But your deeds are legendary as well. A man from Amesbury, who sought a cure for the stone, stayed with us in those guest quarters and pointed you out. With awe, he told us how you had chased a foul murderer up a steep roof at the priory there so God might more easily strike him down." His face glowed with enthusiasm.

Thomas gritted his teeth. Would that tale never die? "As you see, my function was minor. It was God who rendered justice."

The merchant protested that the monk was too modest and then gestured toward the inn. "Will you join me for a jack of ale? The inn is respectable, and pilgrims of all vocations, including clerks with tonsures, find lodging there."

Thomas began to refuse.

"Please, Brother. I would take little of your time and would profit from speaking with you." He pulled a battered pilgrimage badge of older design from his pouch. "As you see, I come here from time to time to worship Our Lady of Walsingham and donate coin to the Holy House of her Annunciation. When I do, I seek edifying conversation with men vowed to God's service. Will you not aid me in this endeavor to grow wiser?"

Thomas' mouth was dry. He longed for good ale after the unfortunate meeting with Prioress Ursell and Father Vincent, followed by prayers and conference with his prioress at the Shrine of the Virgin's Lock.

Although he felt ill-qualified to offer the wisdom requested by this merchant, he did not want to suggest the man speak with Father Vincent. His own dislike of the priest aside, Thomas assumed Durant must have met him before and would have gone to him if he had wished to do so. Perhaps Master Durant did not consider Father Vincent any better qualified to offer godly advice than Thomas judged himself.

Surrendering to his need for ale and not wishing to be discourteous, Thomas nodded consent and followed the wine merchant into the nearby inn.

The rushes on the floor were freshly laid, and the smell of roasting fish for the Lenten meal filled the air with the pleasing aroma of warmed spices. The scent made Thomas long for Tyndal. Sister Matilda's simple Lenten meals were worthy of Eden and brought all who ate them closer to an appreciation of God's generosity to mortals. He wondered what she was planning for the monks and nuns today, then suddenly realized he was getting hungry.

As the monk looked around, he concluded that the wine merchant had been correct about the nature of the inn. Those who served were modest in dress and brought food or drink promptly. Although the men sitting at the tables were jovial, no one was drunk. The tables were quickly cleared and wiped down. Unlike some at other pilgrimage sites, this innkeeper seemed to keep an honest house and gave fair value for the coin he received.

A bench in a corner was quickly found, jacks placed near to hand, and the two men drank deeply. Nodding to each other with mutual appreciation of the refreshment, they fell into that companionable silence common between friends but seldom found with strangers.

Durant of Norwich was pleasant company, Thomas decided. He rarely felt such ease with another and should have welcomed the moment, but this was a man about whom he knew nothing. Studying the merchant seated across from him, the monk chose to be cautious. Despite the merchant's friendliness, Thomas found him puzzling. Perhaps, he thought, that ought to trouble me.

Had Master Durant not been dressed in a robe of finely woven cloth that proved affluence, Thomas would have doubted that such a man could be a successful merchant as he claimed. Perhaps his wine business was so flourishing that a bold manner was not needed, but Durant's demeanor was quiet, almost shy. He did not advertise his wealth, and his clothes were modest in color and design. Were he to guess the man's vocation, he would have said Durant was most likely a scholar or a pious landowner of comfortable means.

While he was regretting his lack of familiarity with the ways of commerce, Thomas realized that the man was gazing at him with a questioning look. Had he asked something for which he expected an answer, or, as the monk feared, was he perplexed at being under such close scrutiny?

Thomas felt his face grow warm with embarrassment. "I beg pardon, Master Durant. I did not hear what you said."

The merchant bowed his head. "It is I who must beg forgiveness for indulging in idle matters. I had heard that you found the body of a Ryehill Priory nun near the bell tower. What a sad experience that must have been!"

"I did so only this morning, before dawn in fact, and already the tale has spread?" Thomas shook his head.

"This inn is close to the priory, Brother. I assume some from here may have been asked to carry the body away."

"I alerted Father Vincent, and he took charge of finding someone from Ryehill Priory to do so."

"Of course. Father Vincent! He must have been praying in the chapel when the nun fell to her death. Perhaps that was why he did not hear her."

Thomas blinked. "Hear her?"

"Scream. I assume she did unless she was dead before she fell." Durant's look suggested he thought it obvious that she must have been alive.

"She did cry out. That is why I rushed to the bell tower."

"And yet Father Vincent heard nothing. His piety is an example to us all. Few leave the world behind so completely when they pray. I am sure you had difficulty drawing him back from his prayers to handle the problems involved in such a tragic death."

"I met him on my way to Ryehill." Apparently, the wine merchant did not share his opinion of the priest, but Thomas was more concerned about something else Master Durant had said. If the priest was known for such devotion, why was he not kneeling at the altar? He was certainly not asleep in his bed. When he met Father Vincent, he assumed he was coming from the priory, but he had no proof of that. Where had the priest been?

"God must have alerted him." Durant took a moment to drink more ale, but his eyes never left Thomas. "There are rumors about the nun's death. Have you heard them?"

Thomas shook his head. He wanted to hear the tales but did not want to appear too eager.

"The story is that Satan pushed the nun from the tower." The man's hazel eyes took on a green cast as he put his jack down on the table.

The changing color of the merchant's eyes disquieted Thomas, and he shivered. Concealing his discomfort with a shrug, he said, "I saw no evidence of the Evil One. The ground was moist, and the exposed floor of the tower must have been as well. As I was told, she was in the bell tower for a good purpose. The cause of this tragedy remains a simple thing. She fell by accident."

"I am most grateful to you for telling me that, Brother. If I hear this slander again, I shall counter it. More ale?" He looked over his shoulder and waved to the serving girl.

"A kind offer, but I must refuse." Thomas rose. "Prioress Eleanor wished me to accompany her to another of the shrines. I must not keep her waiting any longer." A forgivable lie, he hoped, since he intended to visit the priory kitchen and beg food for the street child.

Master Durant thanked the monk for his company, then asked a blessing.

As the man slipped off the bench and knelt before him, Thomas gave him both a blessing and a prayer for the continued health of his wife. They parted after a few courteous words and just as the girl arrived with a small pitcher of ale.

Thomas had only gone a little distance from the inn when he suddenly realized that he and the merchant never once discussed God. Durant of Norwich was interested only in Sister Roysia's death.

How strange, the monk thought, and frowned.

He walked back and looked inside the door at the bench he had shared with the merchant.

The pitcher remained.

The man had vanished.

Chapter Eleven

"They must leave Walsingham." Prioress Ursell glowered like an avenging angel aiming a spear at a snaggletoothed demon.

Father Vincent rubbed his dripping nose. "Prioress Eleanor said she was disinclined to rush the cleansing of her soul and insisted that only Brother Thomas may decide when her penance is done."

"That means little. Her mind can be changed."

"My lady, he is a willful man and yet his prioress did select him to guide her. Perhaps a bishop or other cleric would have chosen more wisely for her, but the Order of Fontevraud is unique in the authority it gives women."

She waved this aside. "Speak firmly with him. As I have heard, he owns no rank in his own priory. As a common monk, he should seek guidance and direction from a priest owning higher merit in God's eyes." She waited, her expression suggesting that the response should be obvious.

He blinked repeatedly.

The silence grew tedious.

"You!" She thumped her hand on the arm of her chair. "Were you not found worthy by a penitent to take possession of a holy relic? Men do not give such precious gifts without asking for a boon in return. Since the man who gave you the sacred hairs from the Virgin's head did not even mention his name, you, with great humility, wondered if it was an angel who blessed you with the gift." She looked up at her staff of office, shut her eyes, and mumbled a prayer.

Father Vincent flushed and bowed his head. "Brother Thomas troubles me." The priest's eyes narrowed with disapproval. "We are all obliged to grieve over our many sins, but I have seen little evidence that he does. The monk does not behave as a penitent ought. When I ask him to join me in prayer, he walks away. For a tonsured man, I have observed little piety and far too much inclination to wander in the streets."

"Stroll amongst the wicked sons of Adam? This is the man that Prioress Eleanor relies upon for guidance?" Ursell's eyes bulged in horror. "Her reputation would suggest better judgment, and her religious rank more prudence. I have heard only high praise when her name is spoken." She hesitated, then thumped her staff on the floor for emphasis. "Yet the high praise of mortal men often polishes the truth so well that deep flaws are hidden." She smiled, tilted her head as if listening to the echo of her words, and then nodded, quite pleased with her phrasing.

"As for Prioress Eleanor, I do not question her piety in coming to Walsingham. To leave her priory for any pilgrimage, she had to seek permission from her abbess and convince her that the journey met a great spiritual need. Once here, she has proved her sincerity. None of her rank has ever walked a mile down the pilgrim road in bare feet as she did." He coughed, and his cheeks became red. "Other than you, my lady! I remember well when you walked along that same path before assuming the rule of this priory. Does that not prove my point that few are so pious?" To judge her reaction, he glanced at her, and then quickly turned his gaze, replete with reverence, heavenward.

She lowered her head with suitable modesty. Neither of them mentioned that she had walked on well-shod feet and only the distance between the Walsingham Priory gate and that of Ryehill.

"As I also learned, she rode a simple donkey, not a good horse, the entire way from Tyndal Priory. All these things point to a penitential humility far exceeding that possessed by the usual pilgrim, let alone one of her noble birth." He cleared his throat and murmured, "Of course there can be no comparison to your own exceptional piety."

"The walk was another ill-considered decision. I have seen her hobble about in pain." The prioress grimaced. "There is such a thing as virtue befouled by the sin of pride."

"I, too, have witnessed that failing in her, yet I must convey a rumor I heard from a pilgrim who resides just west of Norwich. As he told the story, some in the village near her priory claim she was granted a vision of the Virgin last summer. Prioress Eleanor has replied that she is too unworthy for such a gift. Since only Walsingham has been blessed by a visit from Our Lord's mother in our realm, this prioress seems to have come here to humbly beg forgiveness—"

"She doubts visions?"

"It is not lack of faith in visions but rather the location and recipient in this instance. Our site was uniquely favored when the Virgin not only told Richelde of Fervaques that she should build an exact copy of the house where the Annunciation occurred, but even moved the building when it was not put in the proper place. I share Prioress Eleanor's doubt the Queen of Heaven would appear to her as well and that the Virgin would do so in such a remote place as Tyndal village. That worry suggests humility resides in her soul."

Prioress Ursell frowned as she considered this.

"I have seen her praying before the Shrine of the Virgin's Lock more than most pilgrims. Her sorrow is profound, and she has not only donated a candle to our shrine, but coin." He looked very pleased.

"Even if her motive for pilgrimage is worthy, and I do not doubt your conclusions, it is still best that she and Brother Thomas leave us."

Father Vincent twitched with evident discomfort.

"Surely you do not disagree, Father! You know their reputation. If a suspicious death occurs near them, whether or not there is any true wrongdoing, they grow inquisitive. Like dogs, they eagerly sniff about." She curled her hand and bounced it around to suggest a leaping hound. "And like those beasts, they show little concern over the consequences of their unwelcome interest. Sister Roysia's fall from our bell tower is just such a death."

The priest nodded in agreement.

"You do not want them jabbing sticks of idle curiosity into this matter anymore than I." She clenched her fist, winced, and rubbed at a swollen knuckle with her finger. "It took me far too long to reclaim our reputation after the last prioress allowed a nun to flee Ryehill with a chapman." She glared at him. "I have trusted your judgment in these matters, but you know as well as I that we cannot afford any more hint of scandal. Surely it must be simple enough to find a way to make them leave."

Father Vincent licked his lips. "At least Sister Roysia is dead, my lady."

"And yet we must still consider what to do with Master Larcher." Ursell twisted her staff back and forth. The gray light in the room caused the curve of the silver crosier to flicker with dulled radiance.

Shivering, Father Vincent went to the window. Outside, a light rain was falling. The scent of dampened dust in the road, mixed with the smell of wet animals, drifted upward and into the chamber. He grimaced at the odor, closed the shutter, and walked back to face the prioress with his hands in his sleeves.

"Sister Roysia has been duly punished for her sins," he said. "I agree that the craftsman has not, but we would be wise to set the problem of Master Larcher aside until after the departure of this troublesome pair."

Her scowl might have frozen Hell. "Must we wait so long? They have no reason to link the craftsman with Sister Roysia."

"If they should hear or see anything else untoward after Sister Roysia's death, they will certainly remain to pursue their curiosity as you have so well described it."

"Do you think Brother Thomas saw what she had in her hand?" She shifted in her chair, but her look of displeasure did not change.

"He should not have seen it. A tonsured man must never touch any woman, but especially not one who had given herself to God." Father Vincent shook his head with disapproval.

"He must have touched her neck because he concluded it was broken."

"But he did not mention the cloth. That was hidden in her hand which lay under her body. Although his examination may have been inappropriate, he seems not to have done more than he claimed when we questioned him."

"You heard them talking in the chapel. What did they reveal?"

"I could not understand all they said." His voice rose as if he had been accused unjustly of negligence.

"Surely you overheard something! Were they talking about the corpse?"

"I did not hear any allusion to it, but even if they had discussed the death, my lady, they have little cause to pry into our affairs for that alone. Assuming the worst and Brother Thomas did see the torn cloth but failed to mention it to us, he would not have known its origin. The cloth could have come from anything."

"But did he see it? Did he say anything to his prioress?"

"They mumbled. Our chapel is small, and the columned walkway is short. I dared not slip closer lest I be seen."

Ursell's face was marred by fury. "If he did, and another overheard that detail, rumormongers will claim the cloth came from Master Larcher's robe. It is troubling enough that some may believe our nun had a lover. We cannot afford speculation that Sister Roysia's death was murder. I have grown impatient enough with the earlier, idle gossip, Father."

Father Vincent looked down at his feet. "When the two from Tyndal stood in this chamber, I could not have been more persuasive than you that the only conclusion possible was that of a tragic accident."

"If Prioress Eleanor has the distressed soul you claim, she may not shift her thoughts from penance to our sister's death, but I worry about her monk. It shall be your duty to urge them home, but, for now, limit his ability to talk with anyone in Walsingham. Keep Brother Thomas in the chapel where he should have remained from the moment of his arrival. Accompany him to the shrines. Make sure his knees grow raw from prayer—"

The priest reached out with a pleading gesture. "I have tried and failed to keep him where he ought to be. His duty to accompany his prioress may be understandable, but he is drawn outside for other reasons, and although I have argued with him about this, he does not listen."

"You have not told me everything then. What is the true cause of his determined waywardness?"

"He brings scraps from the priory kitchen to feed the whore who tries to defile our Shrine of the Virgin's Lock."

"Whore? He seeks the company of whores?"

Father Vincent waved away her obvious fear. "I have no reason to think he has broken his vows, my lady. If I did, I would have banished him from my chamber and the sacred shrine." The dark lines in his forehead deepened. "The whore is that street creature I caught swyving a local merchant. Although the merchant has contributed to our shrine as penance, she mocked his grief and claimed she was innocent of sin. I quickly recognized her as Satan's minion and pray that God will deliver her soul to her true master soon."

She shuddered. "You must rebuke Brother Thomas! He is blinded by evil if he believes he is providing charity when he gives succor to the Prince of Darkness. Should he continue to disobey you, threaten him!" She pressed her fingers against her eyelids as if that would clear her foggy vision. Her expression suggested weariness. "I shall instruct the nuns in our kitchen to deny him the scraps he takes for that vile creature's maw."

"And the landlord of the inn? Brother Thomas has gone there to seek bits of food as well."

"Remind the innkeeper that we recommend his inn as a proper place for pilgrims to stay. Should that hint fail to gain his cooperation, you might whisper the possibility of excommunication in his ear."

"That is a decision I would not make without advice from a higher authority."

"*Whisper*, I said. Even if you believe this instance may be outside your authority, we are obliged to alert the bishop about the wicked among us. All men know that."

He nodded. "Although I did not hear the monk and his prioress discuss Sister Roysia's death, Brother Thomas did tell her that I had rebuked him for aiding the imp. Not only did he object to my virtuous advice, but she failed to reproach him for doing so." Father Vincent grew thoughtful. "And yet she did remind him that they are here for penance and that he ought not involve himself in matters that were none of their concern."

"A statement that meant either Sister Roysia's death or feeding the evil demon of which you spoke." Ursell looked at the priest. "I am not reassured."

He pointed to heaven. "If God is kind, He may grant Prioress Eleanor the gift of understanding while she prays at the Shrine of the Virgin's Lock. She may see how benighted her monk is and cast his advice aside." But his burst of confidence lasted only a moment before his expression turned doleful.

"As you have taught us, wickedness may overcome virtue when faith is sorely tested. It is irrelevant whether the matter is the whore or our nun's death. I fear the monk's influence over her while she is enfeebled by guilt and sin." She uttered a soft groan of frustration. "You must take him by the hand and direct him firmly, Father. Remind him that God is merciful to the repentant but fearsome toward those who willfully disobey Him. As for her, take the opportunity to preach humility and obedience to those men in God's service who are holier than her monk. She is, after all, a frail woman. You say she longs for forgiveness. She must let you guide her."

"She has acted piously while here. I will try my best, but, unless I can humble him, I may not succeed with her."

Prioress Ursell tilted her head, then flushed with the happy spark of sudden inspiration. "Mention to him that his abbess in Anjou would disapprove of his consorting with whores if word of this misconduct was spread. The Order of Fontevraud is under the authority of the Pope, and the abbess would not want Rome to believe she allowed a man of questionable morals to remain in her flock unpunished, especially one viewed with such favor by her prioress of Tyndal."

He looked uncomfortable.

She ignored him. "This Angevin Order has always been favored by the family of our pious king, but both men and women within it are still ruled by a woman, a controversial practice and thus prone to error." She watched him for a moment. "The abbess surely understands the precarious nature of her supreme authority and that any scandal could be fatal to its continuance. Our problem with Sister Roysia may be pardoned more quickly. We are an unimportant house, a poor one at that and filled only with women, but Fontevraud is an unnatural Order. Any impropriety may mean the end of all tolerance for it."

He carefully duplicated her smile.

"While this worrisome monk contemplates the implications of your words, you must suggest the wisdom of ending their pilgrimage here. Outside his priory walls, Brother Thomas is too exposed to earthly temptations, and his weakness might even infect his prioress with sin. You would do well to remind him of this as well, and that obedience is a virtue."

Father Vincent watched her eyes glitter. He had seen this before and knew he had little influence over her at such times. "How far do you wish me to go in this matter of intimidation?" He began to tremble and could not stop.

"As far as you must to protect the reputation of Ryehill Priory." She sat back. "Now let us return to the question of what we should do with Master Larcher after the prioress and her monk have left Walsingham."

Chapter Twelve

Prioress Eleanor knelt in the chapel, close to the exact copy of the Holy House of Nazareth where the Annunciation took place, and contemplated the meaning of what she had just seen. As she prayed, she began to weep.

After she had left the sacred site and the moment she approached this altar, she was filled with peace. It was the tranquility that caused the tears to flow. Like a woman recovering from a ravaging illness, her body was exhausted, but fresh hope lightened her spirit. The malignant guilt she had suffered since last summer was gone. So was the fear that she had somehow encouraged others to believe she had had received one of God's singular gifts, a vision she was convinced she was unworthy to receive.

When she begged permission from her abbess to go on this pilgrimage, she had specifically intended to worship at this Holy House on the grounds of Walsingham Priory but had rejected the kind offer of Prior William to receive a private viewing. Instead, she chose to wait with other pilgrims, clustered outside the blessed shrine in the chill air, so she might share with them that trembling dread all mortals feel, standing so close to the holiest sites.

When the shrine keeper opened the door and beckoned a certain number to follow him, she was humbled by the anticipation of what she would soon see. He led them at a slow but steady pace past the small wooden statue of the crowned Virgin with a lily scepter, holding her child, and through the upper story of the simple wooden house. Even during this season, when pilgrims traveled less, there were so many longing to view the sacred place that no one was allowed to stop during the passage through.

Compared to the usual bejeweled caskets and relics encased in gold or crystal, this site was as humble as a peasant's hut. The Holy House was meant to be a crude structure, a two-story building created by local carpenters under the direction of Richelde of Fervaques, a woman to whom the Virgin had appeared many lifetimes ago.

According to the legend, the Queen of Heaven came to the widow in a dream and took her spirit to the place in Nazareth where the Annunciation had occurred. During this vision, the Virgin made sure the widow learned the exact appearance and dimensions of the house so well that Richelde could instruct the craftsmen on how to duplicate it. And when the Walsingham carpenters failed to place the structure exactly where the Virgin wished it, they awoke one morning to discover that the completed house had been moved to a different location.

This last detail delighted Eleanor, but it was the plainness of the copy that made the shrine so important to her. This was the home of a simple young woman, a girl chosen to give birth to one who would offer the balm of compassion and peace to a world replete with violence, greed, and hate.

Now that the brief tour was over and she knelt in this nearby chapel, she imagined the Archangel Gabriel with his fearsome expanse of wings. He must have terrified the young Mary, Eleanor thought. Perhaps he was gentler at the Annunciation, hiding his blinding glory that reflected his nearness to God, because he knew the profound grief she would face in the future.

A sharp pain stabbed her heart. Although Eleanor had never borne children, she knew women whose infants had died in their arms. It was a sorrow like no other, and one for which there was little solace. Again the prioress wept, this time for the woman who stood at the foot of the cross and helplessly watched as her son in his agony cried out to God, asking why he had been forsaken. No matter how strong her faith, Mary was still a woman, a mother, and Eleanor knew of nothing that said she had found that moment less than horrible.

Realizing that the chapel was growing crowded, Eleanor rose to her feet and surrendered her place to another pilgrim. As she looked around, she failed to see Mistress Emelyne anywhere. Perhaps the merchant's widow had not yet gone through the shrine, or maybe she was at the springs she had wished to visit.

Walking outside toward the holy wells, Eleanor immediately saw the woman kneeling on the stones in front of the perfectly round pools of water. After her experience at the Holy House, she was disinclined to revive her aversion for this widow. The sentiment had so little cause, she decided, and she tried to understand why she had felt such a thing.

When she and Brother Thomas had joined the company of pilgrims from Norwich, she immediately noticed the widow. In a crowd of humbler penitents, no one could miss the finely dressed woman or her exceptionally well-bred palfrey. The moment the prioress set eyes on Mistress Emelyne, she wanted to avoid her. The woman herself caused no offense, but each thread she wore, every bauble she dangled, and her merry tales of men's foibles bellowed of worldly matters.

Eleanor longed to escape from earthly concerns on this pilgrimage. Not only was she uneasy about the vision some claimed she had seen, but her successful stewardship of Tyndal Priory, deemed admirable and pious by bishop and abbess alike, demanded that she spend more time with accounting rolls than in prayer. This pilgrimage was her time to concentrate on matters of the spirit. The company of this merchant's widow, with her fur-trimmed robe bedecked with a glittering jewel or two, distracted her.

None of this was the widow's fault, and Eleanor was bound by courtesy to speak with Mistress Emelyne when the widow approached her for company. Perhaps, the prioress thought, the woman's companionship had had been forced upon her by God to teach her patience and humility as well as to give her a message

about condescending pride. If this was true, Eleanor feared she
had not been the quickest of students to understand the lesson.

But soon after they arrived at Ryehill Priory, Mistress Emelyne
had shed her thick cloak and fine robe, set aside all jewelry, and
draped herself in a plain linen smock. The stitching might have
been done with a skilled hand, a bit of embroidery around the
square neck, but the garment's cut was simple. From this deed,
Eleanor should have concluded that the widow had come to
Walsingham bearing a true pilgrim's heart, but she still found
the woman too verbose for her taste. Despite the often troubling
passion Eleanor felt for her monk, she found greater peace in
the quiet company of the gentle Brother Thomas.

For a long moment, Eleanor watched the widow kneeling by
the sacred wells, hands clasped over her face and head bowed in
ardent prayer. Mistress Emelyne had spoken of an ailment she
hoped to heal by drinking the waters. The prioress prayed she
had found the cure she sought.

Feeling more compassion, Eleanor joined the widow, lowering
herself to the hard stones that were rendered smooth and shiny
from the many who had knelt there for years beyond reckoning.

The keeper of the wells came up to her with a cup of the
healing water. She accepted it and drank deeply, the icy water
chilling her throat. Quickly, she slipped back into prayer. She
might have asked that the waters cure her of the often blinding
headaches she endured. Instead she begged that the child, Gracia,
be granted a dwelling place where loving arms would hold her
and there was enough food to sustain her in health.

As she prayed, Eleanor grew more ashamed of her unchari-
table feelings toward Mistress Emelyne, whose only sins were
worldly wealth and an abundance of friendliness. Ashamed, she
squeezed her eyes shut. How great was her need to purge herself
of arrogance and unkind judgments!

The widow now slowly rose, her gaze still lowered. Her hands
remained folded.

The prioress stood as well and faced the woman with a more
sincere smile than she had been previously wont to grant.

Mistress Emelyne looked over her shoulder, and then leaned closer to the prioress. "Is it true," she whispered, "that our beloved king plans to visit Walsingham soon before he, himself, invades Wales?"

Eleanor turned her face away so the widow would not see her disappointment. Did this woman really have a more devout nature, or was she so bound by worldly interests that news of kings and wars could distract her even in these sacred places?

But the woman's question pricked at Eleanor. Her father, Baron Adam, had said nothing of this in his last missive from the Welsh border, but, unaware that his daughter planned a journey to Walsingham, he might have omitted the news. On the other hand, she had received no message that the king would visit Tyndal Priory as part of any tour of East Anglian religious sites. If King Edward was planning to visit a shrine so close to her own priory, and she remained ignorant of it, his main purpose was likely quite secular. A stop at any holy site would be brief.

Of course she knew that King Edward had sent an army across the Welsh border. Her eldest brother, Sir Hugh, was currently with Mortimer's troops at Llywelyn's new castle at Dolforwyn. In charge of supplies, Baron Adam was worried about having adequate crossbow bolts, war horses, and carts.

Eleanor looked back at Mistress Emelyne with what she hoped was an innocent expression. "I know nothing about that," she said. "Where did you hear this news?"

The widow's eyes widened with surprise. "The rumors are rife in Norwich, my lady. Since I heard that your brother stood at the king's right hand, I assumed he told you all." Her lips puckered as if she had bitten a sour cherry. "It is time the Welsh barbarians were taught a lesson about their rebellious ways!"

"Sir Hugh would never tell me any details about such an endeavor." Eleanor lowered her eyes with feminine meekness. Her reply was truthful. Her brother had said nothing. It was her father, but she would remain silent about anything he had told her.

Mistress Emelyne nodded and then gazed back at the holy wells. "I care little about wars, battles, and the other affairs of men, events often deemed *great,* unless the actions are taken against heretics and unbelievers. Even the Welsh are Christians, I've been told. Yet it speaks well of our noble king that he might travel to these holy places so favored by his father. Surely God will now favor him on this solemn endeavor." She nodded gravely. "Like King Henry, our present king is a most Christian prince! Did he not go on pilgrimage to wrest Jerusalem back from the bloody hands of the Infidel?"

Certainly his father had been imbued with great faith, Eleanor thought. Although she had not known King Henry III until after he had begun to fail in health and mental strength, her father had told favorable tales of him. Yet Baron Adam, quick-witted though he remained, was still a man who looked wistfully over his shoulder to a time before his beloved wife died in childbirth and his heir returned from Outremer divested of joy. Eleanor suspected that his views of the dead king were deeply colored by those things they shared in more youthful and happier days.

As she considered this further, she wondered if she, too, would have preferred that less bellicose king to the current ruler, no matter how devout Edward was and in spite of King Henry's many faults.

"His father did spend much time here and donated to the upkeep of many shrines," the prioress said at last. "This was one, I believe."

"Then our current king will most certainly visit Walsingham!" The widow's hands fluttered with excitement. "I wonder when he is expected. I did not see any preparations in the town for his arrival. Usually the streets are cleansed until the very earth shines, so that the hooves of his steed may remain unsullied by the excrement of common beasts." Suddenly, she stretched her hand out as if to beg something of the prioress. "I would like to remain if he is to come. Do you not long to do so as well?"

The prioress bowed her head, allowing Mistress Emelyne to conclude that she had responded in any way the widow wished.

Had she to choose, she would prefer not to remain here for any royal visit. Although King Edward and her brother remained friends, Queen Eleanor did not favor the prioress' eldest brother quite so highly. Sir Hugh was inclined to an unseemly reluctance when it came to doing all the queen wished of her husband's courtiers. The most glaring example was Sir Hugh's recent refusal to marry one of her ladies-in-waiting. This refusal by Sir Hugh to comply had caused a quarrel between king and queen, and the king did not like such upsets. Were he to meet with Eleanor, she was sure he would firmly urge her to persuade her brother to honor the queen's desire. That was a request she ardently wished to avoid.

"Oh, do say that you are planning to stay!" The widow's voice intruded on the prioress' thoughts. "I would consider it an honor to serve you if you did."

Whatever your talents, they do not include subtlety, Eleanor thought with annoyance. "You are most kind, Mistress Emelyne, and I am grateful for your offer, but I do not know when King Edward plans to arrive. As you noted, his visit does not seem imminent if Walsingham has prepared nothing in expectation of it. I shall leave as soon as my penance is done. There is much demanding my attention at Tyndal Priory."

The widow grasped her hands together with evident regret. "I grieve to hear that, my lady. May I ask how much longer I may enjoy your edifying company? I feel so fortunate to have met you on this pilgrimage."

Eleanor was stung by a spark of outrage. This woman's tenacity bordered on the perverse, and she resented the way this woman treated her. I am not a saint, whose company gives the devout a taste of Heaven, the prioress thought, nor am I a conduit to the powerful of this realm. If the widow hopes for a meeting with the king as an attendant to this prioress of Tyndal, she will be sadly disappointed.

Eleanor glanced heavenward and hoped God would agree that she ought not encourage this woman with false and worldly hopes. And, she prayed with fervor, I should not remain in her company if, in so doing, she turns her thoughts so quickly to less devout matters.

The prioress cleared her throat. "I do not know the date of my departure. That is up to Brother Thomas and my sub-prioress, who is under instruction to send word if my presence is needed." Eleanor bit her tongue over the last remark which bordered on a lie. Sister Ruth had been given that directive, but the sub-prioress would do anything, short of selling her soul to the Prince of Darkness, to avoid sending for the prioress who had replaced her years ago as head of the priory.

The look on Mistress Emelyne's face suddenly became unreadable. "I beg forgiveness if I have offended, my lady. It was not my intent to pry," she said in a tone that, for her, was strangely calm.

Eleanor assured her that she was not offended in any way, and after the usual courtesies the two women parted.

Watching Mistress Emelyne leave the shrines, Eleanor frowned in thought. This widow had just revealed a sharper perception than the prioress believed she owned.

Then gazing back at the chill waters of the holy wells glittering with promise in the pale light, she felt troubled by that discovery but was uncertain why she ought to be.

Chapter Thirteen

As Gracia sat cross-legged in the clean straw of the stable loft next to the inn, a tear wiggled down her dirty cheek. Angrily, she swiped it away.

The red-haired monk had given her food again. Of the many who believed it an obligation to offer her charity, he was one of the few who had done so with gentleness robed in courtesy. There was no hint of grim duty in his gift, nor any trace of disdain. Perhaps that was the reason she suffered a growing affection for him, or maybe it was his vague resemblance to one of her dead cousins, but the attachment was a dangerous flaw in one who must survive on the streets. Pilgrims went back to the towns they left. Kin died. She had made this mistake of attachment with Sister Roysia, and should have learned from the error.

She scoffed at herself, trying to eradicate the weakness, but this fondness was stubborn and resisted her efforts, retreating to a smaller corner of her heart where it mocked her attempts to banish it. Sliding onto her stomach and burrowing into the dry straw to remain unseen, she tried distracting herself by watching the men who entered and left the pilgrim's inn.

This was not an idle pastime. No one living within a finger's span of death survived without studying the nuances of expression, tone, and actions in those better-fed. And Gracia was a clever student, far more perceptive than her age would suggest. She had survived while others, some older and a few claiming greater wisdom, had died last winter. It was fortunate that she enjoyed observing other mortals. If she missed the games played by children with families that sheltered them, she did not dwell on it.

For her, the inn was a fine school. As she sat at the entrance to beg, she considered various meanings for the interactions she observed. Then she would choose which one she thought was closest to the truth. When the merchant bent forward and clutched his mazer of wine in conversation with a competitor, was he bluffing fellowship to win a good deal, or was this a meeting of childhood friends?

When she was proven wrong, she struggled to discover the flaw in her reasoning. Without giving voice to the knowledge, she was well aware that youth's tender innocence lured Death like a corpse did carrion crow.

Her stomach growled. It was time to beg for food.

Scrambling down from the loft, she walked to the inn. The innkeeper tolerated her presence there, allowing her to sit near the door as long as no one complained. She rarely spoke to passersby. That was unnecessary. Her skeletal form and filthy rags were expressive enough. The charitable winced as they tossed something in the direction of her hand. Others held a scented cloth closer to their noses, looked to the other side, and walked past. Occasionally, a man found her presence offensive, and the innkeeper was obliged to chase her away. When she deemed it safe, she returned to the inn.

As she approached her spot, she noticed a man standing near the entrance. Her eyes were sharp enough to see that his dark clothing was made of fine wool and the needlework was precise and even. Yet he wore no golden chain, bejeweled cross, or rings crafted to catch the light and dazzle the eye. His grayish brown hair was as fine as down, his face neither handsome nor plain. Looking at his well-cobbled boots, she briefly coveted them. A merchant, she decided. He bore no sign of titled rank, but his unmistakable affluence argued against a lowly status.

Despite being a wealthy man, he was unusually mundane. That intrigued her. Those who strode through crowds, red-faced and with clenched fists, told the world unequivocally what they thought and who they believed they were. Others, bowing their heads to hide the state of their souls shining from their eyes, were equally easy to comprehend, although they hoped otherwise. But this man gazed straight ahead without challenge, exuded neither humility nor pride, and walked with modest purpose.

I think he has secrets, she concluded.

Deciding to watch him longer, she edged closer, lowered her gaze to avoid eye contact, and slipped into her usual spot in the dirt by the inn door. It would be interesting to discover what he wished to keep hidden.

The man did not look away from Gracia as others did. Instead, he smiled at her, reached into a concealed pouch, and bent to drop a coin into her hand.

She snatched the gift before it could hit the ground and slipped the coin into a hidden place inside her robe. The movement was swifter than a falcon plunging to catch its prey.

He nodded, as if acknowledging her skill, then walked into the inn and looked around.

Gracia bent forward to better watch.

Raising his hand to greet an unseen acquaintance, he smiled broadly and slipped onto a bench just inside the doorway.

Without moving closer to the door, Gracia could not see who was across the table from him.

"I was hoping to find you," the merchant exclaimed and waved at the serving wench. "Do you prefer wine or ale? I have found the inn's wine to be quite acceptable."

Gracia dared to inch nearer until she was almost at the entrance. Although she feared the innkeeper might send her away if she got too close, she hoped she could remain unnoticed long enough. This spot let her listen in secret with greater ease, but anyone leaving the inn might have to step around her.

She looked about. Few seemed interested in coming to the inn, or leaving it, but that would change. Huddling up to make herself even smaller, she knew she could not stay here long.

"I am not acquainted with you," said the man hidden from view. His tone was petulant and also familiar.

"But I know your reputation, Master Larcher," the fine merchant replied. "Wine, I think," he said to the hovering serving woman. "Your best. I have spoken to the innkeeper and know what he keeps for those who enjoy a fine vintage."

Larcher, the craftsman of pilgrimage badges? No wonder she thought she recognized the voice. Gracia did not like the man. Unconsciously, she rubbed her cheek where he had struck her once when she failed to step out of his path quickly enough.

"I still know you not."

"Durant of Norwich, a merchant of wine, although I invest in other merchandise if I see value in doing so." He let those words hang in the air for a moment. "I come to this town on occasion to worship at the shrine of Our Lady of Walsingham, and have seen your finely crafted pilgrim badges. The nuns of Ryehill Priory are fortunate that they were given the right to the profits from the sales."

"I do not offer a lesser price for direct purchases of the items. They are sold at Walsingham Priory for an honest one."

The merchant indicated understanding. "Yet I think your work might also be sold in Norwich at a profit to you, as well as to me."

There was a brief silence before Larcher responded. "Why should I be interested?"

Durant smiled. "Many vow to go on pilgrimage, a promise they never fulfill. Remember our beloved King Henry III who took the cross, swearing to go to Outremer and restore Jerusalem before his attention was directed to Gascony? He failed to fulfill his sacred vow, although he must have wished otherwise, but was left with the symbols of his oath. Surely we would not say that his promise was false because he was prevented from honoring it exactly as sworn. Was God not kind to him when He inspired his son to go in his stead? That must have brought peace to King Henry's soul."

Durant nodded as the woman put the jug of wine on the table. He pulled it to him, sniffed at the contents, then poured a modest serving for himself and more for the craftsman. "And so we are taught that oaths may be fulfilled in many ways. Should not the honest man have that symbol of intent to comfort him, as our former king did, when circumstances prevent him from doing precisely as he wished?"

Gracia watched Durant of Norwich close his eyes, as if in prayer, and wait. He knows his quarry, she thought, just as she knew the badge craftsman would reject nothing until he learned what was being offered and the profit he might expect. As she watched the stranger, she saw his lips curl up in a little smile as if he understood this, and she grew more eager to discover how he would play this game.

"Continue," Larcher said in a lowered voice.

"Why not offer them the opportunity to purchase a badge to remind them of their vow and give them comfort when they cannot do as they had hoped?"

"Walsingham badges in Norwich?"

"Is Walsingham not a famous site? Is it not close to Norwich? Aye, we have the shrine of Saint William, but Walsingham draws far more despite that." Durant shrugged. "Were I to suggest sales of your badges in London, I would not see a profit. London owns too many saints and has many great shrines of its own." He raised his hands to suggest the multitude of sites. "Saint Edward the Confessor is just one."

Gracia twisted a little so she could see the expression on Master Larcher's face.

He was enthusiastically scratching at the stubble on his chin.

She leaned back. She had seen Larcher do that before. It meant he smelled the chance for profit. The man from Norwich was winning his argument.

Durant poured more of the deep red wine into the craftsman's mazer, then a splash into his own. "Of course, I would act as your agent in Norwich. A small fee per badge sold would be sufficient. You are the craftsman and thus due the higher percentage."

"You interest me, Durant of Norwich."

"King Edward, as I have heard, plans to visit here soon. His father honored this site with many gifts. His son will surely do the same." Again he waited for a response.

Larcher grunted.

"Many would love to combine a pilgrimage with the chance to see King Edward, crusader and man of proven faith. If the badges were sold in Norwich, many might buy them in the passion of their desire, even if they later found they could not fulfill that wish. At least they would have the memento." He chuckled. "As we both know, tales are often told of things that never happened, yet the badge suggests a truth."

This time the grunt was warmer.

"You would lose nothing. Any unsold badges will be returned to you, and these could be purchased here as always. Let us say that you should receive three-quarters of the profit and I a quarter. I have a booth, and I would happily take them back to Norwich with me when I leave." He waited. "You would receive an agreed-upon surety lest I fail to return the unsold."

Larcher began to blink, as if he had just awakened from a dream, and cleared his throat. "You said that more would be sold before the king visits, but do you know when he will arrive in Walsingham?" He looked down at his mazer and gulped the remainder of the wine. "I do not."

"Surely you must. Are you not resident here? I have heard only rumors."

Gracia was surprised to see the Norwich man frown. Was he not close to gaining his wish? What difference did it make if the king's exact arrival date was unknown?

"I fear you have come at the wrong time, Master Durant." The craftsman's voice trembled. "I have no news at all."

Pushing his barely touched mazer aside, Durant rose. "Then I leave you. I shall remain here a few days as I came to visit the wells and Holy House. Should you learn more about the king's proposed visit, leave a message with the innkeeper. When you do, we shall meet to discuss our proposed arrangement further at a place convenient to us both. As you must understand, any agreement depends upon how quickly you learn the date."

Gracia crawled back to her usual spot. She had sensed tension between the men when the issue of the king's arrival was mentioned. She was accustomed to overhearing merchants making deals, and the language used between the Norwich man and Larcher was familiar, but she felt uncomfortable as well as curious about what she had witnessed. Had this discussion been solely about badges, or was something else involved?

Bowing her head to suggest sleep, she opened her eyelids just enough to watch the wine merchant leave the inn. A swift glance as he passed by told her that his expression was devoid of meaning, but his teeth were clenched. As he strode down the street toward Walsingham Priory, his pace suggested anger, an anomaly in one she had concluded was careful about betraying thoughts.

Gracia was perplexed. As far as she could tell, the proposed business transaction between the merchants was a trivial one. The man from Norwich surely had more important matters to interest him or he would not be as affluent as his dress suggested. Why did he care so much about selling a few Walsingham badges in Norwich?

With increasing curiosity, she slipped closer to the door and peeked into the inn. What she saw confirmed her belief that more was involved than the overheard words would suggest.

Master Larcher sat, head buried in his hands, as if he had just learned that a loved one had died. Suddenly, he looked up, reached for the wine jug, poured a quantity of red wine into his mazer, and gulped it down. For a moment, he stared at the empty cup, his eyes narrowing, then slammed it on the table and leapt to his feet with enough force to turn the bench on its side.

Gracia had just enough warning to slide out of his way before he ran from the inn. Without a doubt, this meeting involved a matter of greater import than small profits from pilgrim badges sold elsewhere to soothe men's guilt.

As she considered all she had witnessed, she remembered something else, a detail she had briefly noted. Slipping her hand into the secret place in her robe where she hid gifted coins, she drew out the one given to her by the wine merchant. It was so freshly minted, the edges were smooth and she could feel the details of the king's face. This man either had permission to mint coins or he had gotten these from one who did. Few owned coins with so little wear. This merchant from Norwich, as he had told Larcher, did have interests other than wine.

Deciding to see where this stranger went, she rose and slowly walked down the road. The gift of another coin was possible, but it was curiosity that drove her. She might have misjudged the nature of what she had overheard between the two men, for she was wise enough to know her knowledge had limits, but another possibility occurred to her. Might this be the man whom Sister Roysia had feared would soon come to Walsingham?

Instinctively, she took care not to follow him too closely.

Chapter Fourteen

Prioress Eleanor and Brother Thomas knelt before the Shrine of the Virgin's Lock. The sharp mist had been transformed into a light snow and dusted the town as if the changing season had turned its face back to winter, withdrawing the hand stretched out to a warmer time. Even the pious were disheartened by the weather. No other pilgrims had crept into the chapel, either for prayer or shelter.

Since her last encounter with Mistress Emelyne, Eleanor had felt uneasy, and the chill air in the chapel added to her discomfort. Concentrating on her prayers distracted her but had failed to quiet her spirit. As she rose from her knees, the prioress glanced at her companion and was surprised to see that he seemed distressed as well. There was an unusual scowl on his face.

"What troubles you, Brother?"

He looked up with the guilty expression of a boy caught with his hand in a neighbor's apple tree. "On occasion we have all knelt to God with anger burning inside us," he said as he stood, "but prayer should quench those flames. May God forgive me, but my orisons just now felt as heavy as stones. I could not set aside my fury, and any words I tried to utter sounded like blasphemy even to my flawed soul."

She motioned for him to follow her into the quiet of nearby shadows, and then asked him to explain.

"I find no kindness at Ryehill Priory." His eyes glittered in the gray light.

"We have already agreed that we found little of it there." She waited for him to continue, but he said nothing more. "What has happened since we last spoke?"

"I have had another conversation with Father Vincent."

Although she had seen him driven by anger, she had rarely seen him so furious. One of the reasons she both admired and loved this man was his uncommon gentleness to others, a quality many others had praised.

He struck his hand on the stone wall. "I do not know whether to weep over this man's cruelty or ask God how an imp had so easily taken on the form of a priest."

"Strong words." Eleanor spoke softly and struggled not to touch him with a comforting gesture as she longed to do.

He took a deep breath. "Only a thing without a heart could so stubbornly refuse food and shelter to a child."

"I agree and also fail to understand how he cannot see that we must first feed a child's hungry body and then seek ways to give succor to her soul."

"With your permission, I continue to bring food to this girl while remaining silent in the face of Father Vincent's rebukes." His face flushed as his indignation rekindled.

What more could this priest have done to anger Brother Thomas so? Eleanor wondered. She urged him to say more.

"When I last asked the cook in the priory kitchen for a soaked trencher and bits of cheese, she refused to give me as much as an eggshell. I was shocked, and then saw tears flowing down her cheeks. When I asked her the reason, she said that Prioress Ursell had forbidden any in the kitchen to give me food, no matter why I claimed to need it. Clearly the cook would have chosen otherwise, but she was bound to obey her superior. I did not argue."

"What a strange command for the prioress to give. We knew Father Vincent had condemned the child, but I wonder what cause Prioress Ursell has to sentence Gracia to death?"

"The tale grows darker. Next I went to the innkeeper for scraps. He also refused me and explained that Father Vincent had threatened him with hellfire if he gave me the food I asked. Unlike the nun from the Ryehill kitchen, he was more perplexed than grieved. I was tempted to explain that the priest was stricken with a hellish obsession, one he should have rejected, but I silenced myself in time. Dare I cast blame on anyone who bends to the command of one who claims to speak for God?"

Eleanor felt a moment's discomfort. Had she not gone against a priest's wishes, an act by a woman most would condemn? She straightened her back, reminding herself that she was a prioress in the Order of Fontevraud. As such, she was the earthly representative of the Queen of Heaven. Surely she had that right to oppose Father Vincent. And the Virgin was a mother, Eleanor decided, and must smile on her longing to save this child.

"Finally I said that Father Vincent must have his reasons for this warning, and I would require nothing that might put the innkeeper's soul in danger."

"Despite those words, I know you have not surrendered, Brother." Eleanor looked around but saw no lurking shadows. "I believe you have found a way around this prohibition. Confess it. I shall most likely praise, not rebuke, you."

"I fear I have acquired the sin of gluttony during this season of Lent, my lady. After the last meal, I worried that I would grow hungry before the next and slipped my small trencher into my sleeve to nibble upon later. I confess I also added bits of fish from the table."

Eleanor put a hand to her cheek in mock horror, but her cheeks grew rosy with the effort not to laugh at her monk's cleverness.

"But I did win the war against Satan. Soon after I left the refectory, I saw little Gracia. My conscience surrendered to virtue, and I gave her all that I had stolen."

"And by that act of charity you have been cleansed of the vice of gluttony, Brother. I am sure Brother John will agree when you tell him of this after our return to Tyndal." But her smile quickly faded as the sadness of the child's life overwhelmed her. "Well done!" she whispered. "Unlike others in this priory, you have followed Our Lord's commandments."

"I wish my thievery had resulted in a happy ending to the tale."

"I pray no one took the food from her."

"Father Vincent saw to whom I gave the scraps, screamed at me to snatch the offering back from her hands, and rushed at us. I stood between him and the child so she might flee with her small meal. In a rage, he clutched my sleeve and pulled me toward the chapel. Since I did not want him to hurt the child, I did not resist, concluding that it was better to suffer his rebukes than allow him to harm Gracia by word or deed."

"That was both compassionate and wise."

"Once we were in private, he accused me of consorting with wicked daughters of Eve, disobeying prohibitions meant to preserve my vow of chastity, and being so filled with evil pride that I would not listen to the wise counsel he gave me in God's name."

Eleanor started to protest but fell silent. Her face grew hot with anger over both the treatment of the child and the unjust accusations suffered by her monk.

"Once again, he demanded that I obey him in this matter of Gracia and remain in the chapel to pray, as he would expect any penitent pilgrim to do. If I longed to visit other shrines, I should do so only in his company. Were I to continue to disregard his instruction, he vowed to report my wickedness to Rome, saying that I was unchaste, disobedient, and showed signs of being the minion of Satan instead of any servant of God."

Eleanor stiffened. "Circumventing my authority in this matter is disdainful enough. To ignore the right of our Abbess Isabeau d'Avoir to render judgment in any complaint is arrogant beyond comprehension."

He bowed his head. "I told him that, my lady." Thomas was not fooled by her calm tone. He noted the whiteness of her knuckles as she gripped her hands together.

"And his reply?"

"That you must be blinded by the Devil since you had not put a stop to my wicked deeds." Thomas wondered if he was imagining the growing warmth of the air surrounding them. If not, the cause must be the fire of Prioress Eleanor's now evident rage. "As for our abbess at the mother house in Anjou, he was sure she would understand a priest's right to go directly to Rome with such a grave matter." He had rephrased the priest's actual remark which suggested more strongly that men would always have authority over women in crucial spiritual issues.

"Being descendants of Adam and Eve, we all require guidance to avoid mortal sin," she said after a palpable moment of silence. "That includes Father Vincent." Her eyes narrowed.

Thomas prayed he would never commit a crime worthy of suffering the effects of her profound outrage. A little voice hidden deep within him expressed delight that this priest had.

She glanced heavenward and sighed. "But in order for me to conclude whether or not he has any merit in his accusations…"

Thomas froze.

"Fear not, Brother. I find no fault in anything you have done." A brief smile appeared as she overcame her anger. "Indeed, this ignorant man is unaware that our founder, Robert of Arbrissel, brought many magdalenes to a chaste life by walking boldly into brothels where he preached most gently to the women there. His great virtue was his armor, and he had no cause to be afraid of temptation. If Father Vincent fears someone he denounces as a whore, either his faith is weak or his body suffers from temptations he hopes will never be known."

The rumor that he might have been a nun's lover remained unspoken in the silence of the chapel.

She looked toward the door of the shrine. "I must meet this child, Gracia, who is surrounded by such controversy before she has even reached womanhood. Do you know where to find her so that I may pose questions and determine why she has been so condemned? Like you, I doubt her part in the coupling was willful. Even if it were, God is always merciful if the heart longs for it, but if the sin was forced upon her, we must offer great comfort."

Now understanding her intent, Thomas was relieved. "We can find her, my lady. She often begs near the inn close by and in quieter places when she must avoid those who wish her ill."

"Then Father Vincent shall denounce us both for seeking the company of one he deems beyond salvation. Let him go to Rome, if he is so unwise. There he will be revealed as the heartless fool he is. I stand by our founder's teaching and example. All manner of mortals must be offered God's love, but most especially children." She looked up at him and smiled. "As for my ability to recognize wise counsel, Brother, I am firm in choosing yours over that of this feckless priest. Have no doubt about it."

Murmuring gratitude, he bowed.

Prioress Eleanor then walked toward a cluster of women who had braved the muddy road to pray here. They now rose and stood, hands clasped and eyes lowered, before the altar.

With affectionate pride, Thomas watched his prioress approach the women. Pride might be a sin, but he suspected this was one of the few times God would not condemn it.

When he had first arrived at Tyndal Priory, unmanned by abuse and mad with sorrow, he concluded that the decision to put him under a woman's rule was meant to continue his humiliation. He might have found an older woman with knowledge of the world more acceptable, having been raised by such a person, but this tiny prioress was young and convent-reared.

Wretched though he was, but having no choice in the place of his exile, he had managed to retain enough wit to obey her as required. And so he had learned how wrong he had been to doubt her. Some men, both secular and religious, might often look askance at the hierarchy within the Order of Fontevraud, but Thomas had found the blessing of calm in the curse of women's rule.

The prioress was speaking softly to one woman with a solemn expression and sobering years. Then the woman bowed, pleasure briefly sparkling in her eyes, and she accompanied Eleanor back to where Thomas stood.

Now that the Prioress of Tyndal had the attendance proper for both her vocation and rank, the three walked into the street and sought the girl accused of greater sin than any child ought to own.

Gracia, however, proved too elusive to find.

Chapter Fifteen

Master Durant was not pleased. His visit to a lay brother at Walsingham Priory had proven no more useful for his purpose than the discussion with Master Larcher. As he approached the inn, he was met with a sight that troubled him even more.

Prioress Eleanor and Brother Thomas were engaged in earnest conversations with several men and women, both townspeople and strangers on pilgrimage. How odd for a monk and prioress to be so occupied, he thought.

Although he knew he should discover their purpose, he concluded it would be unwise to openly sate his curiosity. Inquisitiveness was a failing common to all mortals, and satisfying his would not bring him undue attention, but he did not want to be questioned himself, lest their interests touch upon things he had no wish to discuss.

Circling the outside of the crowd, he entered the inn as quickly as possible to avoid notice. His decision proved wise, for he soon learned much from the innkeeper without endangering himself.

Most of the inn's patrons had gone to the shrines. The remaining few stood in the doorway and watched the activity in the road. Durant sat on a bench some distance from the door and ordered wine. He was hungry, and the serving woman went to the innkeeper to ask if the Lenten meal was ready.

The innkeeper walked over to the wine merchant. "I can offer you a root vegetable stew now," he said with an apologetic tone, "but the fish is not yet roasted. I don't like to serve it cold or overcooked, and the midday meal is some time off for most, in particular those who are worshipping at the Holy House."

Durant smiled and accepted the kind offer of stew, then expressed his appreciation of the man's concern over the quality of the fare he offered. Gesturing at the wine, one of the innkeeper's best, the merchant asked if he would join him in a cup.

The man agreed with enthusiasm. Finding a mazer, he slid onto the bench opposite, poured himself a generous amount, and asked, "Did you learn any news from those outside?" Sipping the vintage, he briefly closed his eyes with pleasure.

The steaming bowl arrived. With a sigh of satisfaction, Durant breathed in the warm scent of spices. "I was curious but confess I was too eager for some of your good fare to tarry long enough to find out." Taking a bite of the fragrant root vegetable stew, he nodded with unfeigned delight. "Someone knows a good spice merchant," he said with a grin, then asked, "What started this commotion in the street?"

"The prioress and monk from Tyndal Priory near the North Sea seek the child named Gracia who often begs outside the inn door."

Durant widened his eyes in amazement, then summoned the serving woman to bring another small jug of the same wine. When she did, he poured more into the innkeeper's cup. "Are they hoping to rescue her soul?" He asked the question with a pilgrim's eagerness.

The man's eyes were sparkling from the wine, and he took another long, appreciative swallow. "I can think of no other reason they would want to speak with her." He shook his head sadly. "It is well if they do, for they seem like gentle folk. Our Father Vincent hurls curses at her as well as stones."

"A child, you say? What evil has she done to warrant such harshness?"

The innkeeper shrugged. "The priest calls her a whore. There are rumors she has paid for food with her body, and perhaps that is true. I never saw her lure men but do not follow her when she leaves here. To my knowledge, all she does is sit quietly outside my inn with her hand outstretched. I pity her and let the girl be, most of the time."

"Has she no kin or does she beg for them as well?" The wine merchant took another bite and savored it with a sip of wine.

"Her family was poor, but not beggars, and all but the girl died with last summer's tragic fever. She has no one to take her in. The nuns of Ryehill struggle enough to feed themselves, and they hire no servants. The monks of Walsingham Priory are occupied with pilgrims and the tending of the sacred sites. They have no place for a girl."

"No one cares for orphans in Walsingham? That is most unusual."

"That fever killed many. The merchants have given shelter to their own so their charity is stretched thin. The religious have few scraps to offer compared to the number of mouths open for bread. Some poor boys with strong backs were taken in by Walsingham Priory to work, but most of the poor children became beggars and many of those died in the last winter."

Durant sipped his wine. "Yet she lived. Does she do so well at begging?"

"She's clever and must find places to stay warm." He bent his head toward the stables. "I suspect the groom lets her sleep in the straw. He thinks I do not know, and I let him believe it. But she won't live much longer even if she has gone as feral as a cat." His expression darkened. "Most girls in her situation do sell themselves to men. I might have found some place for her here, but I have hired all I can of others whose families have died. Now that she has been accused of whoredom, I dare not or I would lose custom from pilgrims." He bent his head toward Ryehill. "The nuns know I do not countenance the vice, and they send travelers here with that understanding."

Durant lifted the jug and refilled the man's cup. "Father Vincent must have cause to accuse her."

"He claims he caught her lying with a merchant in that chapel where he houses his new relic."

"A fine acquisition of which he is rightly proud. I can understand why he was angered over such a sin committed there."

The innkeeper snorted. "There is a tale about that relic, but the priest would not be happy if he heard it."

Durant sipped his wine and winked. "You might tell me before I leave Walsingham. I swear to take the story far from the ears of townsmen." He grinned and then said, "I hope the merchant of whom you speak was not Master Larcher. I had some pleasant conversation with him."

The innkeeper leaned forward and murmured, "I won't mention the guilty man's name, but he was not the badge craftsman. That one was too busy swyving a nun."

Swallowing a gasp of shock, Durant let his spoon fall into the bowl of stew.

The innkeeper's reddish face deepened in color, and he quickly changed the subject. "I take you for a kind man, Master. If you will, give the child a coin. She's never caused trouble outside our door and is thin as Death. Even if the priest is right and she has gone down the Devil's road, I would rather she find God's forgiveness and live."

Someone called to the innkeeper from across the room, begging his attention. He downed what was left in his mazer, promised to tell the tale about the relic to the merchant later, and went to speak with the man who had summoned him.

Durant slowly finished his meal alone, as he preferred it. Turning pensive, he considered what he had learned, drank a final cup of wine, and climbed the steps to his room.

There he opened his shutters, stood to one side where he might remain out of easy sight, and looked down on the activity below.

Chapter Sixteen

Master Durant rubbed at his eyes. The sun was shining directly into them.

He realized he had been watching by the window for longer than he had imagined. The sun may be weak, he thought, but it has greatly changed position since I first stood here.

Although he had learned little of value from his spying, the time spent had been worth the effort for other reasons. As a good companion amongst men, he eagerly got needed information from carefully planned conversations, but he pondered the implications of it better in solitude.

From the fewer voices heard below, he assumed the religious had finished their questionings and he could safely reveal himself. He peered down from the window.

The small clusters had broken up and moved away. The monk was talking with animation to his prioress. An older woman of sober mien stood next to her.

Durant walked away and sat down on his bed. Prioress Eleanor and Brother Thomas could be seeking Gracia for a Godly purpose, he thought. Had Sister Roysia not fallen from the bell tower, he might have assumed that was the case and questioned their intent no further. But considering that unfortunate death and the reputation of this pair, he was certain they had some other concern.

What about this girl had caught their attention?

She had certainly interested him. After his conversation with Larcher downstairs, she had followed him on his way to Walsingham Priory. Although she kept some distance behind him, she did little to remain hidden. This puzzled him. If Larcher or another had sent her with a message, she would have called out or run up to him. Had someone wanted to know who he might be visiting in the great priory, she would have been told to remain invisible, although choosing one so young to follow him was a clever trick if done with skill. He had decided to call out and beckon her to him, but Gracia had fled.

She did not lack wits, and Durant dismissed the assumption that she had followed after him to acquire another coin from his pouch. When he gave her the last one, he had looked down into two unusually intelligent eyes. There was no reason to leave her lucrative place by the inn door where many pilgrims, inclined to charity, passed. This child might be young, but the street had educated her well. To live this long by herself, she must be a clever student. Following one merchant who had tossed her one coin was unwise.

Most certainly she had not followed him to sell herself or she would not have run away when he summoned her. The innkeeper's sense of her was probably right. Durant thought it unlikely that Gracia was a whore.

His curiosity still included the question of whether or not her survival had been helped by someone who paid her for information. Since he learned from the innkeeper that she had no living kin, she was not working on behalf of a brother, father, or uncle. That did not mean that a stranger was not dangling food in exchange for tales.

Durant dismissed the idea that she was an assassin. Had she been a young boy, he might have been more suspicious, but a dagger thrust from such weak hands as hers would do little harm to an alert man. And, no matter how clever, neither boy nor girl of such youth was old enough to have honed skills only those aged by years of treachery possessed.

Nonetheless, she had followed him for a purpose, and he had not seen her since she ran from him. She could be in the pay of an enemy to provide something, even if he did not know what it was. As unlikely as that might be, Durant never deluded himself that his opposites lacked cunning.

Now this monk and his prioress were seeking her. At least they did so openly, an argument against the conclusion that they were in someone's pay themselves.

He smiled. Others might believe that those vowed to God rejected worldly affairs. He knew differently. Bishops went into battle wielding maces, and priests used clubs against those they deemed enemies of God. Priors and abbots were expected to own and use skills to gain influence and wealth.

The lords of heaven and earth had long wrestled together for a man's allegiance. No man dared ignore the will of God, even kings who might blind themselves to it for a time, but men of the Church were no less able to turn with impunity from the demands of secular lords. The lesson of Thomas Becket was one well-learned.

Durant stood and began to pace. He must think more carefully about this pair. Might they be very clever, acting in plain sight so their true motives were better hidden? After all, the child had followed him on his way to visit his other spy in Walsingham Priory. Had they sent her to find out who this person was? What were their loyalties?

He felt himself grow tense with fear and willed himself to calm so he might regain his reason.

Assessing the allegiance of the Prioress Eleanor was easy enough. Her family had supported King Henry III when many thought that decision ill-advised. Around the time of that most recent barons' war, it was irrelevant to most whether or not de Montfort secretly longed to take the throne from an inept king and his apparently feckless son. The Earl did not need a crown, only the skill to wield power effectively. But the prioress' father, Baron Adam of Wynethorpe, had been fierce in his loyalty to an anointed king, whatever Henry III's failures. It was even rumored that he actually liked the man.

In hindsight, Baron Adam had been right, as had been the baron's eldest son, Sir Hugh. The brother of Prioress Eleanor had followed Edward to Outremer where close acquaintanceship with death burned away their lush dreams of youth and made the pair leaner men in both body and spirit.

Prince Edward had left for Jerusalem already aware that he must never allow the barons to believe he was a weakling like his father. King Edward returned to England with the same shifting gaze he owned as a youth but with a better knowledge of how to keep those barons from being a trial to kings. Thus Edward had become a deadly man, but he had also learned a warrior's loyalty. Those who had fought by his side in Outremer were brothers. That included the prioress' eldest sibling.

No, Durant decided, Prioress Eleanor would join her family in their allegiance to this earthly king. In her loyalties, God would be foremost, but King Edward was his anointed ruler. Leader though she was of her priory, the prioress was also a woman and one who honored her father and loved her brother.

The merchant peeked back down at the road. The monk was still talking to a burly man whose thick arms suggested he was a blacksmith by trade. The prioress and her attendant had left.

Brother Thomas was a different problem. Durant need not ask if the monk's faith was so profound that he only longed to pray, having fully embraced the priory walls that surrounded him. His efforts to hunt down murderers, rather than spend hours in a chapel, suggested that Thomas still clung to the world. The merchant had also heard how conscientious the monk had been in his covert work for the Church under the direction of Father Eliduc, a man with a reputation for choosing men with promising skill and proven cleverness. But was Thomas willing only to serve the Church and his prioress?

When Thomas was released from his duties by Father Eliduc, the monk seemed content to follow the direction of his prioress. That suggested a man who took his vows of obedience seriously,

an impressive submission considering the unusual Order to
which he had been assigned.

The merchant gazed at Thomas for a long time. Some mocked
the tonsured men of Fontevraud's Order, claiming they lost their
manhood when they submitted to a woman's rule, but this monk
looked more like a knight with his broad shoulders and lean,
muscular body. There was nothing womanish about him, unless
his eyes, as gentle as a doe's, betrayed some feminine weakness.

Durant swiftly drew back from the window. Squeezing his
eyes shut, he cursed himself for letting his thoughts wander from
his purpose. "What are the monk's loyalties?" he muttered, biting
the ends off each word.

Being a man who collected rumors and secrets, the merchant
knew that Thomas was the bastard son of a man who unques-
tionably supported King Henry, but his mother was unknown
and probably of little worth. The monk had never been close to
his father, although the man had acknowledged his son's talents
and paid for the schooling needed to insure a comfortable future
for the boy. Such a background led sons either to loyalty or to
treachery.

As for owning a profound longing for the priory life, Durant
knew why Thomas had become a monk at Tyndal Priory instead
of an influential clerk in the service of a high ranking churchman
or even the king. For this reason, he suspected Thomas owned
only the common acceptance of Church teaching despite his
willingness to follow his prioress' orders. Her own adventures
in pursuit of justice probably satisfied his desire for action and
allowed him to make use of his singular talents as a spy.

But were there to be another rebellion in the land, Durant
had learned nothing about Brother Thomas to suggest where the
man's secular allegiance might lie. It was possible that Brother
Thomas had no firm opinions on such worldly matters and
would choose to follow his prioress in hers. It was equally possible that he might be willing to follow the direction of another,
a man who could offer him a position that was not reliant on
the whims of a woman or on a legitimate birth.

Which possibility was the most likely? With no clear loyalties, Thomas made the wine merchant nervous.

Durant walked to the sweating ewer placed near his bed and poured himself a mazer of bitter ale. It suited his mood better than wine.

Savoring the taste, he set aside thoughts about monk and prioress for the moment. Master Larcher was another problem to consider.

The man had discovered nothing of use. This might be due to Sister Roysia's questionable and untimely death. Or perhaps Larcher's failure suggested that a fatter pouch of coin had been pressed into his hand by the other side in this delicate matter of a king's assassination.

Durant put down the mazer and studied his hands. They trembled.

He was paid to be the cleverest one in any war between men of opposing factions. But was he? He always feared he would lose these battles, even though he had yet to do so.

Pride whispered that he must win. Humility suggested he would one day fail. His pounding heart longed to believe the former was right, yet feared the latter was more likely. To be the constant doubter was his most persistent weakness. He clutched his hands together to steady them, but his palms were sweating.

He looked up and watched a lazy fly circle the room. On a whim, he dipped his fingers in the ale and flicked some at the creature.

The drop hit his mark.

Amazed, he watched the fly fall to the floor. Believing it would die, he felt an odd grief for this thing without a soul and hoped it would meet death in drunken peace. As he stared at the fly, it began to crawl, then suddenly rose into the air and flew out the window, steering a wobbly course.

He laughed, relieved that he had not killed it, and then wondered if this was meant to be lesson for him.

Like that creature, he could not foresee everything in any given situation. There would be surprises and uncertainties. Yet he need not fail if struck with the unknown. He must simply pause, gather his strength, and take off in another direction. It was paralytic fear that killed a man, not the arrival of the unforeseen. He must never forget that the man who survives is the one best able to cope with whatever comes out of the shadows.

Picking up his mazer, he walked back to the window and looked down.

Brother Thomas had left as well. Had he and his prioress learned anything that might lead them to the elusive and quick-witted Gracia?

He sipped the ale as he stared at the quieter road. He should engage Brother Thomas in his own cause, he thought. That would be a bold measure, and it did not matter what the monk thought of King Edward. If carefully directed, Durant might use the man in place of the incompetent, perhaps treacherous, Master Larcher. If he was clever enough, he could obtain the information he needed and let the monk go on his way, none the wiser about the service he had performed for the merchant and his master.

Durant smiled, feeling a rare contentment. It was a good plan.

Chapter Seventeen

Prioress Eleanor hesitated at the door leading to the bell tower, held her breath, and listened carefully. Looking over her shoulder, then down the hall, she confirmed there were no witnesses to what she was about to do.

She grasped the looped rope that formed the handle on the door and cautiously opened it. The squeaking of the hinges was barely audible, but to Eleanor it was as loud as the squealing of angry pigs. Quickly slipping inside, she pulled the door closed and began climbing the stairs.

Although the prioress was a small woman with tiny feet, the steps were too narrow for easy walking. It was a dangerous climb, and, despite her care, she slipped once. The coarse rope along the wall saved her from a nasty fall.

How clever, she thought. Castle stairs were designed to keep an enemy soldier from effectively swinging his sword at a defender standing above him. This priory stairwell to the bell tower was equally well-planned to keep any man from climbing it unless he crawled slowly on his hands and knees. If another person had been with Sister Roysia in the tower, it was unlikely to have been a man, unless there was another entry besides these stairs.

Halfway to the top, Eleanor stopped to catch her breath. For a moment, she suffered a twinge of guilt. As a guest in this priory, she had no right to abuse their hospitality by wandering about at will and prying into their affairs. It was rank discourtesy.

If someone, especially Prioress Ursell, were to discover her in the tower and demand an explanation for her presence, she was unprepared to offer any.

The justification that she had taken the wrong door, and then discovered the fine view of the Walsingham shrines from the height of the bell tower, was so feeble it was an insult to utter it. Not only did everyone in Ryehill know that Sister Roysia had fallen from this place, but they were probably aware that Eleanor and her monk had the reputation for involving themselves in questionable deaths. When the prioress of Tyndal chose to go to the bell tower, she might as well have announced to them all that she believed the death to be murder and that those who ruled Ryehill were either incompetent or entangled in the crime.

Eleanor knew that she would not be here now had she not been so angered by both priory and priest. As she first told her monk, they ought not to pry into something that was neither their responsibility nor concern. Father Vincent's actions, along with Prioress Ursell's apparent collusion, had caused her to reverse her argument.

Anger is rarely a good reason for doing anything, she thought, but hers was born from indignation. There had been maltreatment of an innocent, or rather two. Her monk had committed no sin worthy of being reported to Rome, and she doubted Gracia had done anything to warrant curses and a slow death from starvation.

It seems Brother Thomas has been right, she thought. Although God was doing it obliquely, He was pushing them into this investigation.

She sighed and climbed higher. Prioress Ursell still had reason to be outraged if she caught her fellow prioress exploring where she had no reason to be. Were the situation reversed, Eleanor would be offended over a guest's rude and equally arrogant presumption. Thinking about the insult to her monk and the crime against a child, however, she felt less empathy for the prioress of Ryehill.

Reaching the end of the stairs, she pressed against the wooden panel above her head. It was light in weight. She pushed it to one side, climbed out of the stairwell onto the tower floor, and looked around.

The area was not large. The bell itself was enclosed in a high wooden frame, braced by crudely cut timber. A ladder rose into the loft, presumably to access the bell and wooden headstock for repairs. Although the bell was in shadow, she noted it was a small one and easily rung by a nun. The sound would be lost amidst the deeper tones and melodies from the Walsingham Priory bells, but this bell was only intended to alert the priory nuns to the hours for prayer.

Now that she was here and had seen the space, what did she expect to learn about Sister Roysia's death? All evidence, pointing to either fair or foul causes, would have vanished for equally acceptable or illicit reasons.

A cutting wind attacked from the northeast and bit with the sharpness of a dagger through her woolen habit. Backing away, she sought shelter in a protected corner, and then looked behind her just in time.

The wall there was only waist-high. Falling to her knees in terror, she edged closer and looked straight down into the street. The trembling that struck her had little to do with the cold wind and much to do with the realization that Sister Roysia must have fallen from this spot.

Quickly, she crawled back and braced herself against the tower containing the bell. Closing her eyes, she tried to banish the image of the horror on the nun's face as she fell to a certain death. The soul might long for the afterlife, but the mortal body was terrified by the process of dying.

She opened her eyes. Had she heard a noise other than the wind? But as she peered around, she did not see anyone who had joined her in this place, and the sound of the coming storm muted noise from the road below.

"Surely that was only a welcoming tower rat," she muttered. The weak jest did calm her, but she was certain she had heard something and decided to see if it had come from an inquisitive rodent or a curious mortal.

The wooden panel leading to the staircase was where she had left it. If a nun had climbed to the tower, she could not have left so quickly, nor would she likely have done so without speaking. Yet the prioress grew more convinced that someone was nearby.

Remaining on her knees, she crawled slowly and silently closer to the open stairwell entry. She held her breath and swiftly peeked over the edge.

A girl was sitting just a few steps down. Seeing the prioress' face, her eyes widened as if she had just seen a ghost. "Forgive me, my lady! I meant no ill."

"Nor did I think you had," Eleanor said, trying not to laugh with relief. "I am not a nun of this place but rather a pilgrim to the shrines here. My home is Tyndal Priory on the North Sea coast where I am prioress."

The child shifted uneasily. Despite the wind and fresh air, her movement sent a waft of foul odor from her long unwashed body.

"You have nothing to fear from me, for I have no authority here, but I would learn who you are and why you have come here." She smiled. "Is it the view?" She hoped the jest would calm the child.

"When I saw you, I thought you were Sister Roysia, or else her shade for I know she is dead." She wrapped her arms more tightly around her bony knees.

"I doubt the good nun's spirit would have any reason to do you harm. I have heard she was a good woman."

The child stared at her, and then asked, "Are you alone, my lady?"

Eleanor glanced around and nodded.

"I meant to ask if you were accompanied when you came to Walsingham."

"One monk. Brother Thomas is his name. We arranged to come with a party of other pilgrims." The prioress suddenly looked on this girl with new interest. *The approximate age is right*, she thought, *and the girl's eyes shine with quick wit.* "Is your name Gracia?"

The child slipped down another few steps as if to flee, but then she stopped and looked back up at Eleanor. Her expression suggested a mix of uneasiness and curiosity.

"Brother Thomas has told me of your plight, and we have been seeking you."

"For what reason?" The girl's eyes took on the look of a cornered animal.

"You deserve an honest reply, but I beg you return the favor before I give it," she said, making no move toward the child but instead sitting slightly back of the entrance.

The girl studied her, her gaze swiftly taking in as much as she could see of the small woman sitting above her. Then she nodded.

"Why do Father Vincent and Prioress Ursell dislike you so?" She held up a hand. "I know the story of the merchant's rape, but God demands we succor those who have been wronged. He is the defender of all who have no one else in the world to protect them."

Gracia folded her arms but said nothing.

As the silence lengthened, the prioress let the girl stare. Others would have grown impatient with the delay, or deemed her behavior uncouth, but Eleanor suspected that this child was taking in every nuance of her expression and listening again to every word the prioress had uttered. The experience was unsettling, but there was neither threat nor true discourtesy in the study. Gracia was simply assessing danger, her skill honed beyond anything a child of such youth should need.

The prioress' heart ached.

"You do not believe I am the Devil's spawn?"

"When Father Vincent questioned you, you claimed the man forced you to lie with him. Is that true?"

Gracia slipped up two steps closer, pressed her back against the wall of the stairwell, and bent her head before murmuring, "I told the priest that my entrails bled, and then I asked him why I would willingly suffer that."

This was more than Eleanor could bear, and she stretched her hand toward the girl. Tears began to flow down her cheeks.

Gracia hesitated, then placed her bony fist into this strange woman's palm.

"If you told the priest that," Eleanor said, her voice rough with emotion, "why does he treat you with so little charity?"

"Because I knew that he helped Master Larcher meet in this tower with Sister Roysia."

Shocked, Eleanor almost drew back but stopped herself. She did not want the child to think she had been offended. "Will you tell me more?"

Keeping a firm hold on the prioress' hand, Gracia scrambled out of the stairwell and tugged at Eleanor until the prioress followed her to the opposite side of the tower. The girl stood near the low wall and pointed downward. "Look there, my lady."

Frightened that she would be greeted with another sight of the dizzying void, Eleanor edged slowed forward.

"It is not so far." The child smiled and raised her other hand. "You may take both of these to steady yourself."

Eleanor almost said that she was too small to pull a grown woman back should she slip, but Gracia's offer revealed a kind heart. She murmured gratitude instead.

And so the prioress knelt by the wall, calmed her fears, and carefully peered down. To her surprise, the distance was not so terrifying. The priory roof was just below. The distance was great enough to cause injury, if a man were to fall, but unless he rolled off the roof, the fall should not prove fatal.

As she gazed across the roof, she noticed how close the houses on the other side of the street were to the priory. If she judged correctly, a man might safely jump the short distance between house and priory roof. The question remained how he might climb the tower. Taking courage, she looked down at the stones of the tower. There was nothing to give a foothold for climbing.

She stood up and pointed toward the roof and houses. "Please explain what this means."

"One of those houses is empty, my lady. The family died in last summer's fever." Gracia pointed to a house. "In the back of that house, there is a ladder that rises to the roof. From there, a man can easily reach the top of this priory."

"But from the priory roof to here?"

"A rope," the child replied. Then she urged the prioress to follow her back to a corner of the tower and pointed out a coiled rope lying there.

Eleanor knelt to study it. "Sister Roysia knotted this well enough so he could climb from the roof to the tower?"

The girl nodded. "Sister Roysia left it here, claiming it was meant to replace the one for ringing the bell should that one fray. When she arranged to meet Master Larcher, she secured it to a timber brace inside the bell tower itself and tossed the rope over the wall. The badge craftsman had strong arms and hands. He had no difficulty climbing it."

"Then the story is true that they met for an unchaste purpose."

Gracia firmly denied it. "They talked," she said.

"And why are you so certain?"

"I was here when they met."

Eleanor looked around in amazement. "How did you get up here?"

"Ryehill Priory has few nuns and no servants. I had sometimes seen the front door open and crept in without being caught, then hidden in this tower. But Sister Roysia once saw me outside and, having heard the story of the merchant's rape, suggested I might henceforth find the priory entry unsecured and unattended while the nuns prayed at night before their rest. It is easy for me to swiftly climb the stairwell, and I could sleep in safety. I hid in a dark corner when the nun ascended the stairs to ring the bell. She never tarried when the wind was pitiless."

"But Sister Roysia and the craftsman must have remained longer, and surely they saw you." The prioress gestured around the tower. "There is no place so dark that a sharp eye could not penetrate."

"For someone of my size there is, my lady. As you discovered, it is easy to remain just below the tower entrance and remain unseen. I know of other places for concealment as well."

"And did you observe them often?"

"They met only a few times, my lady, but I was here when they did with but one exception."

This is quite extraordinary, Eleanor thought. Although she once allowed a nun to meet with a monk, who had been the woman's husband in the world, and was confident that their encounters were chaste, she remained doubtful about Master Larcher and Sister Roysia. Yet this girl was not ignorant of sexual matters, being both poor and abused. "What did they talk about, child?" The answer to this question should give her a better idea of the circumstances.

Gracia shrugged. "Stories that Sister Roysia overheard from those who visited Prioress Ursell. I could not always hear details but understood the intent. The first time they…"

Suddenly they heard a sound like a door slamming.

Eleanor froze, but no one emerged from the entrance. She walked over and looked down the stairwell. It was empty. Perhaps she had not shut the entrance door firmly enough, and she prayed this happened often enough with such an ill-fitting door that a passing nun would think nothing of it if the wind sucked it shut.

Then she looked over her shoulder, intending to continue her conversation with Gracia.

The child had disappeared.

She called softly to her but got no response. Where could the girl have gone?

A quick glance confirmed the rope remained coiled in the place she had last seen it. Other than the wind, there was no sound in the bell tower, a place that had suddenly grown ominous and lonely.

From deep in the bell tower, a raven screamed a warning from a hidden roost, then swooped down at the prioress. She fell to her knees. The bird swerved and flew away.

Eleanor shuddered and decided she would look no further for the vanished girl. It was time she left herself. Backing down into the stairwell, she carefully replaced the wooden slat over the bell tower entrance. The descent seemed to take forever, but at last she returned to the door.

It was firmly shut.

I am sure I left it that way, she thought, then carefully listened for any noise on the other side. Praying it was safe, she slowly pushed the door open.

No one was in the hall when she emerged.

As Eleanor returned to the room she shared with others, she grew increasingly curious. How had Gracia escaped?

Chapter Eighteen

Larcher laid the pewter badge on the table and admired his intricate work. It glittered like old silver in the pale beam of light flowing from the window above. Impatient, he began to pace around the empty audience chamber at Ryehill Priory. He had made a great effort to finish the badge for the prioress of Tyndal as requested. Where was Prioress Ursell?

Twitching with annoyance, he looked around as if the woman must be hiding somewhere just to infuriate him. He had no time to wait for her to grace him with her presence. Kicking at the rushes, he muttered a curse unsuited to a religious setting.

The chamber door swung open. Outside, two women held a brief conversation before the prioress of Ryehill entered with a small nun in tow.

He glanced at the attendant, half expecting to see Sister Roysia. A chill shook him as if a ghost had touched his arm, and he began to sweat with rank fear.

"It is about time you finished that badge, Master Larcher," the prioress said as she seated herself with a muted thud onto her dark wooden chair. "Let me see it." She pointed to the item.

He bowed, then reached for the requested object and passed it to the prioress, taking care not to touch her.

No longer brightened by the outside light, the badge looked dull.

Ursell felt the weight of the badge in her hand, scowled, and hefted it again. Then she stretched the object out at arm's length to study each nuance of design.

The silence in the room felt far heavier to the craftsman than this intended gift for the prioress of Tyndal. Master Larcher's temper was growing short, and he longed to go back to his shop. The apprentices were surely growing slack in their labor without the threat of his arrival and the whip he always held in his hand. As he nervously watched the prioress, her glare suggested displeasure. He fingered the details of the Virgin in the badge, and decided he would first stop at the inn for a soothing cup of wine.

"I saw the look you gave my current attendant," Ursell said, lowering the badge and bestowing her disapproving look on the craftsman instead.

Her voice made Larcher think of the Archangel Gabriel's horn announcing Judgment Day. He swallowed, but his throat remained too dry to speak.

"She will not succumb to sin like Sister Roysia did." The prioress waved her hand toward the shadowy figure by the door. "I have made sure she understands the horrors of hellfire for any bride of Christ who breaks her vows."

Although he could not be sure, the craftsman thought he heard a muted cry of pain from the unnamed nun. "I do not understand, my lady," he whispered.

"You both thought I was a fool, Master Larcher. I knew of your meetings in the bell tower." She waited, then hissed, "I pray that Sister Roysia's death has opened your eyes to how a wrathful God punishes vile sinners."

"What meetings? What sins?" As if expecting a dagger blow, he crossed his arms across his chest.

Ursell sneered. "I smell your lie. Your sweat reeks like a sow in heat. That is the reek of unholy lust."

"Lust?" He straightened, and his pallor began to fade. "I felt nothing of the kind for your nun, nor did she for me."

"How dare you insult me and add that to your many sins!" Clutching her staff, she rose from her seat and approached the merchant. "Lest you think me an innocent, know that I left the world understanding all too well what wickedness is common in it. You met Sister Roysia in the bell tower and coupled with her like a dog." She stood so close, her spittle sprayed his face. "There is no other reason for a man and a woman to meet covertly."

He wiped his cheeks and stared at her, unable to speak.

The prioress raised a fist in front of his nose. "Deny it as the Evil One demands, but God knows what you did there."

He bent to one side and reached over to touch her staff of office. "On this I swear. God may strike me now if my hand ever touched your nun with lust."

Pulling the staff away from him, Prioress Ursell stepped back. "I hear the Devil's voice coming from your mouth."

"We did nothing of which you accuse us."

"Do you deny you met each other in the tower?"

"Bring me the witness!"

"That accusation you dare not deny. I am not so easily fooled by your weak attempt to divert me, Master Larcher." She carefully placed her staff between them. "You met, you coupled, and you killed Sister Roysia for the sin you forced upon her in her woman's frailty."

"If someone has told you this, they lie! We were chaste, and I most certainly did not kill her." He cursed himself for his phrasing. He had as good as admitted to one of her accusations.

"Then you did meet. How did you get into the bell tower?" She bent forward, her voice shaking with fury. "Tell me that, confess your sins to Father Vincent, and you might escape Hell. Sister Roysia burns there now, screaming in agony, for what she did. Do you wish to join her? Lust never burns as hot as those flames."

"I deny these accusations, my lady. I am innocent. If the dead nun burns, she does so for reasons I know nothing about." A brief smile teased at his lips. "I have naught to confess to Father Vincent that he does not already know."

She slammed her staff on the floor. "I must know how you got into the tower!"

He glared at her for a moment, then pointed to the badge she had dropped on the table while she raged at him. "That badge I now give to you as a gift, my lady. Such generosity should prove my innocence. I have been maligned by some enemy. I asked for a witness, you did not reply, and you refuse to name the person. I can only imagine the reason and none speak well for the truth of your accusation."

She stepped back and stumbled against the table edge.

He grew confident and smiled. "Perhaps you wish to find another craftsman to make your badges, although no one else in Walsingham has the skills to provide the volume at the speed you require." He waved his hand at the door. "I shall leave you now to consider the implications of your allegations. When you realize your error, I may forgive you for your attempt to throw excrement on my character, but in the future I shall expect you to give me a far better price for my work than you have heretofore."

With a gesture filled with mockery and confidence, he bowed and marched out of the chamber.

The door thudded shut.

Prioress Ursell glanced down at the pewter badge cast aside on the table. "This gift has cost me much," she muttered. "May it at least buy my flock peace from meddling, unwelcome eyes and speed Prioress Eleanor and her monk on their journey home."

Then she spun around to face the little nun near the door. "You will say nothing to anyone about this meeting, Sister. Should I hear any rumor suggesting you have ignored my command, you shall be stripped at the next Chapter and I shall personally whip you."

The nun nodded, bowed her head, and silently wept.

◇◇◇

The merchant was more angry and frightened than he dared let the prioress see. When he slammed the chamber door, he closed his eyes. Rage almost blinded him. His head spun, and he stumbled with dizziness. As if he had just eaten rotten meat, his stomach roiled.

"I humbly beg pardon, Master Larcher!"

With horror at the sound of the woman's voice, he flattened himself against the wall. After the charges flung at him by Prioress Ursell over his relationship with Sister Roysia, had he now added to his crimes by bumping into a nun?

"Are you unwell?"

He stared at her, then sighed with relief. This was no member of Ryehill's thin-cheeked religious flock. Although her dress was simple and gathered around her waist by a narrow rope, the merchant noted the fine quality of cloth. Not even Prioress Ursell could afford such attire. In fact, he reminded himself with contempt, the prioress wore a robe that was almost as patched as those of her nuns.

"I suffered only a brief moment of fatigue, Mistress," he said, his smile growing warm.

"I am most relieved!" The woman's hands fluttered with delight before settling into a demure rest. "I believe we are well met, Master Larcher."

"How so? Are we acquainted? If we are, I beg you to…"

"We are not, but I know your craftsmanship. The fame of your work has spread far beyond Walsingham." She lowered her head. "I am Mistress Emelyne of Norwich. My late husband was a prominent merchant of that place." When she looked back at him, her cheeks became a delightful shade of modest pink.

Glancing with approval at her well-rounded bosom, high forehead, and unblemished skin of fashionable pallor, Larcher found himself inclined to please this woman. And, as he admired her further, he noted that she seemed appreciative of his evident regard.

Mistress Emelyne is a pilgrim here and will soon leave, he thought. His leman need never know if he spent a few hours in bed sport with this woman. That the widow was equally inclined to find pleasure with him was unquestioned. Her fluttering eyelashes gave him all the permission he needed.

"Your praise honors me." He bowed.

"I have seen so many examples of your work in pilgrimage badges," she said softly. "Have you not also crafted a fine pewter badge for the prioress of Tyndal?"

His eyebrows arched in surprise. "But you could not have seen it. I just now brought it to Prioress Ursell."

"In the local shops, I heard much talk of your unique skill. All say that any discerning customer would find your personal crafting of fine objects remarkable." Again her cheeks flushed an alluring shade as she dared to glance briefly into his eyes. "Rumors abound that you have recently favored Prioress Eleanor."

He puffed out his chest. "I confess the tales are true."

"Then I would like to order something to remember my visit here as well. In your finest pewter, of course, and I am well able to pay the price for such a fine object."

"A special order would require consultation." He lowered his voice and stepped slightly closer to her.

"I would expect no less," she murmured.

"Will you come to my shop," he asked, "and grace my house by dining with me? My cook is well regarded, and I offer good wine." He mentioned an hour when the apprentices were not in the shop and nothing could interrupt an enjoyable courting. "Discussions of this nature are best done in comfort. Do you not agree?"

"Of course, Master Larcher. We must speak at some length about the order. You are most kind to offer refreshment and hospitality."

After he gave her directions to his shop and home, he left the priory well satisfied with himself.

For the moment, he set aside his worry over Sister Roysia's unfortunate death, his need to hide where he had been that night, and the displeasure of Master Durant. As for Prioress Ursell's curses on him, he was now free of the priest's threats. Someone had told her about his visits with the nun. Had it been Father Vincent despite their agreement?

In any case, he was now convinced that God did not condemn him for the sins he committed by meeting the nun in the bell tower, no matter what their purpose in doing so. After all, why else would his wife have chosen this time to spend a few days with her sister outside Walsingham, a visit that allowed him to share his own comfortable bed with Mistress Emelyne?

Hurrying along the road back to his shop, he chuckled. His servants were paid well enough for discretion, and he was quite pleased by the prospect of such a lush woman to delight his manhood.

He rubbed his hands. He would also make a nice profit on the badge for the widow, enough to make up for the one he had gifted that avaricious prioress.

Without question, God was smiling on him.

Chapter Nineteen

Prioress Eleanor had experienced such joy in the chapel, when her voice became one with the communal prayers of all the priory nuns, that she was reluctant to return to the strident world of mortal concerns. Even a visit to the shrines with other pilgrims would shatter this mood. Instead, she sought the quiet garden of Ryehill's small cloister and avoided all company except that of God.

On occasion, Eleanor longed for hours when she heard no conversation, saw no people, and could kneel at her *prie-dieu* in the silence of her chambers, waiting for God's peace to fill her and His wisdom to instruct her. In those moments, she envied her anchoress who had chosen to entomb herself.

But, she reminded herself, even the Anchoress Juliana had an obligation to the world of men and those who knelt outside her window, begging advice. Perhaps she should not complain that God had inspired King Henry III to appoint her the prioress of Tyndal instead of allowing her to remain a simple nun at Amesbury. What was inspired by God was still a service to Him. That she had done this assigned duty well, bringing her religious house to a more affluent and respected state, was deemed a pious act. Nor was the success an opinion formed by her own pride. It was the conclusion of others, some of whom had no cause to love her.

Sitting on a stone bench, she sighed and looked down at the funnel-shaped yellow Lent Lily near her feet. She gently touched the plant. The bright yellow petals felt so fragile, yet the plant was one of the first to bloom while spring was still an infant. How deceptive appearance can be, she thought.

Because she was a tiny woman of delicate form, many assumed that she was a weak creature. But her aunt, who had reared her at Amesbury, understood her strength of will and passion for justice in all things. As a loving jest, Sister Beatrice often said her young niece was God's pillar of iron.

When Eleanor was old enough to comprehend, her aunt told her to be prepared lest God choose her to bear the burden of dealing with the world so that other nuns would have all they needed to remain strong and pray for souls in Purgatory. Now that Eleanor was even older, she had learned a truth her aunt felt no need to explain: it was the obligation of a baron's daughter to govern priories, not to be ruled within them.

A rustling nearby interrupted her thoughts, and she gasped in surprise.

"Forgive me, my lady! I did not intend to intrude."

Eleanor instantly regretted her expression of displeasure. The young nun who stood in front of her was gaunt, and her eyes were red from weeping.

"My child, what troubles you?" Eleanor put out her hand. "Sit next to me and, if I am able, let me ease your sorrow." And she is almost a child, the prioress thought. Although older than Gracia, she looked younger than her former maid at Tyndal, Gytha, who had just married.

Collapsing on the bench beside the prioress, the nun buried her face in her hands and began to sob.

Eleanor slid closer and held her until the weeping slowed.

The nun sat up and rubbed angrily at her eyes as if they had cruelly offended her.

"Do not treat them so," the prioress said. "They have done you no ill."

"I did not mean to disturb you, my lady." The words came between gulps for air.

"Grief demands comfort, and the need for consolation is never a disruption."

The nun stared at her. "But Prioress Ursell says…" She put a hand to her mouth, realizing she should not finish that sentence.

Words you need not utter, Eleanor thought. From what she had observed, she suspected Prioress Ursell would have no patience with the weakness of sorrow. Looking more closely at the young woman's face, she recognized her. "Are you not the one who summoned me to meet with your prioress after the death of Sister Roysia?"

The woman nodded and turned pale. "I came here thinking I would be alone, my lady. Please do not tell Prioress Ursell we met or that I burdened you with my woes. She would rightly say that my faith in God's power to heal is lacking, and I confess my failure, but I do beg this singular charity of you."

Eleanor patted her hand. "Without asking, you would have that, but tell me your grief. God often heals our hearts faster when heartache is given tongue."

"In truth?"

"I have found it to be so."

The nun quickly looked around before bending closer to the prioress. "I miss Sister Roysia so much!" she murmured. "We loved each other as if we had been born from the same womb. When she died, she took my heart with her to the grave."

"Tell me about her."

A trace of happiness flickered in the young woman's eyes. "She brightened all our lives when she first came here, my lady. She was gentle to everyone, even though she often favored me with her company." She blushed and waved the last words aside as if they were of little importance. "Prioress Ursell soon noticed her sweet modesty and quiet manner and honored Sister Roysia by choosing her as her attendant when our prioress met those from the secular world in her chambers."

"A privilege indeed." Eleanor understood how valuable such a trusted companion was. Now that Gytha was married to the

Crowner, she missed her deeply. "It was a considerable responsibility for one so young."

"Not once did Sister Roysia speak of anything she learned during those meetings. She treated what she heard like a priest does a man's confession."

How interesting, the prioress thought. Here was a nun chosen by her prioress for goodness and discretion, but, after her tragic death, was discussed as if her only virtue was caring about the timely arrival of a bell ringer. And, as Eleanor had since learned, there were rumors that Sister Roysia had a lover, maybe two. The street child, on the other hand, had said...

"She has been much maligned, my lady!" The nun bent close to the prioress' ear. "I weep not only for her death but for the unjust accusations against her."

"Surely Prioress Ursell will put a stop to those."

"Our prioress and Father Vincent believe the lies and do not argue for her honor. Instead, they try to cover up a sin that never occurred."

This was a different perspective. The ragamuffin had also claimed that nothing lewd occurred between nun and man, but surely Gracia would not have been in the bell tower every time they met. "You believe they are in error?"

Again, the nun put a hand to her mouth, but loyalty to her friend would not be silenced. Her words flowed out in a rush. "In this one matter Prioress Ursell is wrong. Please do not misunderstand me! I have no wish to speak ill of our lady. We respect and obey her. She is consistent in her punishments, has no favorites amongst us, and, despite our poverty, has always provided for our needs above her own."

Eleanor nodded. Remembering the poor quality of the prioress' attire, she believed this much was true. Prioress Ursell might be disagreeable, inflexible, and even cruel, but she did not enjoy luxury at the expense of her priory. "You know that Sister Roysia was accused of meeting a man in the bell tower?"

"Yes, my lady."

"Are you claiming nothing untoward happened between them? Or are you saying such meetings never occurred?" She still found it unreasonable to assume the meetings were innocent and felt a flash of outrage. Had Sister Roysia been one of her nuns, she would have punished her severely, either for mocking her vows, if the meetings were chaste, or for the actual betrayal of them.

She frowned, but her face quickly grew hot with embarrassment as she remembered her decision involving Sister Anne and Brother John. She had no right to be so self-righteous about this equally questionable situation. Appearance, she reminded herself, is not always the same as truth.

"Sister Roysia was never unchaste. She never broke her vows!"

"It is true that they actually met?"

The nun nodded and looked away.

Gracia had shown Eleanor how the craftsman had entered the tower, not by the front door but by climbing a rope. Although the prioress believed her, she preferred confirmation of the tale. She also wanted to establish whether this nun had cause for her assertion of virtue or was imagining Sister Roysia's remarkable chastity out of the blind loyalty of friendship.

The prioress gestured toward the cloister walls. "Are these not high? How could any man climb the walls of Ryehill Priory?"

"We have had our scandals, my lady. A nun did slip away many years ago and later returned heavy with child, but Prioress Ursell has done much to reclaim our honor and reputation since she came to lead us. Although our entrance door is not always watched as it should be, we are still vigilant despite being few in number. Never once has a man slipped into our halls unaccompanied. Although Sister Roysia did meet a man in the bell tower, she swore she did not let him in the front door, lest he be observed. She did not want to endanger the reputation of our sisters, but she never told me how he got into the tower."

Gracia had come in through the door unseen, the prioress thought, but a child is swifter and probably less visible than a man. A girl would also climb those stairs to the tower with ease. A man could not.

"What reason did she have for this strange meeting?"

"She did not lie with him. She swore it!"

Eleanor nodded. "Very well, but why do this? It is against the spirit of her vows even if she did not break them in fact."

"She told me that she met with this man for a purpose God would approve."

"How could God bless such a deed, one that any reasonable person would say cast her chastity into question."

The nun shook her head with evident despair. "When I asked, she said she had already told me too much. But, lest she ever be condemned as a whore, she wanted me to know she had honored her vows and served God well."

What a strange thing to say. Did she expect to be caught? Perhaps she believed she would die. Or was Sister Roysia simply mad?

"But she was still alone with him, was she not?" Eleanor tried to think how she could question the nun further but knew it would probably be fruitless. The young woman had already said Sister Roysia refused to say more.

"She claimed she had a witness, someone to provide proper attendance."

Eleanor stared at her. "Who was this witness?"

The nun shook her head.

Was it the vagrant child? If so, how did she arrange for this? Sister Roysia must have involved another nun in this strange activity. It was not this one, in whom the dead nun had confided. Did she have another friend? Might this witness even be the killer?

Eleanor's head was spinning. There were far too many questions. Although she posed a few more questions, she was quickly convinced that the young nun had no more information.

So she ceased the interrogation and turned to consoling the grieving religious for the loss of her friend. When the nun left, she seemed calmer, although sorrow would linger as a raw wound for some time.

Eleanor remained on the bench, no longer in a contemplative mood, her peace destroyed.

She now had confirmation from two sources that Sister Roysia was meeting a man in the tower. Gracia said he was Master Larcher, that Father Vincent knew of the encounters, and that the priest assisted the pair in this dubious endeavor for an unknown reason. Prioress Ursell had learned of this and, fearing scandal, believed Sister Roysia and Master Larcher were lovers. Yet she had not stopped it.

But Mistress Emelyne claimed that rumor also pointed to Father Vincent as the nun's lover. Gracia had only told her that the priest helped the pair meet, but Eleanor had not had time to ask the child if the priest might be meeting the nun as well. Sister Roysia's friend knew about only one man. And there was an unknown witness. Gracia? Another nun? Both?

Rising from the bench, Eleanor shook her head in dismay. She must speak with Brother Thomas about all this. But she was deeply troubled by the most obvious, unanswered question.

Assuming the curious encounters between nun and craftsman had been chaste, what possible reason could they have had to meet, and why in the bell tower? Of all the explanations she could imagine, none excused the disgrace their actions brought to Ryehill Priory.

Chapter Twenty

Prioress Ursell rose from her prie-dieu and brushed dust from her robe. Her nail snagged on the rough cloth and tore a small hole. Glaring at the spot, she knew she must mend it herself. Ryehill was too poor to allow her to hire a maid, and the nun who served instead was a pitiful creature who never cleaned properly and stuck more needles in fingers than cloth.

As the prioress walked into her audience chamber, she was pleased to note the snapping fire in the grate. At least one duty had been performed properly.

The day was as chill as her mood.

Her orisons just now had been personal, and offering her distress to God had briefly calmed her. She had been shattered by the revelation of Sister Roysia's wickedness, a woman she had trusted with any secrets heard and with the knowledge of how she handled them. Letting a nun under her rule have that privilege was a delicate decision. She had erred in judging the woman suitable. Sister Roysia's betrayal had wounded her deeply.

Now she must choose another to stand inside the chambers when she had dealings with worldly men. The one she had picked for the meeting with Master Larcher was useless. Although Prioress Ursell used fear on occasion to achieve obedience, she understood that too much of it bred rebellion, and so she had only mentioned briefly to the nun that hellfire awaited those who disobeyed their religious leaders. After she had met with the craftsman and the nun had fled to the infirmarian, vomiting the little she had eaten at the last meal, the prioress concluded that the woman had no stomach for the duties of an attendant.

Prioress Ursell was too upset to note her own unconscious witticism.

As she considered the possible choices amongst her nuns to replace Sister Roysia, she regretted how few were in her charge. She knew all their weaknesses and strengths, but no name rose to mind. An aged one whose hearing had dulled might be best, she thought, but even her sole elderly nun was blessed with sharp ears.

She heard a rough scratching at her chamber door. The practice annoyed her, and today the balance of her humors was still fragile. "Enter!" she barked.

A nun walked into the room, head bowed, and hands modestly clasped.

"Why have you come to me?"

"Over a troubling matter, my lady."

"Speak, but be brief." Ursell settled herself into her chair and waved the woman to a spot a few feet in front of her.

"I do not judge what I have witnessed, for that is not my privilege, but the incident is one I believe you must hear about."

Ursell hoped this was not another complaint about special friendships or taking an extra bite at supper. Such things were duly punished, and she must be informed, but she had no patience with little frailties today. "Continue."

"The prioress of Tyndal went to walk in the cloister garden after the last Office. There she met with the nun who was so ardently favored by Sister Roysia. You know her as…"

Ursell waved that away. "Your purpose, Sister." Yet she was now interested in what this woman was saying. Studying her, she recalled that this nun had occasionally come to her with offenses that merited more than a minor penance from the guilty one. As she thought about it, she also recalled that she was one of the few in Ryehill Priory not to admire Sister Roysia.

"She has told this guest of our priory that Sister Roysia met secretly with a man in the bell tower, although she also swore that our sister claimed they did not do so for any evil purpose." Her mouth pursed with contempt. "I do not know if this tale is true, but I was shocked that anyone in our priory would say such a thing to a stranger."

"She mentioned this wickedness to Prioress Eleanor, a woman who has no cause to know of it?" Ursell began to tremble. "Were it even true, of course!"

"She did, my lady."

"What else did this child of the Devil say?"

"That there was another who witnessed these meetings."

Prioress Ursell leapt from her chair, her face pale with horror. "Who?"

"This guest, unappreciative of our hospitality, did ask our disloyal sister, but no name was spoken."

The leader of Ryehill Priory began to pace, fury replacing astonishment. "Prioress Eleanor questioned her," she muttered. "She dared to interrogate one of my nuns without my permission or my presence."

"Although I have no right to judge, my lady, I confess I was shocked that this lady of Tyndal behaved in this discourteous manner." She shook her head. "Forgive me if I err, but I believe she ought to have refused to listen to our wayward sister as soon as she understood the nature of the tale. She has no authority here and should have closed her ears to these scandalous words." Looking up, she shifted her gaze to the cross on the wall. "If the tale were true, only you have the right to know of it and render judgment, not a stranger."

"You did well to come to me with this," the prioress said.

As she looked at the nun standing meekly in front of her, she was reminded of herself at that more youthful age. How could she have been bewitched with Sister Roysia when it was this nun she should have chosen for her attendant? There was no adoring crowd around her, and the woman prayed with quiet fervor. Neither disliked nor liked, she walked about the priory with head down and eyes alert. No one noticed her. Yet she had just proven how deeply she cared about the priory's reputation.

Indeed, Prioress Ursell thought, she understands the importance as much as I.

Gesturing for the nun to kneel, the prioress gave her a blessing and graced her with a rare smile. The woman's face betrayed no smugness over the new favor she had found with her prioress, but Ursell was certain she understood that the news had pleased.

"For now, I shall not reprove our untrustworthy sister until I learn how much of her heart Satan has possessed. Be my eyes and ears in this. If she seeks out the prioress of Tyndal again to continue her scandalous talk, come to me at once. Should any discussions of Sister Roysia's virtue be held by any of our religious with anyone, I want the names, places, and details of their conversations."

The nun swore to obey, bowed humbly to her leader, and left in silence.

Prioress Ursell was filled with anger and a longing for retribution. She knew that some in Walsingham had heard gossip of Sister Roysia's sins, but a rumor with no proof may fade away or be countered. Unlike that nun who had returned from the arms of her chapman great with child, Sister Roysia had died before there was similar evidence of wickedness. As for her religious, she feared from the beginning that the story could not be kept from them, but she would forbid discussion of it.

But this chattering sister, this treasonous prattler, had spoken of the scandal to a stranger and presented the tale as truth. The punishment meted out to this creature would be long and harsh. As for Prioress Eleanor, she must find some way of silencing her.

Looking up at the stark cross on the wall near her carved chair, Prioress Ursell swore an oath that this matter of Sister Roysia and Master Larcher would be ended now before the scandal grew like a virulent cancer. When the nun died, she thought the rumors would as well, but she was troubled by the new arrogance shown by the craftsman.

"We are poor enough," she muttered. "We cannot suffer greater loss because of what has happened here."

Walking to the chamber door, she threw it open and ordered a messenger sent to Father Vincent. Master Larcher must be dealt with, finally, harshly, and now. As for this obnoxious prioress from Tyndal, Ursell would make sure the woman learned there was a penalty for insulting the leader of Ryehill.

Chapter Twenty-one

Eleanor knelt beside her monk in front of the altar holding the Shrine of the Virgin's Lock.

The woman who had accompanied her to the chapel finished her prayers and rose to find a quiet corner where she might breast-feed her querulous baby.

After her footsteps faded, the prioress whispered, "I must speak with you, Brother."

"And I with you, my lady. The matter is urgent."

"Give me your tidings first." She looked around. "I see no one too near."

"Gracia is outside," he whispered, "but we must hurry if we are to speak with her. She is afraid Father Vincent will catch her."

"By what miracle have you found the girl?"

"I saw her coming from the stable near the inn and called out. She motioned for me to follow her to a quiet street, and there I asked her to meet with us. She seems frightened, apart from her desire to avoid the priest, but would not explain why. I promised we would not endanger her."

With an apology to God for failing to offer all the prayers she had intended, Eleanor rose to her feet and told Thomas to take her to the girl. "Did she tell you that I discovered her in the bell tower, Brother? I pray I have gained her trust, but fear otherwise. She disappeared before I could ask her everything I needed to know."

"She is clever at hiding, my lady, but she trusts you. She insisted that you be with me if she were to tell her tale."

When they reached the chapel door, Brother Thomas cried out in dismay. The child had vanished.

"I do not see Father Vincent," Eleanor said, gazing down the road toward the priory, "but something must have frightened her away. I doubt she will risk her safety and meet us again."

Thomas looked in the opposite direction. "There! She beckons," he said and rushed away.

Eleanor glanced nervously behind her where the young woman was crooning to her baby while she nursed him in the chapel shadows.

She knew she should not follow her monk alone down the backstreets of Walsingham without proper attendance, but she dared not take a stranger with her lest Gracia flee. If she did not go to the child now, the girl might never help them resolve vital problems, and another murder might be committed. Brother Thomas could not pose all the questions needed because she had not had the time to tell him what she had learned.

Afraid to disobey the rules of her calling, but equally dreading the consequences if she did not, Eleanor hesitated, took one step toward the young mother, then made up her mind not to summon the woman. "May God forgive and protect me," she murmured. If He was kind, the mother would be so occupied with her babe that she might not even notice the prioress' absence.

Picking up her robe so she would not trip on the hem, the Prioress of Tyndal raced down the street after Brother Thomas.

Still ahead of the pair, Gracia veered off the main road and entered a dark street—one that was empty, narrow, and stinking of urine and garbage.

Please stop, Eleanor silently implored the girl. In this less than salubrious part of town, where residents did not pay for cleaner streets, she was grateful for the company of her tall monk.

Gracia waved the pair to a dark niche between two buildings.

Eleanor looked up and shivered. One of the buildings leaned ominously. Should her transgression in disobeying the restrictions of her vocation be deemed wicked enough, she would die with all her sins still upon her if that structure collapsed on her. Silently, she begged God not to punish Gracia and her monk for an offense that was hers alone.

"Why did you flee, child?" Thomas crouched by her side. "Speak quickly," he whispered. "My prioress should not be on these streets, but she comes out of love for you."

Gracia's face was pale. "I thought I saw the merchant in the street, Brother, the one who hurt me." She pulled on his sleeve until he bent his ear to her mouth. "If you need to find me again, the stableman for the inn has now taken mercy on me and lets me sleep in the straw of the loft when there are few horses and only he is there."

Eleanor felt her face grow hot with anger. "Has this vile creature done you any further harm?"

The child shook her head, but her gaze never left the ground.

Eleanor was not convinced that Gracia was telling the truth, but she sensed the girl did not fully trust anyone enough to confide her vulnerability. Kneeling on the other side of the child, the prioress took her hand. "What more have you to tell us? You told me in the bell tower that Father Vincent knew Master Larcher met Sister Roysia there and abetted their encounters."

Thomas stiffened in shock.

"According to one of the women who shares my quarters," Eleanor said to him, "there are rumors that Master Larcher was the nun's lover. Some also say that Father Vincent was as well. With all that has been happening, this is the first opportunity I have had to tell you."

He was stunned into silence.

Eleanor wondered if he thought the priest incapable of the sin of lust or had some other reason for such dismay.

"I do not believe Sister Roysia met with the merchant for any wicked purpose, my lady." Gracia's eyes never stopped scanning the area despite the presence of her two protectors.

"Tell us more about Father Vincent," Thomas hissed.

Gracia turned to him. "After watching the craftsman lower himself from the bell tower and flee to the top of an empty house, the priest caught Master Larcher climbing down the ladder into the garden behind. He made the merchant confess he had been meeting Sister Roysia, and I overheard the priest threaten the man with exposure unless he paid for his silence. He said the prioress would refuse to buy his badges if she knew of this." The child's lips twitched up briefly. "Father Vincent did not say it was payment to him. He called it a donation to the Shrine of the Virgin's Lock in expiation of his sins."

"Did the priest see you, child?" Eleanor had not released the girl's hand and wondered why Gracia continued to look around so fearfully. She looked behind her but saw nothing that would trouble the girl.

"They both did, and that is the reason Father Vincent hates me," she replied. "I laughed and he caught me. I swore I would say nothing. How he gets alms for his shrine is none of my affair. Yet he chose not to believe I would keep my word and has since threatened me with hellfire and rocks. When he caught the man raping me, he used that as his excuse to discredit anything I might say. Now I no longer believe I need keep silent."

Thomas looked at his prioress with a sorrowful look.

"You have said you do not think the merchant and Sister Roysia were lovers," she said. "Can you confirm or deny whether she and the priest were?"

"Sister Roysia did not couple with the merchant when I saw them, nor do I think she would commit that sin. She was a most devout nun, charitable and kind. As for the priest, she never would lie with him even if the Devil tortured her." She glanced over at the monk. "She did not like Father Vincent."

Thomas sighed. "A wise as well as a most virtuous woman."

"Did the priest know they were not meeting to lie together?" Eleanor saw the child's eyes widen slightly and knew the cause was not her question. She glanced over her shoulder. Although she thought a shadow moved, she did not see anyone in the narrow street. Squinting to focus, she decided the movement had been imagined.

"Master Larcher did not argue when Father Vincent accused him of that sin."

"Whatever their purpose was in the bell tower, I think it odd that the craftsman would not protect the nun's reputation," Eleanor said. She shifted her position. "You overheard some of their conversations. Why did they meet in such a strange way and in the tower?"

"Sister Roysia heard many things in Prioress Ursell's chambers, my lady, when visitors came. The nun said that secrets were often whispered while she waited just outside the door on those occasions the prioress was briefly called away. I do not know how she and Master Larcher knew each other. They did not behave as kin, but they were worried about a rumor that an attempt on the king's life was being planned when he came to Walsingham. Before her death, Sister Roysia told the craftsman that an assassin was nigh. Master Larcher begged her to send him word the moment she found out who the man was." She looked from one to the other. "Perhaps you will know better than I what he meant when he said: 'I must send word to my master.'"

Speechless with horror, Eleanor and Thomas stared at each other.

"She gave her word but died soon after." Gracia suddenly stood up, pulling away from the pair. Her next words came in a rush. "I never again saw Master Larcher in the bell tower. Maybe the nun was hoping to meet him the night she fell to her death. Perhaps she learned who the slayer is. I do not know." Without warning, the girl fled into the darkness between the two buildings.

Eleanor and Thomas leapt to their feet and spun around. The monk stepped in front of his prioress, but she managed to peek around him.

The only thing they could see in the gloomy street was a trotting dog in search of scraps. Not far from where the two stood, he stopped at a narrow opening and sniffed, then began to growl.

They did not move.

The dog spun around and ran toward the more traveled road. Nothing in the shadows moved.

Thomas gestured to the prioress to remain where she was with her back protected by the building. Then he edged along the walls toward the spot where the dog had stopped. When he reached the place, he jumped in front of the opening, his fists clenched in defense.

Eleanor's heart pounded like a drum.

Thomas dropped his hands and leaned into the space to look around. Finally, he walked back to her.

"There is nothing there," he said when he reached her side.

"The dog saw something," she said.

"It might have been a rat, my lady, but I think we should leave now." Thomas whispered. "I do not like this place."

"Nor do I, "she replied, "and I do not believe the dog saw a rat."

He bent his head in the direction Gracia had disappeared. "Is the child safe?"

"I pray she is. As for anything overheard, we all spoke too softly."

"I do not know what caused Gracia to flee." He looked back at the narrow space and thought for a moment. "Do you think Master Larcher might cause her harm? He knew she had witnessed the encounter with the priest."

"And she was present when he met with Sister Roysia."

"And thus the girl knew he was seeking an assassin. The merchant might choose to kill any witness to these discussions, especially a street child who could earn coin by telling enemies about his work."

"We must find a way to keep her safe, Brother. She also fears her rapist. I did not believe her when she said he had caused no further grief."

Thomas nodded. "First, let me accompany you back to the priory."

"After stopping at the chapel where I hope the young mother and her child still wait for me. I pray the babe distracted her enough to forget I was even there."

When they reached the road that went by the chapel, he hesitated to look over his shoulder and mark the spot where the dog had growled and the alley where Gracia had disappeared.

"Do not seek evil spirits alone, Brother," Eleanor said, almost putting her hand on his arm but quickly drawing back. "I fear for your soul if you do."

"I obey, my lady," he said, but his expression suggested he longed to do otherwise.

As the pair disappeared into the Shrine of the Virgin's Lock, a figure slipped out of the dark street they had just left and into another narrow space between two buildings that had a view of priory and chapel.

When the prioress, monk, and nursing mother reappeared, the phantom watched, until they reached the door to Ryehill Priory, then stepped deeper into hiding and became one with the shadows.

Chapter Twenty-two

Master Larcher gazed down on the street below his shop and belched. His stomach was sour.

He had been in a fine mood until he discovered one of his apprentices asleep. The boy had failed to complete his allotted number of badges, and this laxity caused production to fall behind the obligatory schedule. For each day there was a minimum number to finish. Today's requirement had not been met. Since the prioress would use any delivery delay as reason to pay less for the next order, no matter what he argued or threatened, he had personally whipped the offending youth to encourage refreshed enthusiasm for responsibility.

"All these youths care about is drink and whores," he muttered.

He turned from the window and poured himself another cup of wine. The vintage was silky and soothed his rebellious digestion. Drinking it also improved his mood. When Mistress Emelyne arrived for supper later that day, she would surely find the wine perfect.

Absently, he ran a hand through his hair and down his face. In her honor, he had had his hair washed and the stubble on his cheeks shaved. Even without looking into his wife's highly polished silver disk, he was confident the woman would be pleased.

The cook had been ordered to find a good roast as well, although a small one was preferred. This Lenten season might require abstinence on most days, but he told God he would trade a feast day for this one and still honor the forty days of sorrow. As added penance, his priest would probably require him to fast an extra day. He would do so willingly, but the day might have to occur after this order for the priory was complete and Lent had passed.

He licked his lips. The meat would be succulent, as spring lamb was, and would be surrounded by tender root vegetables with spices from Outremer. His cook had told him that Grains of Paradise had been purchased from the spice merchant who swore their peppery origin was from the Garden of Eden itself.

Such pleasant thoughts and the cup of wine warmed him all the way down to his manhood. He chuckled. That pleasure must be saved for last. Even though he was still virile, he believed it wise to restrain himself and, during Lent, went so far as to tie his organ down at night. Indeed, he had recently discovered that he was better able to perform with his favored leman if he swyved her less frequently. His wife did not seem to mind that he practiced abstinence with her.

He set the cup down and shifted his thoughts to another matter.

Sister Roysia's death was lamentable.

The day Prioress Ursell so outrageously cheated him on the new order, he had been quite ill with fear. The slayer was nigh, but he had no name, and his master would soon demand it. Then the nun had given him a sign that she had a message. He uttered the phrases agreed upon at their last meeting, and her reply told him to meet her that night.

Such urgency was unusual, and the meeting was ill-fated from the start. His leman had kept him too long in bed. For once, he had been thankful when his manhood failed to stiffen again at her bidding. He had rushed away but was late for the meeting with the nun. Now he was grateful.

Had he met her when expected, he might have been caught in the tower, after she slipped to her death, and been accused of heinous crimes. Instead, he was still in the road when he heard the scream, saw a man racing toward the bell tower, and wisely chose to flee back to his house.

Unfortunately, he believed she had discovered the name of the one coming to Walsingham to murder King Edward. Her urgency about meeting suggested that, and he had no way of learning it by himself. Although he was never sure how the nun got her information, she was reliable, which was why he suffered Father Vincent's bribery and the trials of meeting in that ridiculous place.

Looking down at his hands, he noted they still had burn marks from the rope used to climb the tower. At least he need no longer bribe the priest to remain silent. The man could say what he liked about lusty nuns coupling with men. Larcher's true purpose for the meetings was safe from discovery. Now that Sister Roysia was dead, no one cared about old sins when there were new ones to talk about.

But who was this assassin? It could be any man, even the wine merchant, although Master Durant had approached him in the proper manner and uttered the expected phrases to prove his authenticity. Yet there was something about the man the craftsman did not trust. Larcher felt uneasy, but there was no time to get any message through to his master and receive a reply. Durant was here and demanded answers soon.

Larcher's master did not like to be contacted, and his own messages to the craftsman were terse. His last one, slipped into a pouch and delivered by a filthy youth, had been: "A man will meet you." A few phrases were given to identify the agent, and that was all. But the enemies of the king had spies as well. The phrases might have been learned by one of them.

He shivered, and his stomach churned again. He must end his involvement in this nefarious trade. Despite the greedy prioress, he still gained enough from the pilgrimage badges that his apprentices made from a cheap tin and lead alloy. But the extra work paid him what he needed to keep his mistress in comfort and eager to welcome him to her bed.

It also paid for a man to watch her to make sure she remained faithful. A few lemans were stupid enough to seek the occasional young stallion to supplement their pleasure, but his seemed wiser than that. Give a woman enough baubles, he had decided long ago, and she would stay with the source. Although he suspected she filched from him, claiming a clasp or ring had been stolen and begging a replacement, he was tolerant. Women always seemed uneasy about their futures, but she had little cause. She was still young. He planned to keep her for a while.

Larcher sighed. So was the wine merchant his contact? He had no choice but to think so, yet he did not like it. Durant was like a ghost, insubstantial in a way no mortal ought to be.

But if he was the man to whom he was to pass on information, how could he bring him the name of the killer he was supposed to provide? The nun was dead. And if he did not succeed in his mission, he knew he might well suffer for his failure and just how painfully. He had heard of men beaten beyond all healing, bar a miracle.

Cursing, he walked back to the jug of wine and poured another cup. Somehow he must find a way to satisfy his obligation. Durant had shown profound displeasure with him, but what could he do? The number of pilgrims, amongst whom a traitorous murderer could hide, was small at the moment. When Easter week arrived, and most labor slowed to honor the death and resurrection, penitents came in swarms. If discovering a killer amongst the other sinners was beyond him now, how could he hope to do so beginning Easter week?

He cursed Sister Roysia for being so careless as to die like she did and leave him such a dilemma. She should have been more careful on the slippery floor of that damned bell tower.

His head swam. His eyes teared. Staring heavenward, he begged God not to let him suffer for his unavoidable failure at this ill-conceived task. Even the promise of Mistress Emelyne's plump breasts did not brighten his spirits.

A knock on the chamber door disrupted his grave musings.

He roared permission to enter.

A man servant nervously looked around the open door. "Master, you have a visitor who begs to see you."

Larcher growled his displeasure and looked at the light outside his window. It was too early for his tryst with Mistress Emelyne. On the other hand, perhaps the guest was a customer wanting to order an expensive piece of pewter.

"Someone I might want to see?"

"A business offer, I was told." The man looked relieved that his master had not thrown something at him.

"Bring the man up."

Master Larcher swallowed the rest of his wine, and then hid the jug. If the client needed refreshment, he would offer him a cheaper but still acceptable vintage.

Chapter Twenty-three

Thomas might not like the local prioress or her priest, but Ryehill Priory was a far safer place than the narrow, dark streets of Walsingham. He was grateful that Prioress Eleanor was now within its walls.

Before he left her, he said he would seek out Master Larcher. After hesitating a moment, she agreed. Gracia's story seemed reliable, but she was still a child. For now, all they had was her testimony, conclusions based on partial information, and gossip from a fellow pilgrim.

The merchant could clarify, confirm, or deny details—if he was willing to do so. Both Eleanor and Thomas feared he would not cooperate. The man may or may not have been a nun's lover, and he was either working to save a king or planning to kill him. He had no reason to answer any question they posed. If Thomas revealed his own knowledge of clandestine matters when he was alone with Master Larcher, the prioress had said, she feared for his safety. The craftsman was a very treacherous man.

Her deep concern pleased him. It was clear she valued his services, and he could not have felt more honored if she had been the king himself. Had she been the king, he thought with amusement, he might have earned a knighthood by now and made his dead father proud of his bastard son. Yet Thomas was content. The respect given by one whom he revered ranked far higher than the rewards granted by mortals in less favor with God than Tyndal's leader.

His prioress also expressed concern for the wellbeing of Gracia. "Larcher knew she had overheard them discussing treason," she had said. "Might he not kill her for the knowledge even if he is King Edward's man and innocent of Sister Roysia's death? Dare he let any untrustworthy witness to his secrets survive?"

"It is unlikely Larcher would kill a child," he replied, but knew the argument was weak. He was unacquainted with the man. As additional reassurance to his prioress and himself, he pointed out that Gracia had long survived due to the swiftness of her wit and feet.

"Yet the girl was afraid of some threat and fled from us," Eleanor said, "despite the protection offered by two adults and before we had finished talking. Although she fears her rapist, I doubt that man would dare approach when we were with her."

His prioress was right, he decided, and Gracia's safety was one more reason he wanted to interrogate the badge craftsman now. Even if he discovered nothing about the nun's death, he needed to learn what kind of person the merchant was.

Larcher might not be the king's man. He could be the assassin himself and have killed the nun because she had learned more about him than he deemed wise. If this were true, Gracia's life was in danger.

Having worked as a spy himself, albeit for the Church, the monk knew that men often lied about their loyalties to obtain information for their true masters. Even if Larcher were loyal to the king, the monk was quite aware that those who did this work did not always obey God's law. Despite his assurances to his prioress, Thomas was uncertain whether the craftsman would or would not kill the child to silence her.

Swearing to observe caution, he and Prioress Eleanor had separated, she to the protection of priory walls and he to the unknown dangers of Master Larcher's house. Before they did, he had begged a blessing from his lady and she had given it, adding a prayer to God for His special protection.

◇◇◇

As he walked down the road toward the shrines, he stopped a carpenter and asked the way to the craftsman's house. This man had been one the monk questioned outside the inn when he and his prioress sought information on Gracia. Proud that the monk wished further information from him, the man's chest swelled with pride and he grew talkative.

As the carpenter described, with impressive detail, each landmark on the way, Thomas' patience was sorely tried. Every turn in the road was matched by the man's torturous twists of body and hand. The monk's mouth ached with the effort to keep his lips smiling with appreciation.

Finally, the tradesman paused to catch his breath. The monk thanked him, and then raced down the road, looking back briefly to wave in gratitude. That thankfulness extended to escaping the man himself.

Master Larcher's house lay closer to the holy shrines, along a street that was wider than the ones he and his prioress had visited with Gracia. A raker was pulling refuse away from doors and dragging it into piles. A short distance away, a cart waited to haul the garbage away. With delight, Thomas noted that the cart horse appeared to be taking a nap.

Suddenly, he became aware that someone was walking close behind him. Veering toward the middle of the road, Thomas spun around and faced the man following him.

Durant stopped, raised his open hands to prove good will and that he held no weapon. "I did not mean to startle you, Brother. I was about to call your name."

You were too close, the monk thought. If you had intended as you claim and meant no ill, you would have called to me from a greater distance. "Master Durant." He did his best hide his nervousness and smiled ingenuously.

"I am honored that you remembered my name." The wine merchant's smile could have meant anything.

"I recall our conversation in the inn. You promised to stop any further rumors about the Devil being involved in Sister Roysia's death. Thus you helped preserve Ryehill Priory's reputation. That was a kind gesture."

The wine merchant bowed, but his gaze only briefly left the monk.

Thomas felt a growing apprehension. This was a puzzling man, one who probably had many secrets buried inside him, but the monk did not know if they were benign or malevolent things. He had seen the prioress' cat kill a mouse with more directness than this wine merchant played with his fellow men. And those mortals, the monk suspected, might well include himself.

"I see we are walking in the same direction. May I join you?"

Thomas was about to reply when the merchant stepped so close to him that he could feel the heat of the man's body. Durant grasped his arm and very firmly pushed the monk to move on.

Glaring, Thomas resisted, forcing the wine merchant to stop. There was no doubt that Master Durant wished to control this chance meeting. The monk was not about to become a willing follower.

Durant dropped his hand, stepped back, and laughed.

This was not the reaction Thomas had expected. Perhaps he had misjudged the merchant, or else the man was cleverer than he had assumed.

"Forgive me, Brother. I am accustomed to the world of commerce. We rarely stand still to discuss anything."

Clever, Thomas decided, but even more certainly a lie.

"I am going to visit Master Larcher and noted that you are walking that way as well. If I have not offended you, I would share that part of my journey in your company." He waved in the direction of the shrines. "I would appreciate hearing about your experiences at the holy sites."

Silently, Thomas uttered an unholy oath. Although he had also planned to meet with the craftsman, he did not want Master Durant to know that. A satisfactory explanation of why he happened to be walking this street did not come swiftly to mind, so he took the offensive before the question was asked of him.

"You have business with him?" He hoped his question did not suggest he was deliberately prying.

"I learned that he is the craftsman who makes the pilgrimage badges for the shrines here." He clapped his hands together in pleasure. "God chose to smile on me, and I met him at the inn where I am staying. In the course of sharing a very pleasant wine, I suggested we might become partners in a business venture."

Thomas looked at him with amusement. "I see that miracles do not always take place in shrines but in the world of commerce as well. That a wine merchant from Norwich sees a reason to join with a craftsman of Walsingham pilgrimage badges amazes me."

A twinkle of what might have been appreciation shone from the man's eyes. "Men who love coin are ever alert to the ways of acquiring more. I see no reason not to tell you that we thought we might extend his sales to Norwich for those planning a pilgrimage here. If a penitent owns the badge before departing, he may be more likely to fulfill his vow."

Thomas uttered a sound that could be interpreted as disbelief or delighted surprise.

"The idea may come to nothing, but the offer of compensation was a fair one to us both. I hoped to meet with him and discuss it further."

The two continued on in silence, each man lost in his own musing.

"What brings you to this part of Walsingham, Brother? It is far from any shrine." Durant's voice bit into the monk's thoughts.

Glancing at his face, Thomas knew the merchant had finished playing games with him. He should not have shown such evident doubt over Durant's explanations. If he wanted to avoid equally overt misgivings from this troubling man about his own purpose here, he would have been wiser to play the innocent.

"I have not been in Walsingham before and thought to spend a little time walking about the town. Monks do not often see the outside of our priory walls." He shrugged. "Improper or not, we always enjoy news of the outside world. I readily confess that I share this weakness, but seeing what some believe are the joys of the secular world only makes me stronger in my vocation." There is enough truth in that, Thomas thought. He and Prioress Eleanor often found too much violence beyond the walls of Tyndal.

"Then we soon part," Durant replied, "and I may not have the pleasure of your company again." He pointed to a house some doors ahead which Thomas knew, from the painfully explicit details he had been given, belonged to Master Larcher.

"It shall be as God wills it," the monk replied.

Thomas would give the wine merchant time to complete his business with the craftsman and hope Durant left soon. It would require stealth, but he might hide nearby and watch for the merchant to leave. Then it would be safe for him to visit Master Larcher.

He looked around. Unfortunately, there was nothing here to give him cause to tarry. Were he to try to hide somewhere, he might be reported. Despite his tonsure, householders did not trust strangers who lingered with no obvious purpose, and thieves never hesitated to disguise themselves. Pretending to be an innocent religious might add to their many sins, but robbers were not usually as rigorous in their faith as they were in their devotion to their trade.

Durant stopped close by the craftsman's house. "Will you give me a blessing, Brother? I am a sinful man but wish I were a more virtuous one." He knelt.

Thomas obliged him but did not add any prayer that God look with favor on this strange enterprise mentioned by the wine merchant. He doubted God would believe he meant such a thing and refused to insult Him by pretending he did.

Rising, Durant smiled at the monk. The warmth of the look seemed genuine and Thomas felt a twinge of guilt. The man still might not deserve his suspicion.

The two parted, the merchant to the door of Master Larcher and the monk to his aimless journey down the street as he tried to decide what he ought to do next.

But Thomas had not walked far before he heard running footsteps behind him.

"Brother Thomas! In God's name, please stop!"

The monk spun around, shocked by the urgency in the man's voice.

It was the wine merchant. Durant's face was ashen. "I beg you to come quickly. I need your help." His voice trembled with emotion.

Thomas nodded. This was unfeigned. Something had happened to toss aside all pretence.

Together the men rushed back toward Master Larcher's house.

Chapter Twenty-four

Father Vincent looked over his shoulder and saw the monk and wine merchant running toward Master Larcher's house. Terrified they would see him, he fled into a narrow alley.

Pressing his back against a wall, he prayed he would not faint. Were he to do so, and someone found him, he would be hard-pressed to explain what he was doing in this part of town. There was no one living here whom he had any cause to visit, except the craftsman Larcher, and that was the last person he wanted anyone to think he had just seen.

Why was he so cursed?

His head spun. Sweat ran down his back and sides. Even he could smell the sour fear oozing out of him. He whined and groaned, then muttered a prayer to God for forgiveness. Realizing he had spoken aloud, he glanced around, hoping no mortal was close enough to hear him.

There was no one around.

Easing away from the wall, he slowly peeked around the corner toward the place he had seen the two men.

No one was seeking him, or at least not yet.

Feeling a modicum of hope, he hurried down the short alley and emerged into an adjacent street.

He longed to run but knew he was wiser not to do so. If a man passed him by, he might remember that haste. If nothing else, the person might be a pious soul and stop him to ask if he could help. Why else would a priest be running unless there was a dire illness or impending death?

Again God showed His favor, and Father Vincent escaped from his questionable route and into the main road to the shrines. If anyone saw him, they would assume he was returning from worshiping at one of them.

Breathing a sigh of relief, he slowed his pace even more. Now that he was safe from pursuit, he could take the time to arrive at Ryehill Priory with the welcome news that they need no longer fear anything Master Larcher might say or do.

Chapter Twenty-five

Durant ordered the apprentices away from Master Larcher's door. Three swiftly fled back to the workshop. One hesitated, looking over his shoulder as if enchanted by violent death. Once the private stairway to the house was cleared of the curious, the wine merchant turned to Thomas. "Let us go up," he said. "I think you can guess what the lads found."

The body of the manservant lay on his back in the stairwell a short distance from the entry to his master's rooms. Thomas knelt by the man's side, but his examination was brief. There was a dagger in the chest of the corpse.

"We must send word to the sheriff or crowner," the monk said, looking down at the merchant standing a few steps below. Thomas put his hand on the servant's neck. The flesh was still warm to the touch. "The murderer left not long ago, although I fear he has escaped beyond reasonable hope of capture."

"We shall call the king's men as soon as we see what lies in those chambers, Brother." With that, Durant leapt up the stairs and past him to the entry door. He did not bother to call out or knock before going inside. The door was half open.

With a final glance at the dead man, Thomas slowly rose and followed. If he had only suspected before that this wine merchant was not all he claimed to be, he could now no longer doubt it.

Yet he followed him into the chambers without hesitation. Listening to his intuition when reason saw no logic, he believed that Durant had begged his assistance without guile. This time, Thomas was certain they shared an interest, if not an exact purpose. Whatever the man's true vocation, the monk decided he had nothing to fear from him in this matter, although he was still unhappy that he had been used to obtain information and even more that he was fool enough at the time not to realize it.

As he walked through the door into Master Larcher's living quarters, he looked around the room.

Durant knelt in front of a dark wooden chest, the three iron locks pulled up, and he was searching through the contents. A few rolls of parchment lay on the floor. A small box was upside down, the contents scattered. The smell in the room was foul, but the wine merchant paid no attention to the cause.

The body of Master Larcher was slumped over a table, his hand next to an overturned goblet, and his head in a pool of vomit.

Thomas walked over to the corpse and touched the neck. Like that of the servant, it was warm.

On the table was a pottery jug. He peered into it. It was half-filled with a wine that had a pleasant smell. The merchant apparently enjoyed fine wines, he thought. Bending to look under the table, he noticed a stain in the rushes on the side opposite where Larcher sat. He knelt, felt it, and sniffed his hand. The spot was still damp, and his fingers smelled of wine.

He glanced back at the table top. There was no second goblet, and the wine spilled from the merchant's cup was dripping next to the body.

When he stood, he saw that there were few household articles to examine. Like many people of his rank, the craftsman established his affluence by quality of craftsmanship rather than quantity of movables. Master Larcher made sure that his prosperity was on display.

Atop a heavy oaken chest, there were two large and intricately designed pewter plates, in front of which rested several well-crafted goblets. Surely, Thomas thought, Larcher had made these items himself. There was also another pitcher, full of wine. This container was made of silver.

He sniffed. Although his experience of wine was limited, the monk noted that this vintage had a harsher odor and suspected the quality was more ordinary than the one near the corpse.

Ignoring the plate, he examined the goblets. One felt damp inside. He sniffed and caught a light scent of wine. Had Larcher invited the killer to drink a cup with him, hospitality that was repaid with murder? Afterward, the man must have poured his own wine into the rushes and replaced the goblet with its fellows on the chest. How odd, Thomas thought, and walked back to the corpse.

He pulled the body back into the chair. There was no blood, no knife in the chest, but Larcher's face was contorted. Bending closer, he looked into the man's staring eyes. They were dilated, and his cheeks bore red patches. Thomas had seen this before.

Master Larcher had been poisoned.

Dipping his finger into the wine still at the bottom of the goblet, he sniffed again. There was no particular odor, although he caught just a hint of something slightly flowery. He wiped his finger on his robe.

"What have you found, Brother?" Durant rose to his feet and shut the lid to the chest with a slam. He did not look pleased.

"This was not a robbery." Thomas gestured around the room. "There is too much of value left, and I see no empty space where an item may have sat. I think the craftsman had a guest who did not want to be remembered," he said. "Yet the evidence of his visit was poorly disguised."

Durant went over to the corpse and did a quick examination. "Stab the servant. Poison the craftsman."

"That knife thrust was skillfully directed into the servant's chest for a swift death. The attacker may have stabbed him after he killed the master and as he was leaving. The servant was lying on his back, facing the chamber door. Surely Master Larcher would have been suspicious if the guest was not announced by the manservant."

Durant frowned. "It was still a dangerous plan. What if one of the apprentices had a question for his master and found the servant's body in the stairwell? Or the apprentice might have arrived after the craftsman was killed but before the servant was. If the servant caught him."

"If the former, he still would have had time to flee. Even if the apprentice saw him, but had never met the killer, escape is easy in town streets. If the latter, both apprentice and servant might have suffered a quick death, although two would have had a better chance of apprehending one murderer. I do suspect the servant was killed last, yet I agree that either plan was imperfect. I doubt the slayer stayed here long." Thomas pointed at the corpse. "That poison must have killed him quickly."

Durant nodded.

"I suspect you know the type well. Lily of the Valley?"

The wine merchant smiled, then examined the contents of the pitcher. "I know the wine. It has a fine flavor but also a smooth texture. If Master Larcher had had more than one cup, he might have preferred the feeling of it more than the taste and swallowed without noticing the sweeter flavor." He glanced back into the ewer. "Someone stewed a potent brew to kill him this swiftly."

"There is another wine over there." Thomas pointed to the jug.

Durant examined it. "A common vintage. I fear it will turn soon and find a better use in the kitchen as flavoring." He nodded at the pitcher on the table. "His guest must have been a special one to be served that." He glanced down at the stain on the floor, and his expression grew sad.

Thomas looked at the silver wine container on the chest, and then back at the more humble one made of pottery on the table. "Is it significant that the better vintage was in a common pot but the lesser in a finer pitcher?"

Durant chuckled. "I fear it means that our craftsman wished to hide the wine's poorer quality by placing it in a very attractive container."

Thomas glanced at the corpse and found he could not laugh at a dead man's foolishness. "Surely now we may send word…."

"Soon." The merchant walked over to an inside door, peered around it, and entered.

Thomas followed. The room was a bedchamber. "You have not found what you are looking for?"

Kneeling beside the bed, Durant started to peer under the mattress. "Nor what I feared I might." He glanced up at the monk.

Thomas swallowed his impatience. "If you tell me what you seek, I could help. It would take less time."

Durant sat back, lost in thought, and stared at his hands.

"The apprentices know we are in these chambers. To remain here longer without calling the king's men would cast suspicion on one of us," Thomas said. "My vocation protects me from many things, but I do not believe yours does. We both want the killer caught, even if our reasons might be different."

"You ask as if you did not fear my cause," Durant replied. His expression lacked all pretense, and his tone was firm as if he had just made an important choice.

"Should I?"

"I know who your father was."

Thomas felt as if an icy hand had grasped his heart. He willed himself to stay calm. "It is not a secret."

Durant got to his feet and waited for the monk to say more.

Thomas took a deep breath. Although he had chosen to remain silent about his parentage since his time in prison, the reasons for doing so no longer seemed relevant. Yet he had never spoken of it, fearing that he would still bring disgrace on the innocent and because he preferred the anonymity of being a simple monk with an ill-defined past. "I am not ashamed of my birth, sire or dam."

"Does your prioress know the circumstances of your birth?"

"When I took vows, I was taken into God's wider family. She is my sister and I her brother. That is the only kinship that matters in our priory."

But Thomas began to feel uncomfortable. In truth, he doubted Prioress Eleanor did know and feared her reaction should she learn his story. What did this man want of him? Now he feared the merchant was jabbing at his soft spots for some malevolent reason.

"But she has not forsaken her earthly kin. Why have you?"

"Why ask these things? Of what merit are they that you take this time to pry?"

"I ask because I must, Brother, but my heart tells me to trust you. One matter more. Do you swear to answer honestly if I promise to leave you in peace even if your reply does not please me?"

Confused, Thomas hesitated and then nodded once.

"Do you follow your family's loyalty to King Edward?"

The question was not what he feared the most—the one regarding his time in prison—but his immense relief shattered his self-control. He replied with a burst of fury. "You think I would admit to treason? You assume I would be fool enough to believe a man who says he would accept such an admission? I know you not, Durant of Norwich. I do not even know if you are a wine merchant. If you are a king's man, prove it. If not, I shall depart now before I break my vows and crack your neck!"

Durant reached deep into his robe and pulled out a tiny document, tightly rolled. "Read this. Since I trust you enough to show it to you, you must trust me enough to believe it."

Thomas unrolled it and read the brief note. His face paled. "If this is true, and the seal suggests it is, why trust me or anyone? You play a dangerous game."

"I know your story, Brother. Not just your kinship but the reason you were imprisoned and your later service for the Church. I am in a position to guarantee you will not betray me."

Thomas turned away as if he had been slapped. It had been many years since he had felt shame this fresh. He ached with it. "Let me be. I have finished my penance," he whispered. "Since that time, I have served my prioress and done so honorably."

"You do not mention God, Brother." Durant's voice was gentle.

"Her word comes from God." He looked back at the wine merchant and clenched his fists. "If you think to silence me by threatening to tell Prioress Eleanor of my past misdeeds and mixed loyalties, then tell her all. I serve her will, not yours."

"I have no intention of doing so and have said what I have for one reason only. Your loyalty to your prioress and the Church is unquestioned. I need you to serve your king with equal fervor."

Thomas knew he could bear no more of this. His head swam with the agony of old wounds torn open. The room stank of foul death. He hated this man and yet he was drawn to him for reasons he had no energy to explore. "I honor King Edward. Bastard though I am, I am still my father's son and his loyalty to the anointed king was unquestioned." He squeezed his eyes shut for a moment, then said, "If I had answered otherwise, would you have let me walk away a free man as you swore?"

Durant suddenly embraced the monk, then gently pushed him back. "I gave my word, and I am, in my way, an honorable man. Had you been traitor to our liege lord—"

"Yours, not mine." Thomas briefly smiled. "Mine represents the Queen of Heaven on earth."

Throwing his hands up with mild exasperation, Durant continued, "I had little doubt of you. Few men can feign loyalty for long when their hearts do not own it. It is a rare skill, and I mean it as a compliment to you that I never believed that to be one of your many talents."

"May we now cease this talk and concentrate on a swift search so the authorities may be summoned." The monk gestured around the room. "What do you want me to do?"

Chapter Twenty-six

Thomas did not need to be told to replace everything with care after he had sifted through. He had searched enough rooms, chests, attics, drawers, and even under floor boards when he was an agent of the Church. As a result, he and Durant finished looking through Larcher's quarters neatly, quickly, and thoroughly.

"Nothing," the monk said, turning to his companion.

"Indeed," the merchant replied, rolling up the last parchment roll and putting it back in the chest. "I had hoped for a name, but I am content that our corpse showed more discretion about his singular duties than I thought him able."

Thomas circled the rooms one more time to make certain all was well. "Surely we may now send word to the king's men."

Durant nodded and started for the door.

The monk followed. "I would advise questioning the apprentices."

"I agree, although I doubt they saw much." He looked over his shoulder and smiled. "You do well at this work, Brother Thomas."

Feeling an unaccustomed warmth, Thomas looked away, but he knew his face was flushing.

"You should talk to the lads. They might tell you far more than they would this strange and curious merchant."

The two men walked out of the chambers. When Thomas shut the door, he noted that there was no evidence of it being forced. All question about whether the killer had been a guest or a man intent on robbery vanished.

"Larcher may have lived over the shop, but this staircase was private," Durant said, carefully walking around the servant's body. "When I arrived, I found one apprentice throwing up in the corner near the stairs. He must have seen the servant, but his reaction chases away suspicion that he killed the man, or even entered his master's chambers. When he saw me, he screamed, fearing I was the murderer. The sound of his distress brought others from the shop. It was then I ran after you."

As they reached the bottom of the stairs, the monk noticed the puddle of vomit. "Will you wait for me to talk to them or are you going to fetch the sheriff?"

"The last, and I shall return with him. That will give you time to pose your questions without interruption, and you can tell me later if you learned any fact of note." He opened the door to the street and began blinking in the weak sunlight as if he had emerged from a profound darkness. "I doubt anyone will think us guilty," he said, turning to the monk. "I came on a matter of business that anyone at the inn might confirm. You wished to speak further with the craftsman, perhaps about a badge for your prioress. We delayed to search for a killer who may have hidden himself in the house."

"Simple and reasonable," Thomas replied.

As he watched Durant hurry down the road, he realized that he was enjoying this brief return to tasks similar to those assigned under the direction of Father Eliduc. But that past work for the Church had been performed as a duty and, as Father Eliduc had suggested, in penance for a sin Thomas never quite accepted as evil. This time, his sole motive was to avenge an innocent woman's death and save the life of a king. As for the latter, the monk had not realized how deep his loyalty to King Edward was, but it was no less than his dead father would have expected of a son, legitimate or not.

Thomas set these musings aside and went around the corner of the house to the workshop entrance. As he had anticipated, none of the apprentices had gone back to their labors.

Several white faces stared at him as he walked in the door.

"We have sent for help," he said. "I fear your master has been killed as well as his servant." He watched for a reaction.

Larcher might not have been loved, but the consequences of his death would be significant for them and the future of their training. With one exception, they were mere boys, and one began to weep. The eldest, Thomas assumed, was the longest in the craftsman's service and most likely to be the spokesman for them all. "Are you near the end of your apprenticeship?" he asked the young man.

The youth nodded. He had a spotty beard and scarred face, marks left from burns when he poured hot metal into the stone molds. "I am John from the High Street. Master Larcher left me in charge when he could not be here."

Thomas asked if he had seen anyone entering or leaving the house by the private entrance.

The lad shook his head. "We have just discussed this. I was here and kept the apprentices busy, Brother. We have a large order for Ryehill Priory and little enough time in which to make the badges. Work keeps us occupied, and we pay no more attention to the world than a monk might in his priory." He winked.

A young man not too ground down by a hard master, Thomas thought and smiled in return. "Why was an apprentice in the entrance?"

"Master Larcher had not been down to the shop this afternoon. Although we were delayed in completing the day's allotment for Ryehill," he said, glancing at a small apprentice hiding under a table, "we have individual requests as well as a large order from Walsingham Priory itself. I sent the lad to seek instructions on what design we should do next in the hours of light left in the day."

Noting John's look at the boy, the monk motioned for him to continue. If the craftsman was as harsh as Thomas suspected, he was glad there was one here who owned more benevolence. John would make a good master in his time.

"I heard the boy cry out and, with club in hand, rushed to discover the cause. A couple of the other apprentices followed without similar protection." He shook his head. "Boys are curious creatures and often own too little sense."

Unless she had a journeyman son, the monk thought, Larcher's widow should be grateful for this fellow's help until the continuation of the business was settled. The youth was wiser than many men of greater years.

"When I got there, I found one who called himself Durant of Norwich comforting our lad. This man had discovered the cause of the commotion. Then he swore he would take responsibility and sent us back to the shop. I saw him call to you. We know nothing else, Brother."

"Who found the servant's body?"

John pointed him out and waved the lad forward. Bending close to the monk, he whispered, "Be gentle. He is of a timid nature and now owns a belly to match."

A small, thin boy approached who shook so badly he could barely stand. The lad reminded Thomas of Gracia, but she had a bolder look. Looking into the eyes of the young apprentice, the monk was reminded of a young deer facing his hunter.

Thomas crouched so he would not loom over him and put a hand on his shoulder. "I know you went to seek the advice of your master. Tell me what happened when you got to the door of his private entry."

"It was open. I knocked. No one came. I walked in. I did not see the servant. I called out. No one answered." The boy's face turned a pale green.

Thomas squeezed his shoulder. "Well explained, lad! Now nod if I am right about the rest." He lowered his voice. "You walked up the stairs."

The boy nodded.

"You saw the servant lying outside the master's chambers."

He swallowed and looked away.

"I know you saw the dagger, but do you recall if the door to the rooms was open?"

The boy shook his head, then raced outside.

Thomas heard him retching. Turning to John, he smiled. "He answered my questions well and was very precise."

"He is the second youngest in the shop but very careful about details, Brother, and an honest lad. I have never caught him doing anything but what he was assigned."

"Did anyone else go up the stairs after you came to the boy's rescue?"

"None of us did. As soon as the lad saw the blood and knife, he fled to summon me. Before he could reach the shop, he vomited. After that, the merchant arrived and dismissed us. I watched the man. He immediately summoned you and did not climb the stairs first." He hesitated. "I doubt he had time to go upstairs before I arrived. Our lad said the man from Norwich held him while he vomited."

Thomas nodded, then spoke with the other apprentices, calming the fearful and answering the questions of others who chose to hide their terror behind curiosity.

John went out to talk with the boy who had found the corpse.

Before long, they heard the sound of men approaching. Thanking John for his help, the monk warned him that the king's men would question them further and suggested the child be spared that. "He knows nothing that you do not," Thomas said.

"I shall become the finder then," John replied. He looked around at the other apprentices. "As we all agree?"

They nodded

"But there will be no jests about my weak belly!" He grinned.

He will also be a good father when he becomes a journeyman and can wed, Thomas thought, and left the shop.

◇◇◇

Durant's expression was as grim as the scowling leader of the armed men.

Thomas guessed this was the sergeant, who served under the crowner, and that he would not be pleased to be called to this crime. The murder of a prominent man was a troublesome thing for those charged with enforcing the king's law. When a man living in the poorer alleys of the town was killed, the death might be forgotten if not quickly solved. But the town leaders would demand a hanging for Master Larcher's death and a swift justice at that.

The monk waited until the merchant had led the party into the house and then emerged alone shortly thereafter. "Are we needed?" he asked, suspecting they were not.

"Let us depart, Brother. Did the apprentices have any information?"

When the monk told him of the conversation, Durant nodded. "I now agree with you that the manservant must have been stabbed as the killer was leaving and that Larcher knew the murderer or he would not have offered him such a fine wine."

"If the poison killed him before he could cry out, I would agree."

Durant directed the monk to a quieter part of the street, away from others who were passing. "You know that I am an agent of the king. I am here because an assassin has been sent to Walsingham to kill King Edward when he arrives to worship at the shrines. Larcher was my contact, and his duty was to discover who this person was. Sister Roysia was one of his sources of information."

"A nun?"

"She was Prioress Ursell's companion when the prioress met with those who came on pilgrimage. We have another set of ears in Walsingham Priory, but the nun was the better source." Briefly, he smiled. "There are those who will tell a woman much because she does not have the ear of God like a priest does. I was often amazed at the news I got from Sister Roysia through Larcher."

"Her death was not an accident then."

Durant raised an eyebrow. "Did you ever think it was?"

"She had a piece of torn cloth in her hand when I found her body." He looked meaningfully at Durant's robe. "Well-woven and of somber color."

"It was not mine, nor was it Larcher's." He grabbed the monk's shoulder. "You must trust me, Brother. Search my room at the inn if it will satisfy you, unless you think me clever enough to destroy the robe first."

"I do."

"I would not kill someone as useful as Sister Roysia. That you might believe more readily. As for Larcher, there was nothing about him that was subtle, even in attire. He loved to dress in cloth that equaled the quality of his wine. You noted the color of the robe he was wearing when he died. It was not somber."

Thomas conceded, and then added, "I saw a man in the street who hid in the shadows near the bell tower the night she was killed."

"That was me. I saw you kneeling beside the corpse."

"If Larcher was—"

"I saw a man flee when he heard the scream and believe it was the craftsman. I did not completely trust Larcher, nor did the man who sent me here. From the information I was given before I arrived, the craftsman believed the nun hoped soon to learn who the assassin was. I chose to follow him and, if needed, get the information without the need for further messages. Later, when I met with Larcher, he confessed he had gotten no information from her before she died."

"And you have learned nothing from your other sources?"

Durant shook his head.

"You think the murderer is in Walsingham?"

"The deaths of the nun and the craftsman suggest that is the case."

Thomas rubbed at his eyes. "Then we have little time. If the killer is here, the king must be coming soon."

"That is my conclusion, although the precise date is unknown even to me."

"Do you wish my help in discovering the name? I cannot promise success, but more of us in the hunting party bodes ill for the prey we seek."

"I would be grateful, Brother, but it would be preferable if your prioress were not involved." He held up a hand. "I respect the allegiance you owe her. If needed, tell her what you must and do as you think best. I trust your judgment and your discretion."

Thomas swore it.

"I shall ask the neighbors here if they witnessed anything, before the king's men do." The merchant glanced over his shoulder toward the craftsman's house. "And one or two others."

"And I will seek more information where I think it safe to do so."

"May you find that child, Brother." Durant grinned at the surprise on the monk's face. "I thought her clever but wondered if she had a questionable master."

"If she had, she might be fatter."

With a laugh, Durant embraced the man he now seemed to trust, promised to meet him soon, then hurried off.

Watching him walk away, Thomas knew he had agreed to do this for the sake of the king. As for the wine merchant's allegiance, the monk had seen proof that the man worked for King Edward, and he did not doubt that Durant would kill anyone without hesitation if the need arose. Such ruthlessness made him uneasy, yet there was something about the man that drew Thomas to him as much as caution urged him to keep his distance.

Thomas prayed that his decision to join Durant in this endeavor would not prove deadly.

Chapter Twenty-seven

From the shadows of a narrow alley, an indistinct figure watched the armed band enter the craftsman's house.

The assassin shrugged. There was little to fear from the king's men. They would find nothing.

With a war raging against the Welsh, King Edward needed money. A special levy was likely. Merchants had fat purses to thin. But why should they pay a new tax to kill a distant foe when their immediate safety was threatened? Fretful mortals grew less eager to pay for wars when violence was amongst them, and the craftsmen of other towns had occasionally risen against the king's collectors with some success.

For this reason, the king's men had cause to keep the wealthy merchants content. It took time to seek an elusive killer, thus haste would be favored. The traitor was confident that the sheriff would drag one of Larcher's apprentices away for hanging, an easy sacrifice to the needs of this king's war.

Durant of Norwich and Brother Thomas were more worrisome.

Of least danger might be the monk. Staring at the tall man, whose red-gold hair sparkled even in weak sunlight, the slayer knew Thomas was as quick-witted as he was handsome, but surely the man would never guess who had killed the foolish merchant. The monk and his prioress were accustomed to those who slew out of greed, jealousy, or fear. They had no experience of men who shed blood so the land might be rid of a dishonorable sovereign and, in due course, graced with a nobler king. But the assassin had no quarrel with the two religious. If they had the wisdom to stay apart from this matter and leave Walsingham soon, they both could live.

The wine merchant was a different problem. From what the traitor knew of his work for King Edward, the man should die, and perhaps he would. Yet there remained the possibility that his services could be bought. Many who served one master for jewels and equally glittering promises would be willing to obey another if the bag of coin was heavier or the rewards more tempting.

Durant was clever, skilled, and too valuable to be lost if his loyalty could be transformed into a wiser one. If not, the slayer concluded, a knife in the throat while he let himself be pleasured in a dark alley would be a simple task. Apart from a few, most spies did not long survive the turmoil of dark plots.

The murderer tensed.

The monk and wine merchant were leaving.

Slipping deeper into the alley, the traitor pressed against a wall and further pondered what should happen next.

Durant would seek witnesses who might have seen someone approach the private entrance, although he probably suspected that would be a waste of time. To let oneself be noticed was the work of an amateur, and Durant must know his quarry was no apprentice in these matters. Still, the man had no choice but to ask his questions, and the assassin was pleased that this futile search would keep the wine merchant busy.

As for the monk, it was probable that he would also look for information elsewhere. Talking to the little beggar was his most likely choice, and she knew nothing. Had she, she would have been strangled by now, a crime any reasonable person would attribute to the dangers of living on the streets.

Peering around the corner, the killer confirmed that no one was approaching this alley and decided it was safe to leave as well.

Some would say it was unwise to remain in Walsingham after killing the craftsman and advise escape. But that counsel failed to take into account what was involved in the greater goal of killing a king. Not only was it necessary to stay until the king came to Walsingham, but fleeing without good cause sparked interest. By themselves, the king's men might not recognize a fugitive as a murderer, but Master Durant could and would not hesitate to point a finger in the right direction.

Mistakes in the execution of lofty deeds must never be made. Even little ones could be fatal to the purpose. Careful though the assassin had been, there was one thing that had not been done, something that should have been destroyed after the death of Sister Roysia.

But discovery of the nun's body had been unfortunately swift. There had been little time or privacy to take care of the matter then. Ryehill Priory might be small, but the nuns did occasionally walk the hall outside the tower door. Escape without detection from the bell tower had been paramount.

With all the nuns at prayer, now was the right moment to remedy that error.

If anyone had been standing outside Master Larcher's house just then, they might have seen a vague shape become one with the darkness of that narrow alley leading to the nun's priory. Perhaps they would have asked, in this town of sacred shrines, if the creature they witnessed was mortal at all. Might it be a damned soul still seeking absolution when there was no longer any hope of it?

Chapter Twenty-eight

In their tiny private chapel within the priory, the nuns of Ryehill softly intoned the words of the Office. The chant, which usually calmed her, stabbed at Eleanor's ears like pricking thorns. To dull the pain, she pressed her hands against the sides of her head.

A nun glanced at her with an anxious look as if closing her ears to the chant meant the prioress of Tyndal was struggling with Satan.

Eleanor ignored her. This was the start of one of her terrible headaches.

With the turmoil after the death of Sister Roysia, she had failed to take her daily doses of feverfew prescribed by Sister Anne, and she was about to suffer for that negligence. Her stomach roiled, and she silently berated herself.

The life of King Edward was in danger, and a nun had been killed. This was not the time to flee to a dark room where she prayed she might endure a pounding so fierce that it promised to burst her skull like a stone shot from a trebuchet. She must try to lessen the severity of this illness.

When she had joined them all at prayer, she chose to kneel away from any direct sunlight in the back of the chapel. She should have realized then that the sensitivity of her eyes to a paltry light did not bode well. Soon she could not bear the pain from the flickering candles, let alone the weak sunlight from the one window, and she began to feel nauseous.

Eleanor rose. Out of the corner of her eye, she saw the frightened nun cross herself. The prioress quickly slipped out of the chapel.

The hallway on the way back to the pilgrims' chamber was empty. Briefly, she hesitated at the ill-fitting entry door to the bell tower. It grieved her that Ryehill was so poor that the only proper door it could afford was the one seen by the world.

But she quickly walked on. The pain had grown too much to bear no matter how much she longed to concentrate on prayer or to seek more clues that might lead to a killer. She must find the feverfew that Sister Anne had put in linen packets for the journey.

When she entered the guest chamber, no one was there. The woman and her child, who so kindly accompanied her to meet Brother Thomas at the Shrine of the Virgin's Lock, had returned home with her husband. Only she and Mistress Emelyne now shared the quarters, although the nuns had laid down several new straw mattresses for the pilgrims who would arrive in droves during Easter week. The relative peace of seeing the shrines without the crowds would soon end.

She was grateful she had chosen this quieter time to visit the pilgrimage sites. The very thought of the coming hubbub caused the throbbing in her head to increase unbearably.

The feverfew was in the chest where she and the widow kept their few personal belongings. It would not take long to find the carefully apportioned herbs. Little would be left in the chest now that the other pilgrim had gone. Eleanor took hold of the heavy lid and raised it.

The articles inside had been disturbed. Apparently the young mother had not respected the rights of others to share the space and left all in a tumble. Desperately, Eleanor dug through the things in the chest to find the feverfew. A stronger wave of nausea hit her, and she swallowed several times, desperate not to vomit.

Then one item caught her attention. When she pulled it out of the chest, she saw something that so stunned her that it numbed her pain.

It was a robe, finely woven and of somber hue. As she examined it more closely, she saw the ripped sleeve. A piece of cloth was missing. This had not been left behind by the woman and her child, too poor to have owned clothing of such fine workmanship.

She gasped.

From behind her, a hand reached around and clamped her mouth shut. Something very sharp bit into her back.

"I see you have found what I hoped no one would, my lady. In particular I prayed that God would save you from this, for I never slay unless I have no other choice."

Chapter Twenty-nine

Thomas stood outside the walls of Ryehill Priory and looked up at the sky. It was light blue with a wisp of clouds to dull the color. How deceptive, he thought. The promise of fair weather could turn into a howling storm with little warning beyond the ache in an old man's bones.

A voice called out to him. The wine merchant approached.

Thomas reminded himself that it was not just the weather that could be deceptive. "You look pleased, Master Durant."

"I found one witness, Brother. Someone was seen leaving Master Larcher's house before we arrived."

"That is good news!"

"Perhaps it is not. The man said it was Father Vincent."

Thomas was shocked. "The man is malevolent, but stoning innocents is his favored cruelty. I doubt he would poison the craftsman who made badges for this priory."

Durant bent closer. "Look behind you. I think we shall have an opportunity to find out."

When Thomas turned, he saw the priest and prioress in close conversation at the door to the priory. The pair did not look happy.

"Is it wise to confront him with Prioress Ursell? Might he be more willing to confess his sins if alone?" A small voice whispered in the monk's heart that it would be good to humiliate the merciless priest. Another tiny murmur suggested he should be kinder than the man he loathed.

"I would like to see how he explains himself in front of her. If he is a killer, it is the duty of the Church to punish him." The wine merchant gave him a wry smile. "If not, but his transgressions are grievous enough, I have heard that Prioress Ursell whips erring nuns. Perhaps she will be allowed to assist in his penance."

Although the monk was disinclined to believe the priest would murder two people with poison and knife, he knew the man was capable of allowing someone to die with deliberate neglect. Was it not murder to let Gracia perish for lack of food, or unthinkable cruelty to withhold comfort from a battered child? His heart hardened. "Let us confront him then and press him without mercy."

The two religious stepped back from each other the moment they saw Brother Thomas and Master Durant approach.

Remembering his first meeting with them, Thomas wondered how the pair would try to hide evidence of foulness committed this time. Bile seared his mouth, but he could not summon charity.

Father Vincent scowled. "You were missed at prayer, Brother."

"I take the blame for that, Father," Durant replied. "Brother Thomas and I met on the way to Master Larcher's house." He glanced at the monk with a grateful smile. "And I asked if he would walk a while with me to answer some theological questions."

Father Vincent became as pale as snow.

If Thomas was not mistaken, Durant chuckled softly at the sight of the priest's dismay.

But the wine merchant's eyes grew cold. "When we reached the craftsman's house, I entered." He bent his head to one side and waited, gazing at the priest. "I was greeted with such a horrible sight that I was obliged to summon Brother Thomas back before he returned to the chapel."

The prioress started with surprise, her expression suggesting puzzlement as she looked at the priest.

Father Vincent swayed on his feet.

"Master Larcher and his manservant had been murdered most cruelly." Durant turned to the prioress and waited.

Thomas continued to watch the priest.

"His servant as well?" Ursell cried out. "May God have mercy on their souls!"

"And for that reason, Brother Thomas was not in the chapel for the last Office. He was tending to the souls of two slaughtered men."

"Has the guilty one been caught?" Ursell put a hand to her mouth, and her eyes rounded in terror. "Master Larcher made the badges we sold to pilgrims. Death has grown too fond of our priory."

"I feel unwell," the priest murmured. "I must…"

As he addressed the prioress, Master Durant's sharp smile might have cut flesh. "There is a witness who saw Father Vincent leaving the craftsman's house just before we arrived."

The priest covered his face and slid to his knees.

Horrified, the prioress shouted at Father Vincent. "You lied to me! When you claimed we no longer had reason to fear him, you led me to believe you had spoken harshly to him, threatened him with hellfire, and made him eager to protect this priory from his wrongdoings and those of our nun. Did you kill him?"

Vincent began to whimper.

Although Thomas felt no pity for this trembling creature, he had a duty to offer counsel to all, even those he despised. He walked over to the quivering priest and knelt in front of him.

"The Church will not hang you for your sins," he said, "but you will never see your beloved shrine again, nor, should I think, God's sunlight. Now is the time to stop honoring Satan with your lies and tell us all that happened." He glanced up at the prioress whose face was splotched with the colors of both wrath and fear. "As well as putting yourself in danger of hellfire, you have led this good lady, the prioress of Ryehill, into mortal error with your falsehoods. You must speak the truth for her sake as well as your own. If you do not do this, your soul will drop into the lake of fire when you die."

A rivulet of urine began to twist around the priest's knees. "I have sinned. Oh, dear God, I have sinned, but I am not a murderer." He bent over until his forehead touched the damp earth. "Believe me! And, may it please God, forgive me!"

"You were seen leaving the house just before we found the bodies," Durant said in an even tone, his expression suggesting he felt no more distress for the priest than he might for boys playing in a quiet street.

"I was there. I confess it!" Vincent looked up, his forehead smeared with mud. "Have mercy and believe me when I say that I, too, found the bodies, but I am innocent of killing the men."

"Convince me, priest," the merchant said. "The circumstances do not argue in your favor."

Father Vincent tried to look outraged. "I am a man of God. How dare you question my word?"

Durant laughed. "Yet you did not summon the sheriff or alert anyone else to what you had discovered. We did. Why did you fail to perform this duty if you were innocent?"

"God's law rules me! Not the king's."

"Such a declaration from you is ill-advised," Thomas hissed, "unless you want witnesses called to reveal how poorly you observe God's laws."

"Who would dare…?"

Prioress Ursell's head was twisting back and forth, first to stare at her priest and then at his accusers. Although her first inclination would have been to defend her fellow religious, her scowl proved she was changing her mind.

Thomas stood. "All know how you favored a man who raped a child because he gave you donations for the shrine while she was denied the comfort of mercy. Was this because she had no gold to give you? Many say so and even wonder why God has allowed this to happen. And we have witnesses who report that your dealings with Master Larcher were dubious at best."

"Dubious?" This time the prioress moved away from the priest as if she had just discovered he was a leper. Glancing at the puddle surrounding him, she sniffed, then grimaced in distaste.

The priest waved his muddy hands heavenward. "God knows my reasons were praiseworthy. My heart was pure!"

"Pure?" Durant noted what Thomas had just suggested about dealings with the craftsman and used it to strengthen his attack. "There is nothing *pure* about murder. Perhaps you had reason to kill Master Larcher to keep the truth of your arrangement with him hidden."

"What dealings, Father Vincent?" The prioress stepped forward and rammed the butt of her staff just in front of his knees. "What have you done?"

He gazed up at her, his mouth opening and shutting like a pike lying on the edge of a fish pond.

"The truth," she snarled. "The bishop will hear of this if you do not tell me. Have you done something to endanger the good name of Ryehill Priory?"

"It is your nun that fouled that, my lady." Vincent's voice rose in pale imitation of moral indignation.

"A sin you were eager to abet," Thomas replied.

Prioress Ursell stared at the monk, then looked down at the priest. As she considered the implications of what she had just heard, her look took on the expression of a hawk eyeing its prey.

"How dare you!" Father Vincent squirmed. "He who is without sin may cast stones. You have much to answer for, monk. A lack of piety—"

"How dare I? It is easy, Father," Thomas continued. "You were overheard talking to Master Larcher whom you caught climbing down from the bell tower. Do you want a repetition of your exact words?"

"Lies!"

"I think not. You told him that violating a bride of Christ was worse than adultery and that his soul would go directly to Hell. When he begged you not to reveal their meeting, you told him that there was a price for your silence. Shall I continue?"

"No! It is all lies. A misunderstanding!"

"Lies or misunderstanding? I believe there is a difference, Father." Durant glanced at Thomas.

"I think you must tell the whole story, Brother," Prioress Ursell said with a voice so quiet that sailors would say a sea storm must be brewing.

"I grieve that you must hear this tale from a stranger, my lady." Thomas bowed his head to her. Despite her earlier incivility, he was beginning to realize just how much Father Vincent had duped her. As Prioress Eleanor told him, this woman, like any leader of nuns, had good reason to fear scandal, and this priest had brought that curse down on her head for his own selfish motives.

"I lament more this wickedness you have uncovered," she replied, "and do not condemn you for bringing it to my attention."

The monk nodded, then looked back at the priest. "You made a pact with the craftsman. He would donate generously to your shrine, and you would do nothing to stop the meetings in the tower with Sister Roysia."

"It was that child, demon from Hell, who told you this, wasn't it?" Vincent raised a fist and shook it. "A lying, whoring—"

"The tale comes not just from her but others in the town," Thomas said. All he knew, apart from what Gracia had witnessed, were the stories Mistress Emelyne had told his prioress, including the one about Father Vincent being the nun's lover himself. He did not believe that but preferred to spare Prioress Ursell an additional humiliation for no purpose. If the priest believed the tale of his bribery was more widespread, he might confess, and Thomas would be content. This was not a secular matter, subject to the king's justice. A confession would satisfy the Church, precise evidence would not be needed, and Father Vincent would be punished.

Prioress Ursell gasped. "You told me about their sins but said I must not stop the pair from meeting." Ursell looked away. "You forbade me to punish Sister Roysia, swore you would deal with the craftsman's wickedness but needed time to do so in a way that would not harm the priory. A simple woman, I obeyed you." Her voice faded into a whisper. "I trusted you."

Thomas thought he saw tears on her cheeks. Despite her faults, he caught himself pitying her for an instant.

Father Vincent was not quite defeated. "The craftsman threatened to spread rumors that I was Sister Roysia's lover. Does not that make him the more sinful man?" His voice rasped. "The whore heard this and must have aided him in the wickedness."

Prioress Ursell's mouth dropped open.

The wine merchant's eyes twinkled. He seemed pleased that the craftsman might have been cleverer than he had thought probable.

Thomas shrugged. He had chosen to keep that story to himself. If the priest wanted to wallow deeper in the pigsty, let him do so.

"It was his revenge. He told me that when last he paid…" Realizing what he had just admitted, Father Vincent shut his mouth.

Prioress Ursell was no fool. "You are guilty of taking bribes, letting this wicked affair continue, and putting my priory in danger of condemnation. You should have stopped Master Larcher and come to me with his threatened and vile accusation. I could have dealt with my sinful nun."

"And for this petty greed you killed the craftsman and his innocent servant?" Durant shook his head in disbelief.

All this, the monk hoped, might finally push the priest into confession.

"No! I admit I took bribes to benefit the Shrine of the Virgin's Lock. I confess to that, but I did not kill anyone. I went to Larcher's house to force him to remain silent about the affair for the good of Ryehill's reputation and to stop telling the stories that I had broken my sacred vows with a nun. I found the servant and the craftsman dead. I fled in fear. I—"

The prioress snorted in contempt. "How little you cared for our reputation before."

"Sadly, my lady, the situation is far graver than that." Master Durant stepped closer and lowered his voice. "Shall we meet in your chambers?"

Prioress Ursell looked dazed, as if she might crumple under the weight of one more horrible revelation, but she stiffened her back and nodded, turning to lead them into the priory.

As they reached the entrance, a white-faced nun appeared at the door. "My lady, come quickly!" Unable to say more, she began to weep.

Gracia pushed past the young woman and raced up to Thomas, grasping his sleeve. "To the bell tower, Brother. I fear Prioress Eleanor has been murdered."

Chapter Thirty

Brother Thomas' fingers left bloody streaks on the stairs and wall. Silently cursing the tiny steps to the bell tower, he clawed his way up, proceeded by the street child and followed by Master Durant and Prioress Ursell.

When he finally burst through the entrance, Gracia pulled him by the hand to the low wall surrounding the bell tower.

"There!" The young girl pointed at the priory roof below them.

Thomas saw the body of his prioress lying there. Grief may have scalded his eyes with tears, but fury dried them. In an instant, he forgot all vows and swore he would personally tie the killer's limbs to four swift horses and let them tear the man apart. Then he heard a sound, looked down at the child beside him, and saw that she was weeping too. His heart shattered, and he could no longer contemplate violence. Squeezing her hand, he bent down and whispered words of comfort.

Prioress Ursell gestured at the staircase. "I will go back to the priory and send for help. If there is any chance that she might be alive…" She looked back at the men, clearly debating the propriety of leaving them there, then shook her head and disappeared through the entrance.

Gracia looked up at Thomas. "Prioress Eleanor may be alive, Brother. The fall is not as far as that suffered by Sister Roysia."

Durant leaned dangerously over the wall and pointed. "Look!"

Following the direction of his finger, they saw someone stumbling along the priory roof toward the houses beyond.

"It is the murderer," Gracia said.

Suddenly, the merchant noticed the rope dangling over the edge.

Thomas did as well and reached out for it.

"No, Brother, let me give chase. This is my particular enemy," Durant said and grabbed the rope.

Gracia screamed at him. "It will break with your weight!"

Durant blinked, then saw the cut in the rope. "I am grateful for your warning, child." Then he, too, ran for the stairwell entry.

Thomas followed.

"Stay here, "Durant said, putting a restraining hand against the monk's chest. "I will seek the killer and swear to bring him to justice." His look softened. "You have vows to keep, Brother Thomas, and a child to comfort. I promise that the end of this matter will satisfy you." With that, he eased down on the top step. "It will be faster to slide," they heard him say with a light jest as he vanished.

Although he knew Durant was right, Thomas clenched his fists in helpless frustration. Then he turned to seek Gracia.

To his horror, she had leapt up on the wall and was balancing precariously.

He rushed to the child and put her down on the safer tower floor. "Do not endanger yourself like that!"

"Then look at the roof yourself." Her face was pale, but she was smiling. "I think I saw our lady move."

Kneeling at the wall, he looked down and realized that his prioress had shifted onto her side. "She lives!"

Crying out with joy, Gracia clapped her hands.

Now he saw Eleanor struggling to sit up. "Stay where you are, my lady," Thomas shouted. Fearing she would slip off the roof if she moved too much, he waved franticly to get her attention. "Prioress Ursell has gone to seek aid. They will come soon."

Eleanor looked up and raised a hand.

Suddenly, a ladder rose from the street and was braced against the priory walls. Two figures began the climb. One was a man, but, to Thomas' amazement, the other was Prioress Ursell. Even in this situation, he thought, the prioress of Ryehill was determined that there should be no real or imagined impropriety.

Unable to know whether to laugh or cry, he sat back on his heels and began to do both.

Gracia put her arm around his neck and laid her head on his. "Come, Brother," she whispered, "let us leave this place."

Wiping his cheeks, the monk stood, touched by her comforting when he should have been the one to ease her pain. "You have something to tell me about this." He gestured around the narrow space of the bell tower. "While we have no witnesses near, reveal what you know and then we shall depart."

She pointed upward into the bell tower itself. "I was hiding near that bird when she brought Prioress Eleanor up here."

He looked up. A raven had a nest in the roof above the bell. The creature glared at him.

Suddenly, he grasped what Gracia had just said. "You are saying that it was a woman who tried to kill Prioress Eleanor?" Now that he thought about it, he realized that the figure they had just seen was very small for a man, yet he and Durant had assumed...

"I do not know her name. She is a pilgrim staying here. I saw her with our lady when she went to visit the shrines at Walsingham Priory."

Was that Mistress Emelyne who had ridden close by his prioress' side from the moment they met the pilgrimage group on the road from Norwich? How could she have been the one? As he recalled, she was flighty, verbose, and too eager to please someone of high rank. He shook in his head in amazement. This woman was a murderer and even the assassin?

"Could you describe her?"

"I could not see her face at first, but she matched your prioress in height and was plainly dressed. At one point she did look up, but I was in the shadows on the ladder above the bell and wrapped my clothes around me to escape notice. It was then I recognized her as the woman who so often sought the company of Prioress Eleanor. Before she had always been bright-faced and her voice high-pitched, but when the two emerged into this place, her expression was angry. Her voice dropped so low I could barely hear her."

He nodded. Might this widow be a man in disguise? No, he thought. A woman might pass as a beardless youth, but a grown man could not hide his beard.

Hearing voices, he looked down on the roof below. Gracia urged him to let her see as well so he held her while she peered over the edge of the wall.

Three were now on the roof. The man stood at a respectful distance while a nun worked on the prieress' arm. Ursell stood on the ladder leaning against the house and watched.

He whispered reassurance to Gracia, then urged her to step back. As he continued to watch, he leaned over a bit more, trying to find Durant, but he could not see into all the streets. The figure they had witnessed crossing the roof was gone.

"Do not bend out so far, Brother."

He stepped back as his heart thumped with increasing happiness. His prioress was alive and could move. Perhaps Durant had caught the attacker. Grinning, he said, "Continue with your story of what happened."

"When they arrived, I did not know why they had come here, but I felt I should not let them know I was here too. So I watched. Then I saw that the pilgrim held a knife against Prioress Eleanor's back." She winced. "I was frightened and did not know what I could do to help." She looked down at her thin body. "I am fleet if I need to run, but my teeth are too poor to bite and I have no heft."

"There is no blame in realizing what you cannot do." Taking her hand, he felt how fragile her bones were. She desperately needed feeding, he thought. When this matter of murder and assassination is done, he would not leave Walsingham until he had arranged a home for this girl.

"The woman said that she regretted what she must do but had no choice. If only our prioress had not found her torn robe, she would have lived." The child looked up at the monk. "Does that mean anything to you? She held a garment in her hand. The sleeve had a piece torn from it."

"It does," he said with sadness. All had thought a man had killed Sister Roysia, so concerned were they over the presumed affair between Larcher and the nun. Instead, it was a woman, claiming to be a pilgrim. It grieved him that someone had traveled to Walsingham, alleging she sought forgiveness for sins but was instead intent on committing them.

"She pushed our prioress toward that pillar and ordered her to tie the rope as she directed. I wondered if I might drop on the woman's head, knocking her to the ground, but she never came close enough. It would not have helped if I had simply fallen from my hiding place and startled her." Again she looked at Thomas for confirmation.

"You were right. You are too small to struggle with a grown woman who holds a knife. You might have injured…" He stopped for a moment, realizing that the child had referred to Prioress Eleanor as *our prioress*. It touched him deeply. "You made the only decision you could," he said simply.

"When the rope was tied, and the woman tested its strength, she raised her hand and hit our prioress on the head with the hilt of the knife. I think Prioress Eleanor raised her arm to defend herself but not soon enough. I saw blood flowing from the spot where she was struck." She covered her face in her hands. "It all happened so fast, Brother!"

Thomas picked her up and held her close while she sobbed. "You could do nothing," he repeated until the weeping ceased, then he put her back down but held on to her hand.

"She dropped the knife and pulled Prioress Eleanor to the edge of that wall and pushed her over the side. Then she tied the torn robe around her waist, grabbed the rope, and was over the side herself in an instant. It was only then that I could climb down from my hiding place."

"It was you who cut the rope with the discarded knife?"

"I wasn't quick enough. The rope is thick, and I did not have the strength to cut faster. Before I could slice through, I felt the rope go slack. When I looked over the wall, the woman was standing on the rooftop. Prioress Eleanor had fallen near the edge, and the woman began to move toward her. I screamed for help. She looked up, saw me, and fled. I ran down the stairs to seek a nun who would alert Prioress Ursell."

"You saved Prioress Eleanor's life. Had the woman discovered that our prioress was still alive, she would have pushed her over the edge of the roof onto the street. After one fall already and that blow to her head, our lady surely would have died."

Gracia's eyes widened. "Do you think so?"

He nodded. Assuming Prioress Eleanor was not critically injured, the child's cry for aid might well have saved his lady's life.

Pulling Gracia into his arms, he hugged her. "May God give you all blessings," he said. "Poor mortal that I am, I shall beg His mercy comfort you for all eternity because of what you did."

As if he were her father who had just returned from a long journey, she snuggled closer to him.

Chapter Thirty-one

Thomas eased himself slowly down the stairs while Gracia followed, reminding him to take care and that his injured hands would need tending. It was a good lesson, he thought, that she, who lived her own life on the edge of death, cared about the needs of another mortal.

When they reached the bottom and entered the hallway, he saw a nun waiting by the door, her head bowed. He recognized her as the one who had rushed to summon Prioress Ursell with Gracia by her side. Thomas put his hand on the child's shoulder as assurance that he would protect her if there was any dispute about her continued presence.

"Sister?"

She looked up.

"You are weeping," he said. "What grieves you?"

"My sorrow includes the violence done to Prioress Eleanor, Brother, but begins with Sister Roysia. Is this tragedy part of hers?"

"I fear it is," he replied, "but the slander hurled against the good nun has been proven wrong."

"Are you Sister Roysia's friend whom she called her most beloved?" Gracia suddenly asked.

The nun flushed, then nodded.

"There is a message I vowed to deliver to that nun, Brother." The girl looked up at him with a worried expression.

He reassured her that there was no offence in this.

"Sister Roysia remained true to her vocation," Gracia said, turning to the nun. "She swore me to silence about her meetings with the craftsman but feared for her life. If she should die, she said I must tell you that she did this to save the life of God's anointed king. Each time she met with this man, excluding the first, I hid in the bell tower so she might not be alone with Master Larcher."

The nun gasped.

"Were you there the night she died?" the monk asked.

Gracia shook her head. "I knew nothing about this last encounter. The decision to meet must have been made after the hour when I walked by the priory to see if the front door was open. I found it locked and assumed Sister Roysia had not been able to find a way to let me in so I might sleep safely in the tower. That night, I found shelter in the streets."

The young nun reached out and hugged the child. "Thank you for telling me this!"

Thomas waited while the two talked, but finally his growing concern overcame him. "Have you heard anything about Prioress Eleanor?"

The nun's face was almost luminous after the news she had just received from Gracia. "Forgive me, Brother, for my selfishness. The infirmarian has gone to attend her, and the messenger told her that your prioress is injured but alive."

He almost leapt with joy but restrained the impulse as unseemly. "Then I shall go to her as well." He glanced at the vagrant child and urged her gently toward the nun. "Will you take this child and make sure she is fed, Sister? I have heard that Prioress Ursell denied her scraps, but this girl saved my prioress' life."

The young nun looked down into Gracia's eyes and a smile tickled the corners of her mouth. "No one would dare deny her sustenance now, Brother." She looked at the monk. "Prioress Ursell must certainly agree." She reached out a hand and took the tiny and very grimy one in hers. "Come with me. There is soft bread and cheese in the kitchen."

Thomas bent to whisper in Gracia's ear that he would come for her soon with news, then he smiled at the nun and rushed out the priory door.

A crowd surrounded the ladder from which Prioress Eleanor had been lowered off the roof, but Thomas edged his way through the men and women with ease, whispering that he served the lady lying on the ground. Many simply honored his calling, when they saw him, and stepped aside without hesitation.

As he reached the empty space at the center, he saw Prioress Ursell pounding her staff of office into the earth as she stalked the perimeter and glowered at any who dared move closer. Oddly enough, she reminded him of Moses with the shining face after he had climbed down from the mountain in Sinai. It was a strange image, but he meant it as a compliment.

Looking around, he did not see Father Vincent. That did not surprise him.

As he walked toward Ryehill's prioress, she stopped. Her look changed from that of a mighty prophet to one of a mortal filled with shame. Honoring her office and taking mercy on her humiliation, he humbly bowed to her. "May I have permission to go to Prioress Eleanor's side?"

Biting her lip, she nodded. "Most certainly, Brother. She will welcome your comfort." Her voice was tense with a rare excess of emotion.

As he approached the small figure lying on the ground, he saw a lean nun kneeling beside her.

The Ryehill infirmarian glanced over her shoulder. With a look of gentle understanding, learned from many years caring for the sick, she nodded. "Welcome, Brother Thomas. Our lady was just asking for you."

Trying to maintain a properly somber mien, he knelt close by and swallowed his tears of relief.

"I shall be a short distance away," the infirmarian said. "She is weak and needs rest. If I may advise, please do not stay here long. We would like to take her as soon as possible to the priory for the complete care she needs."

This infirmarian was older than Sister Anne at Tyndal, but she reminded him of his friend, a woman who cared more about healing than judging any sin that might have caused the illness. He swore to keep his visit brief.

As the woman rose and walked away, he wondered how many nuns went to her for comforting when discipline and the harsh life at Ryehill grew too hard to bear.

"I am grateful you are here, Brother." Prioress Eleanor's voice was surprisingly strong.

"God was kind to us all at Tyndal Priory, my lady, when He kept Death from snatching you away." Her arm was in a small splint, he noted, and bound close to her body. Blood still stained her face. He hoped the infirmarian had used comfrey for better healing.

"Your prayers would give much comfort to this frightened soul," she said with warmth.

"I offer them with all my heart," he replied, "but I grieve that you suffered this and I was not there to protect you." She was pale but had smiled at him as if he truly was the one person above all she longed to see. He swatted at an errant tear on his cheek.

"You are Tyndal Priory's own Galahad," she said, her eyes twinkling. Then she grew more serious. "Has anyone seen Mistress Emelyne? It was she who killed Sister Roysia and confessed it to me. I found her torn robe in the chest where I had stored herbs sent with me by Sister Anne. The widow carried that robe when she took me to the tower. Perhaps she dropped it there? I think we might compare the hole with the cloth found in the nun's hand."

He shook his head. "I fear she may have escaped, my lady. We saw her on the roof, and a wine merchant sped off to capture her."

"A wine merchant?"

Thomas felt his mouth go dry. He cleared his throat. "I was on my way to speak with Master Larcher and met Master Durant on the way. Since he had some questions of theology, we walked together. It was he who found that the craftsman had been—"

"I heard he was killed. That, too, was done by Mistress Emelyne." She winced. "I realized she planned to murder me as well when she grew eager to brag about the details of her cleverness. She is the assassin waiting to kill the king, Brother. You must send word." Again she winced, clenched her teeth, and uttered a moan of pain.

A figure cast a shadow over Thomas. He looked around and saw the infirmarian.

"Brother, your prioress is in pain. I beg that you let us take her to the priory so I can offer her a soothing draught. She needs to sleep and suffer less so the healing can occur more quickly." She smiled. "And, lest you fear otherwise, I used both comfrey and mallow leaves on that wound."

He looked back at Eleanor.

"We shall speak soon, Brother. Pray for me."

"I shall." Giving her a blessing, he rose.

The infirmarian motioned for the bearers to come forward. Gently lifting the litter, they carried the prioress away. At the head of the party was Prioress Ursell, her staff of office glittering in the pale sun. The infirmarian followed behind, watching to make sure the trip was accomplished with as much gentleness as possible.

Thomas looked up at the sky. Late in the season though it was, he wondered if the hazy light meant a late snow. He hoped not.

"Brother Thomas!"

Master Durant ran to his side. The man was sweating, and his eyes were dark with anger. "The killer has escaped." He spat out the admission as if it were rotten meat.

"Prioress Eleanor said that it was a woman and her name is Mistress Emelyne, a merchant's widow of some means from Norwich. Gracia also recognized her as the pilgrim who accompanied my prioress on the visits to the shrines. The widow was a member of the same party we joined when we came on pilgrimage."

Durant raised an eyebrow. "I find it strange that she claimed she came from Norwich and owned such wealth. I know her not, Brother, and I should."

"She confessed much to Prioress Eleanor before she tried to kill her. My lady says she is the assassin you seek."

"How diabolically clever to use a woman," Durant said and suddenly looked weary. "The king shall be told." He fell silent and his gaze grew distant with thought. Murmuring something Thomas could not hear, he bowed and abruptly walked away without another word.

Thomas watched him disappear and suddenly felt bereft. If this was the last he would see of the merchant, he would have preferred a different parting. Then he shook away such thoughts.

He had prayers to offer for his prioress' recovery, and he turned toward the road leading to Walsingham Priory. He would never again kneel at the Shrine of the Virgin's Lock.

Chapter Thirty-two

A dusting snow was falling outside, but there was little need for a fire in the chambers of the prioress of Ryehill. The anger flowing from Prioress Ursell was hot enough to fry the Devil.

Thomas almost felt sorry for Father Vincent. Almost, he thought, for I shall never forget what he did to a child.

The prioress of Ryehill nodded to the monk. Dark circles, like the ashes of mourning, were etched under her eyes. "You have much to tell us. I may fear your news, but I must learn each foul truth." She glanced at the priest who knelt before her like the penitent he ought to be. "It is my duty."

"I shall keep the tale brief, my lady. You have been betrayed by those whom you had reason to trust, but not by the ones you were led to believe had brought shame on this priory."

She stiffened but did not blench.

The priest muffled a whine.

"Sister Roysia was murdered, not by Master Larcher, but by one who came to Walsingham as an alleged pilgrim."

"Not by her..." The prioress gulped and then mumbled, "her lover."

"She brought her virtue into question by meeting Master Larcher as she did, but he was never her lover. She remained chaste, although a few might question if she did so within the spirit of her vows."

The priest looked up in horror. "But..."

"Silence!" Ursell slammed her staff on the floor. "The sooner I hear all from Brother Thomas, the better for this priory and even you."

"When Father Vincent caught the craftsman climbing down from the bell tower, he assumed the man had entered the priory for carnal purposes. Larcher let him believe this but refused to give him the name of the nun until Father Vincent tricked him into revealing that it was Sister Roysia."

"And you might have stopped these meetings then," the prioress hissed at the priest. "I said as much at the time."

"We had no choice," the priest howled. "Who would make the badges if not this man?"

She looked at the monk. "I take full responsibility for my part in this. As a frail woman, it is my duty to follow the greater wisdom of a man of God, and this priest insisted I obey his wish to delay action." Her eyes narrowed. "Yet I should have known he spoke with Satan's voice. That I allowed the impropriety to continue is reprehensible." She waved her hand at the priest.

"I fear that Father Vincent did take bribes from Master Larcher as payment for his silence and permission to continue the meetings."

"This is true? I have prayed that you were wrong." She looked at Thomas as if longing to hear he had lied.

The priest's expression suggested he had just seen an avenging angel with a flaming sword standing over him. "Not bribes, in truth," he mumbled, trying to soften his previous confession. "Donations."

"A witness has come forth. A reliable one." He would not mention Gracia's name. Confident she was telling the truth, he feared he might strike this foul priest if he again called her a whore.

It was the prioress who silenced Father Vincent before he pursued the identity of the witness. "I take your word, Brother, for you have proven yourself to be an honest man." She glared at the priest. "Had I been told the truth, I would have dealt with both nun and craftsman as God demands, even if you chose otherwise. Bribes! How dare you?"

"The money was needed to feed your nuns." He whimpered.

Her eyes widened in horror. "I would have appealed to the Bishop of Norwich, Roger Skerning. We serve God with righteousness here, and I would not have touched one coin you obtained in that manner."

Thomas had saved the worst news, a tale Master Durant told him after hearing it from the innkeeper. The man recalled a relic seller, who had stayed at his inn in the winter. When the relic seller enjoyed too much wine on his last night, he had boasted of his lucrative deal with Father Vincent. Although the innkeeper did not doubt the sacred nature of the item acquired, he told Durant that he knew the priest had paid a great sum for a few hairs from the man's large collection of strands.

"There is more, my lady. Do you recall when you suddenly had less income for the care of your flock? Was it around the time your priest told you about the new relic?"

"No!" Father Vincent began to beat his fists on the floor. "I only borrowed money from the priory for this relic. I knew it would bring greater rewards, well worth the minimal suffering of fewer mouthfuls of food...."

Prioress Ursell's eyes blazed. "Miscreant! You stole money to pay for that relic, then told me how few alms there were during the winter and that we must make do with less? One nun died because our infirmarian could not pay for the herbs to treat her." She bent forward and snarled at the priest. "You lied when you said a penitent had given you the relic and suggested the gift might have been from an angel. I was blinded by your pretty tale and mistook the Devil's work for God's! "

The priest put his hands over his eyes.

"The money he received from Master Larcher was intended to pay back the price of the relic, or so I believe." Thomas said softly.

Sitting back, she looked at Thomas, her ire turned to sorrow. "I shall inform the bishop. The relic will be sold."

Father Vincent sobbed.

Ignoring him, the prioress shifted uneasily. "You swear that the merchant and my nun were not lovers. If that is true, I would know why they met in such an unseemly fashion." She whispered the last sentence.

"I give you my word that Sister Roysia never broke her vows, my lady." Thomas bowed his head to gain himself time. He did not want to explain as she required but could not avoid doing so in part. Durant had given him permission to tell what he must but begged him to keep as much secret as possible.

The monk straightened. "The king is planning to visit this town soon, and one of his courtiers learned that an assassin had been sent to kill him while he was here. Master Larcher, who was the king's man in this place, was told to discover the traitor's name. Since pilgrims stay in the priories here, and impart news while visiting, he was to contact specific religious in the Walsingham priories, whose loyalty was unquestioned and were in the best position to overhear important information. These sources were told to report anything to him that might lead to the capture of the assassin."

Father Vincent and Prioress Ursell looked equally horrified.

"Sister Roysia was one, but she could neither read nor write and verbal messages sent by courier were unsafe. She suggested to the craftsman that they meet in the bell tower when she had news. Master Larcher was often in your chambers, my lady, and she could give him a signal at one of these frequent meetings. By the phrases spoken, she indicated time. She let down the rope. He climbed it and they talked."

Looking ill with grief over all she was hearing, the prioress groaned.

"Sister Roysia called on the child, Gracia, to hide in the tower while she met with the craftsman so she would have proper attendance."

The priest opened his mouth to protest, then thought better of it.

"Why not tell me of this?" the prioress whispered.

"The good sister did not want to endanger any of Ryehill's religious with this perilous knowledge, including you, my lady. Having seen the child in the streets, she offered to let Gracia sleep in the tower if she would come on those special occasions when a signal was given."

He hurried on, hoping neither priest nor prioress would ask for details he did not want to divulge. After all, they need not know that the nun had chosen to give shelter to Gracia every night after the rape in defiance of Father Vincent's curses. Some of those nights also coincided with the meetings. "Sister Roysia gave her oath to one of the nuns here that she had never broken her vows, even if others condemned her for lewdness. If need be, that nun will confirm that."

"There is no doubt that Sister Roysia was murdered?" A tear fled down Prioress Ursell's cheek and was brusquely swept away.

"She was. I believe she learned that the assassin had arrived in this priory and sent for Master Larcher so she might reveal her name. The assassin met her in the tower instead and pushed her to her death."

"*Her?*" Father Vincent's mouth gaped.

"Mistress Emelyne, the woman who also tried to kill Prioress Eleanor, was in the pay of the king's enemies. She confessed all to Prioress Eleanor before she tried to kill her."

"A woman!" The prioress gasped.

"Who better to hide her mission?" Thomas looked down at his hands. "She claimed to be a merchant's widow from Norwich and was part of that band of pilgrims we joined on the way here. Prioress Eleanor found her torn robe in the chambers they shared here. The missing cloth was in Sister Roysia's hand." He looked at Ursell, daring her to criticize him for failing to mention he had even seen the fabric. "I have confirmed that the piece matches the hole in the garment." Since he had not trusted Prioress Ursell to let him have the evidence, he asked the infirmarian to retrieve it for him. It was a favor he would keep secret.

"We harbored a traitor." Prioress Ursell nervously rubbed her neck. "Even the Church will not protect us from condemnation. King Edward stands in high regard for his service in Outremer."

"You did so without knowledge, my lady, and it was, after all, your nun who died trying to save his life. Prioress Eleanor herself will swear to your loyalty, proven by Sister Roysia's death, and beg that King Edward grant you rents or property to make up for the loss of income from the pilgrimage badges. She cannot promise her plea will be successful, but, as you know, her brother enjoys the king's favor."

This time tears of relief did pour down her cheeks. "You and your prioress are compassionate beyond measure, Brother." Then she turned to Father Vincent. "As for you, I shall inform the bishop of how you betrayed your calling, tried to cast shame on this priory, and how you lied to me while robing yourself in holy merit. The relic will be sold for the benefit of the poor." She shuddered. "I would not allow one morsel of food bought with the proceeds to touch the lips of any of my nuns. It would pollute their souls." She rose. "Plead for mercy, priest, for I now cast you from my sight and will beg for a praiseworthy man to replace you. May you be thrown into a dark prison for the remaining of your miserable…"

But Thomas did not stay to hear all her curses, and escaped while she was still uttering them. He had a child to tend and a wounded prioress to comfort. The less he saw of this pair, the better, although he admitted that he had found a small redeeming aspect to the dour Prioress Ursell.

Chapter Thirty-three

Durant turned away from the window of his room at the inn and smiled at the monk standing at the open door. Gesturing to the table, he said, "I ordered food, Brother, with the hope you would join me."

"That is a feast." Thomas sniffed the air, pungent with herb-rubbed and roasted fowl. An abundance of steaming root vegetables glistened on a small platter. In the middle of the table, a pewter jug sat with two goblets nearby, suggesting a good wine was to be part of the meal.

"I fear my tastes were formed in the markets of Norwich and the vineyards of the Aquitaine, not in the kitchens of a priory."

Thomas laughed and was happy he could do so. Durant knew his past too well, yet the monk sensed he had nothing to fear from this man, although others surely did. He was also pleased the merchant had summoned him again. "Nor, as you well know, were mine, Master Durant. Yet I am surprised you and your wife were not captivated by the miracles created by Sister Matilda, overseer of our priory's kitchen, during your stay at Tyndal Priory. Her version of monastic simplicity does not lack earthly delight."

An ill-defined expression passed quickly over the wine merchant's face, then he nodded. "I do recall the meals there. They were remarkable. Sadly, my opinion was skewed because ale was served, not wine, and I am better acquainted with the grape."

Thomas grinned. "The ale is a local marvel. Had you stayed longer, you might have learned to prefer it."

With a laugh, Durant bowed. "Please sit and let me pour some of this wine. The innkeeper is well-stocked with items that satisfy all tastes, and today is a feast day. I find his wine very pleasing." Durant poured a deep ruby liquid into each cup and handed one to the monk.

Thomas raised his. "To the King of Heaven and the king of England."

"Well said, Brother."

And the two raised their goblets to the respective lords.

After Durant had insisted on serving the monk, then himself, the two men sat and ate in a silence that both found comfortable. Occasionally, one nodded in appreciation of the cook's skill with bird or turnip, but they savored the offerings as men of taste might.

Refusing another helping, Thomas sat back and sipped his wine. "To what do I owe this invitation? Do not think me ungrateful, but I have served as you do, only for a different master, and know there are reasons for everything."

"You are both correct and in error. I do have a reason, but I also missed your company." The merchant blushed.

Thomas raised an eyebrow, then felt foolish. He saw vulnerability flicker in the man's eyes, a betrayal of weakness he had not expected. "I am glad you did," he said gently. "Not many knowing of my imprisonment and ancestry would be so kind."

Durant looked away. "The rank of your sire puts you far above me."

"And that of my mother places me far below." The monk waited a moment. "Shall we agree that their union and the lack of God's blessing on their bed places me somewhere in the middle of God's greatest creation?"

"Still, I see your kin reflected in your eyes."

Instinctively, Thomas shut them. "I may be a changeling for all you know and own no kinship with those you mention." He reached out a hand. "Shall we agree that I am simply Brother

Thomas of Tyndal Priory and due honor only as I best serve God?"

Durant took the offered hand. "You should have served the king. Did you take vows out of profound conviction?"

Thomas did not pull his hand away, finding comfort in the man's touch. "I did not, but I discovered a home and true calling at Tyndal Priory. Prioress Eleanor is a wise leader, and I am happy in her service."

"God has given you peace?"

"He granted me what may be the greater gift, that of patience." Thomas realized that the merchant had withdrawn his hand. Looking up, he noticed that Durant's eyes seemed to have changed color from green to a soft brown. "Peace comes from a purer faith than I own."

The merchant sipped at his wine, as if considering a new aspect of it, and then nodded. "How does Prioress Eleanor?"

"Her arm was broken, but the infirmarian at Ryehill is skilled. She said the break was an easy one to set, and there is no sign of corruption in the flesh of the outer wounds."

"You sound surprised to learn that the nun here is competent." Durant chuckled.

"Are you not as well? Did you think anything good could come from that priory?"

The merchant shrugged. "Sister Roysia gave her life to save God's anointed king."

"That she did, and surely God has found a place in Heaven for her soul, but we failed to arrest the traitor."

"That was my news, Brother."

Thomas sat up. "You captured her?"

Durant poured them both more wine. "We were given her body." He held up a hand to delay any questions. "I think God must have arranged this strange form of justice."

"Can you tell me what happened?"

"Mistress Emelyne, or so she called herself, joined a party of pilgrims returning to their homes along the road leading to London."

"Not back to Norwich then."

"She was never from that place, Brother. I knew no one by that name, rank, or wealth, and discreet inquiries proved me right. Her masters provided all she brought here to establish her identity as a merchant's wealthy widow." He smiled. "At least Ryehill Priory has her fine horse and a few gems to sell for holier purposes. They will be allowed to keep them."

"Please continue. I should not have interrupted."

"Not far from here, in a part of the road overhung with trees, that traveling party was attacked by men on horseback. Outlaws, the poor pilgrims believed, and feared for their lives as well as their purses. Yet the men robbed only one of the more affluent and then cut the throat of our assassin. Suddenly, with no warning, they vanished back into the forest. By the time the pilgrims found help, the outlaws were long gone and Mistress Emelyne quite dead."

Thomas looked at him for a long time. "Not outlaws, if I were to guess. King's men?"

"Would the king not want her alive to reveal the names of those who sent her?"

"Unless her master was known already, and her silence was of greater value than her voice."

Durant laughed. "Clever, Brother!" He bent forward. "Shall you believe me if I say that I know nothing more about her or her master?"

"You did not say 'I swear,'" the monk replied. "It matters not if I do or do not. I doubt I will learn more than you have told me."

"The king has many enemies, and some have coin enough to pay for a cunningly hidden assassin."

Thomas raised one finger. "With this war I suspect the Welsh have little coin to spare, but they are a clever people." He raised another. "The Muslims proved their talents with the man who stabbed King Edward in Acre, a servant the king had learned to trust, but I question whether they would send another so deep into the lands of Christians." He studied his hand for a moment and then raised a third finger. "The estranged and disinherited from the last rebellion, a few of whom are in the courts of unfriendly kings…"

Durant cleared his throat.

The monk looked up from his hand.

"Do not try to discover the truth," the merchant said. "It does not matter. The woman is dead and has been buried without a name in a grave no one shall find."

Sighing, Thomas swallowed the last of his wine and refused more.

Durant looked at him with sadness darkening his face. "I thank you for not mentioning my name to Prioress Ursell. If you have told your own prioress, she will know it is best if she does not tell anyone else of my involvement in this matter."

"Surely the king would like to use you again in his particular service."

Durant did not reply. Instead, he said, "The king shall be told how loyally you both served him in this matter."

"My name need not be mentioned. Instead, I would ask a boon on behalf of my prioress."

"What favor does she wish?"

"Be kind in your report on Ryehill Priory. Father Vincent is a man with a shriveled soul but is not a traitor, and Prioress Ursell was distraught to discover she had unwittingly harbored the woman. It was a Ryehill nun who gave her life for King Edward. A gift to feed and clothe the nuns would be welcomed."

Durant stood. "As Prioress Eleanor wishes, I shall make sure they suffer no more than they have through their own bad judgment and will suggest that the priory ought not to starve after the loyalty they have shown."

"I am thankful for your hospitality, Master Durant." Thomas rose from the table. "Tyndal may be grateful as well when they discover I have eaten too much here to eat there for many days."

Durant walked to his window and stared down at the road. "I shall leave here soon. In truth, I did intend to make a pilgrimage part of my purpose here. That duty I have done as well as my work for the king." He turned to face the monk. "I wish we could join forces again, Brother."

For a moment, Thomas hesitated, and then said what he thought. "If God's will unites with that of King Edward…"

"And your prioress…"

"If God demands a justice that the king does as well, I know she would be willing to lend my poor efforts."

"We think too much alike, Brother." Durant smiled and then strode toward the monk and knelt. "Will you give me a final blessing that I may share with my wife?"

When Thomas had done so, Durant rose and suddenly pulled him close, kissing him gently on each cheek.

It was an instant only, but Thomas felt an emotion he had not felt in years. It was the hint of joy, a feeling so unfamiliar he almost did not recognize it.

Durant stepped back and murmured, "After all we have done together here, are we not like brothers? I have none from my mother's womb who remain in this world."

"Nor have I any kin who would call me such," Thomas replied, his voice hoarse.

"Then shall we exchange a kiss as brothers might who long to share the joy of each other's accomplishment in a worthy endeavor?"

Thomas shut his eyes, his heart pounding so he could hear little else, but then he looked at Durant. "Yes," he said.

The merchant took the monk into his arms and kissed him softly on the lips. "Thus we have honored our efforts as brothers of choice with a common goal," he whispered in Thomas' ear.

The monk knew he must have uttered a reply, but all he cared about was the brush of Durant's breath against his cheek.

The merchant stepped away. "I must beg this of you. Return to your prioress as I shall to my wife. Take Prioress Eleanor my good will and that of the king, who will surely honor her as he does her brother, Sir Hugh. And I shall share the blessing you have given me with my wife in Norwich."

Thomas stared at him, noticing that the merchant's face was pink. But from the heat he felt in his own cheeks, he feared his own were of like hue.

Durant spun around and strode back to his window. "Now go, Brother," he murmured. "As you are bound to serve God, please go."

Chapter Thirty-four

Prioress Eleanor sat in the high-backed chair of Prioress Ursell's audience chamber and listened to Brother Thomas convey the latest news.

Prioress Ursell had insisted that she take these quarters. Her immediate reaction had been a kind refusal, but Brother Thomas called on the infirmarian to provide the obligatory stern-faced authority. Together they argued that Eleanor must accept if she wished to speed her healing and return to her own priory sooner.

She conceded. Now she was glad, even though Prioress Ursell was obliged to retreat to a harder bed in the company of her nuns.

Today was her first extended time out of bed. Most of her injuries were minor annoyances, but her wounded arm throbbed and she lacked her usual vigor. As she looked at her monk, she saw his concern, smiled to reassure him, and then discreetly tried to find a more comfortable position to ease the broken arm before she commented on what he had just said.

"I do not believe the story of the accidental brigands, Brother. The attack was too convenient, and their unwillingness to injure or steal from others is unnatural for those who live on havoc and theft."

"If the band had meant only to silence her, they accomplished that effectively, my lady. We should be grateful that the innocents in the traveling party did not suffer because a traitor chose to hide amongst them."

"One merchant might disagree, but otherwise the outlaws showed uncommon charity, a kindness that speaks well for those who sent them." Once again, she shifted her arm into a different position. Using that as an excuse, she looked around.

Prioress Ursell's current attendant, a young nun with solemn manner, stood by the door with head bowed, but Eleanor was certain that her ears were alert to anything of interest that might be said. "I wonder whom Mistress Emelyne served." She smiled at her monk and tilted her head toward the nun. "I assume that no one knows."

"I have heard no rumors," he replied, cautiously signaling that he understood her meaning. "Are you healing well?"

"Quite so, with the help of a little comfrey and then yarrow for the bruises and cuts. To ease the pain of my arm, the infirmarian adds a few drops of poppy juice to that fine wine sent by a generous wine merchant from Norwich."

Thomas blinked, his cheeks turning a light pink. "Kind, indeed."

"Prioress Ursell has a fine healer amongst her nuns, one who is eager to improve her skills and has asked many questions about our hospital. I promised to pose them to Sister Anne on our return. Perhaps we can copy one of our herbals and send it back, in gratitude for the care here."

Thomas looked away.

Eleanor knew his thoughts. In his opinion, Ryehill had no right to a gift after the evil it had fostered and the arrogance with which it had treated her. But we must agree, she thought, that the infirmarian has shown competence and much kindness to me.

"Gratitude for simple things as well as the great ones is a lesson I may take from this pilgrimage, Brother," she said, in reply to his unspoken concern. "The journey here, despite the interruptions, has been a good one."

"You have found the peace you sought?"

"I had at the Holy House, but before I lost consciousness in the bell tower, I felt something indefinable." She grew pensive. "I saw nothing, nor heard a voice, but I was filled with tranquility. Had I died in that fall, I believe I might have faced God, content that I no longer carried one sin with which I have been burdened. Whatever some may claim about the events of last summer, Our Lady of Walsingham has let me know that I am not to blame for those conclusions."

"We saw great wickedness that summer."

"Perhaps some in the village learned compassion."

"We may pray that is so, but never again do I want to be surrounded by so much hate as I was the day I stood in the midst of the mob screaming for a family's blood."

Lost in their own memories of that time, they fell into a long silence.

Outside, birds sang of hope and joy. In the near future, they would be building nests for their eggs and seeking food for the chicks born. The air gave hints that flowers and leaves would soon burst out to chase the color of death from the earth. Spring, it seemed, had arrived in time for Easter week and the large number of penitents who would travel here, including King Edward.

"I shall not stay for his arrival." Eleanor looked at her monk, knowing he would understand her reference.

"And if you are not sufficiently healed by then?"

"We must arrange something so I can return to our priory. I'll not remain in Walsingham, even if the journey back is slowed by my injuries." She glanced at the nun by the door. "My presence would be a distraction. Courtiers, inclined to generosity, might give to Tyndal because of their respect for my brother. Ryehill, in this instance, needs the gifts to survive, far more than we, especially from the king."

He studied her for a moment, then his expression grew gentle.

How well he knows me, she thought, and understands that I also yearn to go home where I feel safe. The prioress did not need a painful arm to remind her that her pilgrimage had almost proved fatal.

Glancing at Prioress Ursell's attendant by the door, Thomas said: "I have sent the requested message to our king, including your prayers that he will be generous to this place."

"But we have one other important matter to resolve, Brother."

"I had hoped we were in concurrence on that issue, my lady."

She smiled at his eagerness. "Does she wait to be called?"

"She stands outside the door."

"Then bring her in."

Thomas asked that the door be opened, and the nun who had been Sister Roysia's friend entered, holding Gracia by the hand.

The child knelt and folded her hands. She was now dressed in a simple robe and did not reek of the streets.

"I bathed her, my lady, and have untangled her hair." The nun looked down at her thin charge. "Sister Roysia said she was a good child, although grown too feral." Her brow furrowed with worry. "I have made sure she has been fed, as Brother Thomas required, but she does not eat much."

With thanks for her gentle care, Eleanor dismissed the nun and told the child to rise and sit by the chair. "Tell me of your kin, child."

Gracia hesitated, glancing at Thomas.

He nodded.

"They are dead, my lady. I have no family on Earth."

"And who were they while they lived?"

"Honest but poor. I have no siblings left. All died with the last fever."

Eleanor reached out her good hand. "You lived. God has a purpose for you."

With some hesitation, Gracia took it. "If so, He has a strange way of showing it."

To the girl's surprise, Eleanor laughed. "He often does. I wish you had not suffered as you have, but I believe that torment may have ended."

Thomas grinned.

Gracia looked wary as only a child can who has forgotten the experience of kept promises.

"Would you like to return with us to Tyndal? I do not inquire whether you have a calling for the religious life, nor do I require it."

Gracia started but, instead of drawing back, grasped the prioress' hand more firmly.

"You are young and need the care of good women."

"I must serve, my lady. I shall not live on charity."

"I did not ask you to come to our priory to labor in the fields."

"I must do something to earn my bread. I have begged in the streets long enough."

This might be pride, Eleanor thought, but the form was an honorable one, not a sin. "First, you must gain strength, and then I insist you suffer the trials of education."

Gracia nodded with eagerness.

"When you have lived with us awhile, you may decide whether to continue within the walls or find a life without, but you shall not go forth without skills and the good health to survive."

"My lady, I have no love for the world. There is too much violence, and I fear it. May I remain as a servant to your nuns?"

"You are too young to decide, my child."

"But you shall not force me to leave if I do not wish it?"

"I give you my word. When hunger becomes a vague memory and you have gained all that is needed to live in the world, then you, and only you, may decide whether to go or stay."

"And I shall never again have to see that merchant who raped me?" She began to weep. "My lady, he threatened to strangle me if he ever came upon me while I was sleeping. He believed I would spread the story of what he had done and vowed that I would not live to do so. I could run from Father Vincent's rocks, but I could not stay awake forever!"

With profound unhappiness, Eleanor watched the girl tremble and cursed those who would cause any child such terror. She squeezed Gracia's hand and longed for two good arms to hug her. "I swear it. You need not be afraid of him any longer and shall sleep without fear." In silence, she promised God that she would protect this girl if she had to give up her own life to do so.

"May I ask two last questions, my lady? I do not want to try your patience."

"I like questions. If I cannot answer them, I shall say so honestly."

"May I change my name from *Gracia* to *Felicia*?" She looked over her shoulder at the door. "Sister Roysia's friend told me that I was most fortunate when Brother Thomas took responsibility for my care. She said the word in Latin was *Felicia*."

"I agree to that, but only if you choose, in time, to take vows. *Grace* is an attribute of God, and thus *Gracia* is a sacred name."

"May I begin my service to those within the walls of the priory very soon?"

"When you are strong enough, you may." Eleanor's eyes twinkled. "Do you have some work in mind?"

"Whatever is most needed, my lady." She straightened her back. "I can run quickly and remember exactly what I am told…"

"Do you like cats, my child?"

The girl looked perplexed. "They taught me much when I watched them in the streets. God made a clever beast when He formed the cat."

"If you are to serve me, you must be gentle with the great orange creature who shares my quarters. I have named him Arthur, but he is no pampered thing. He keeps the kitchen free of vermin."

Gracia gasped. "You wish me to serve you, my lady?"

"My maid has just married, and I need a young woman who is discreet, clever, and observant. You own those qualities, and the duties are not hard. Would you mind the task?" In fact, Eleanor thought, this child was only slightly younger than Gytha was at the time she became her maid.

When the girl began to weep, these tears were joyful. Prioress Eleanor slipped from the chair, knelt next to her, and, with one arm, held her fast.

Chapter Thirty-five

The crowd of happy pilgrims traveling back to Norwich was a noisy one. Some sang; others prayed aloud. The day promised to be warm, and a sweet-smelling breeze brought gladness to those souls, recently cleansed at the holy shrines.

Master Durant's palfrey shared the general eagerness to return home, but its rider was more reluctant. The merchant slowed the pace until he and his mount dropped to the rear of the traveling band. Finally, he turned his horse around to look back at the town of Walsingham.

With an equine snort and shake of the head, his palfrey protested the delay but complied. After all, this master had always been kind.

The outline of the town was softened with a morning mist. Bells from the priories and churches rang the hour of the Office. The sound was haunting. To Durant, it was also bitter. He bowed his head and prayed, once more admitting to God that he did not yet regret all his sins and most especially those committed after his duty to King Edward was done.

The previous night, his last in Walsingham, he had slipped from the inn in the darkest hours to an alley off a narrow street and sought that place he knew well. There he and another man found each other. Each avoided the gaze of the other as they drew close. To see was to remember. To remember might bring madness—or perhaps the contemplation of questions displeasing to kings and bishops.

Their kisses had been hard and brief, the fondling desperate, but for an instant afterward they held each other as mortals do when both wish their act meant love. Then the man had fled, and Durant walked back to the inn, stifled moans from other dark corners echoing in his ears.

In the hazy light of this morning, he shook away the memory and patted his restless horse on the neck, letting the creature trot back to the pilgrims who had not traveled far down the road.

Promising that this would be his last look back, he gazed over his shoulder at Walsingham. His heart felt as if someone was carving bits of flesh from it with a dull knife, but his pain had nothing to do with what he had done last night. The cause was Brother Thomas.

Pressing a hand against his chest, he groaned and rode on, forcing his thoughts to think about what must be done on his return to Norwich and his wife who was waiting for him.

In truth, he loved her. Early in their marriage, they had agreed to lie together only to beget children, as the most pious often did. When their only babe died, his wife suffered more than he, and he had grieved deeply enough. Her dark moods seemed to descend when she was deemed most fertile, and she confessed she could not bear to couple with him for the pain it caused. Unlike most husbands, he had taken this news with gentle concern and never complained about her failure to pay the marriage debt. Over time they grew closer, except for the sadness of having no laughing children. That was a grief they shared.

Then she heard about the reputation of Tyndal Priory for healing. At her urging, they traveled there where she received herbs and a balm that eased her moods and numbed the pain of intercourse. Now she was eager for him to give her a child.

In part he shared her joy, relieved that she no longer suffered and that she might bear children. She was a good woman, competent in the house and business, faithful and dutiful, but he did not yearn to couple with her like other men did beloved wives. He had been happiest when they shared affection but not passion.

He sighed. In the past, he had found it easy enough to return to those necessary deceptions after his missions for the king had ended and he had his night of relief. This time, he dreaded it, in particular the joyful expression on his wife's face. It would not be easy to lie with her, even to beget the child they both wanted. He would do so, but there was a difference now. Durant of Norwich, wine merchant and spy, had fallen in love with a monk.

He was also terrified. It was one thing to seek the occasional encounter with men he did not know, and even refuse to confess it until he must, but his soul howled at the blasphemy of wanting to lie with a man vowed to God. Yet he also knew that he might be willing to suffer an eternity of hellfire for one night in the arms of that auburn-haired monk. It was that truth which frightened him most.

Tears rolled down his cheeks, and he sobbed quietly, bowing his head to hide his agony. One night? He would prefer it be a lifetime.

A mother in the band of pilgrims heard his sobs and asked what comfort was needed.

He shook his head and tried to smile.

Now assuming his tears were joyous, she bent to her young son and pointed out that man who wept because he found God's forgiveness and was cleansed of his sins.

Durant wiped his cheeks dry. If that explanation made her son hesitate before committing some cruelty, then let the boy believe it.

Whatever his heart wanted, his longing for Brother Thomas was doomed. Even if the monk shared his lust, if not his love, he would never lie with Durant. He had taken vows, oaths he honored, and had made it clear that he found solace in the priory. After all Thomas had suffered for the one time he had lain with a man named Giles, Durant also knew he would never try to seduce him. That would be an even graver sacrilege.

The merchant urged his horse to a faster pace. When he returned home, he would try to bury his sorrow with the reward from the king in that cracked vessel near the privy. Then he would lie with his wife, as they must do to bring forth the child they longed for.

But when I do, he thought, I shall imagine I am in the arms of an auburn-haired man, with no tonsure, who happens to go by the name of Thomas.

Thomas hurried down the street to meet Prioress Eleanor at Ryehill Priory. Although her arm would be long in healing, she had insisted they plan their return to Tyndal Priory as soon as possible. A cart must be found to carry her and the child, she said. Adam, her donkey, would be spared the burden of her weight on the journey back. As they imagined the beast's expression of contentment when told the news, they had both laughed.

When he passed the inn, he hesitated, and then walked on. The merchant would not be there. He had told him that he was joining a large group of pilgrims returning to Norwich very early that morning. The thought that he would never see Durant again grieved him.

He looked back at the inn. Complex and troubling though Durant was, Thomas liked him. Were he to be honest, he felt something more, an emotion he could not quite define. Surely not love, he thought. He had felt that only once, a devotion for which he had suffered in prison and then endured mockery by that very person who had been as eager as he in the coupling.

But the pleasure he had found in Durant's company was more than the simple enjoyment of working with him to save the king's life, although that was part of it.

Did he long for a more secular life? He had not always liked spying for the Church, rooting out those who worked against the best interests of the proclaimed faith, but he did enjoy solving mysteries when he and his prioress were called to do so.

Although he still did not own a deep faith, he no longer regretted taking vows. Tyndal was his home, and he had friends who brought him joy, both inside the priory and without. Before this pilgrimage to Walsingham, he had married Crowner Ralf and Mistress Gytha, two people he loved far above himself, and he looked forward to baptizing their children. Whatever his initial reluctance in joining the Order, he had found some peace. He no longer looked at any woman with lust. In Prioress Eleanor, he had a worthy liege lord, and she was pleased with his service. Sister Anne gave him the love only an elder sister of the flesh could and had taught him much that helped in healing bodies.

No, he said to himself, I would not leave the priory to serve the king as Durant does, even if I were promised a rare forgiveness for abandoning my vows.

Meeting Durant, however, had changed something within him. He had lusted after other men, a few had even evoked tenderness in him, but he would never forget the kiss he had willingly shared with the merchant that night in the inn. The difference, undefined and insistent, between Durant and all those other men gnawed at him.

Suddenly Thomas stopped, frozen in amazement at what had just occurred to him.

With a sharp intake of breath, he realized that he no longer grieved for Giles.

Were he to meet him on this street, this man he had loved since boyhood, he would not weep, nor would he suffer. He might offer him a blessing, praying that he had found contentment and that his remaining years on Earth would be joyful, but he would not long for a kiss or an embrace. If Giles offered either, he would comply without grief or desire. Giles had become a memory, both pleasant and sad, but the festering wound was healed.

Gazing upward, Thomas asked God why this had happened. As usual, He remained silent, and yet the monk sensed, more than heard, a soft whisper in the light breeze caressing his face.

"It matters not if I fully understand," he murmured. Although he had denied that he had found peace when Durant asked, he felt it now. With an inexplicable conviction, he also believed that his meeting with this merchant was the cause of it. Perhaps, he thought, he and I will meet again.

Then he hurried on to Ryehill Priory, as eager as his prioress to return home.

Author's Notes

Walsingham was a famous East Anglian pilgrimage site during the Middle Ages, on a par with Canterbury and even Santiago de Compostela on the continent. There is some debate over when the Holy House was first built under the direction of a local widow, Richelde de Fervaques. Some claim it was 1061, but J. C. Dickinson gives a compelling argument for the earlier part of the twelfth century. In any case, the Church and faithful believed it was the only site in England where the Virgin Mary had visited; thus the wells and the Holy House of the Annunciation on the grounds of Walsingham Priory would have been a suitable pilgrimage destination for Prioress Eleanor had she been real herself.

The tale of the Holy House being moved is part of the legend. When the house could not be successfully finished by the local carpenters, Richelde undertook a nightlong vigil, hoping to receive an inspired solution. Early the next morning, she looked outside to see five angels leaving the finally completed house which had also been moved to a spot deemed more suitable by the Queen of Heaven.

When Richelde's son, Geoffrey, returned from crusade in the mid-1100s, he founded Walsingham Priory to enclose and protect the Holy House. From descriptions left, the two-story structure (approximately 23 feet, 6 inches by 12 feet, 10 inches) looked more like an English dwelling than anything from

Nazareth, but, despite the rich gifts left around it, the house was as simple as Prioress Eleanor described. All was destroyed during the reign of Henry VIII, who had been a devotee in his earlier life, but the shrine has been recreated in modern times and remains a popular pilgrimage site today.

While Canterbury badges were considered superior in quality; Walsingham produced many more badges, according to archaeological evidence. The badges were contracted out to craftsmen, and most were the cheapest blend of tin and lead. Stone molds were used to form them, a craft that required much skill. Sadly, not much is known about the men who made these molds in the late thirteenth century.

Among the other relics in Walsingham was a vial allegedly containing dried breast milk from the Virgin Mary, although she was not supposed to have left any part of her earthly existence behind when she ascended to heaven. One other relic of note was St. Peter's knuckle bone, although Erasmus, in the early sixteenth century, concluded that the saint must have had been a giant if such a huge bone belonged to him. I have been unable to confirm that these specific items were in Walsingham in 1277. There is evidence of *relics*, but the only documentary proof of these two specific ones is from the 1290s. I opted to assume that Geoffrey probably brought these two objects back from crusade.

The famous Slipper Chapel, where pilgrims left their shoes to walk the rest of the Pilgrim's Mile to the Holy House, did not exist until the mid-1300s, but there was a tradition of removing shoes and walking some distance long before the chapel was built. Prioress Eleanor followed the custom.

Ryehill Priory, Prioress Ursell, Father Vincent, and the box containing strands of Mary's hair never existed. But Ryehill with its financial problems was typical of many religious houses in the era. Since priories and abbeys had to be self-supporting, and the smaller ones often lacked rich patrons, the leaders of places like Ryehill usually struggled to feed and clothe their monks or nuns. Some monastics actually starved, their bodies discovered dressed in tatters.

Edward I did go on pilgrimage to the Walsingham shrines at the time mentioned in this story. He visited on Palm Sunday of 1277 while on a journey to acquire 200,000 crossbow bolts from St. Briavel's Castle for his men invading Wales. The story behind his attachment to the Lady of Walsingham, whom he believed had inspired him to move from his chess game before a large piece of masonry fell where he had been sitting, is true. How she got the message to him is unknown, but he became even more devoted to her shrine than his deeply religious father, Henry III.

As for threats to King Edward's life, he may have become one of England's more highly regarded monarchs after his death, but he had plenty of enemies in his lifetime. The idea of a plot to kill him is not unreasonable.

He had angered many during the second Barons' War under Simon de Montfort, selling out friends and bonding with former enemies to survive. Nor was he beloved by those in the Holy Land against whom he fought. Before Edward returned to England after the death of his father, Sultan Baybars (most likely) sent an assassin to kill him in Acre. Although the king never went back to the Holy Land, he frequently said he wanted to do so. Those who hoped he might never travel again to Outremer surely considered ways to keep him from fulfilling that dream. As for the Welsh and the Scots, they did not love this warrior with a penchant for invasions.

Many learned quickly that Edward was far more dangerous than his less bellicose and more easily manipulated father. It should not surprise if they spent much time praying that Edward I would not have a long reign, while seeking some way of making sure he didn't

Throughout history, there have always been spies. Although the system in thirteenth century England may not have been as sophisticated as the one in place during the reign of Elizabeth I, every side had eyes and ears in every other camp. As for women acting as spies, they existed. During the de Montfort rebellion, a woman named Margoth, disguised as a man, alerted Prince

Edward that the troops at Kenilworth under de Montfort's son, Simon, had taken few precautions to protect themselves. Thanks to her good information, Edward attacked the young Simon's army with devastating effects, and the battle at Evesham became a victory for the royalist cause. How she was compensated, why she did this, and what happened to her afterward are unknown. Once she performed her task, like the most successful of spies, she disappeared from view.

It is difficult to prove the sexuality of those historical characters from the Middle Ages whose behavior might lie outside the socially approved. We do not have Facebook for daily confessions. We lack secreted videotapes of what really happened in those medieval haylofts, and we can't interview the people themselves. So we make assumptions, perhaps correct, maybe not, but we do the best we can with the often imprecise but surviving evidence. The same problem exists in creating fictional characters who are intended to represent credible behavior and people in an era.

From tales, poems, riddles, histories, and legal records, we know that the average medieval heterosexual had sex at times and in ways forbidden by the Church, got abortions, acquired divorces and committed bigamy, formed long and often acknowledged relationships unsanctioned by the requisite officials, and even used contraceptive methods known at the time. We also know, from many sources, that society has always justified forbidden practices, ignored them, or simply redefined them into socially acceptable ones when there was a compelling reason to do so. The Victorians may have been masters at ignoring the obvious or skillfully reinventing the meaning, but they did not invent the art. We humans have always been flexible when it suited us.

So what about gay people? Unfortunately, we do not have a lot of indisputable information about the practices of medieval gay men and women, especially those who successfully survived, and even formed longtime relationships, without suffering religious or secular punishments.

Criminal records are always problematic. They say a great deal about one person or an individual event but less about what was going on in the broader world. Church punishments and admonitions are also flawed. The term *sodomy,* for instance, has many definitions, most of which do not refer to homosexual practices at all. As for common social practices, such as sharing a bed or even forming a bond of brotherhood, none are evidence of homosexual behavior, but to say that sexual relations did not take place within them is equally inaccurate.

In order to create a portrait of a medieval gay man or woman, we should start with the nature of certain social expectations and consider implications. The most important one is medieval marriage and the fact that it was rarely a love match. In the middle to high social ranks, it was primarily a contract intended to bond families for political and economic reasons as well as to stabilize society and produce the children expected for all the above reasons. Although love was not the initial impetus, there was a general hope that it would develop or that the partnership would at least become tolerable. Marriage, for the secular society, was also a way to define when a boy became a man.

Durant of Norwich, no matter what he felt about other men, would probably have married unless he chose the religious life. Quite likely he wanted children. In his case, he was fortunate enough to marry a woman with whom he formed a compatible relationship, and they were both eager to have a family. But marriage left him unsettled and vulnerable to seeking elsewhere for the deep bonding he lacked with his wife, a situation also common with heterosexuals in less than satisfactory marriages. Like many medieval men in his situation, he had recourse to male prostitutes as well as other men who also found solace in secret.

For those who argue that Durant could not be gay because he slept with his wife, cared about her, and was eager to have a family, I point to the extensive documentary evidence from other eras during which homosexuals hid to avoid persecution and were as ignorant as their heterosexual counterparts about their equal part in the human condition. The story of Oscar

Wilde may be the most famous, but one of the richest sources comes from the post-World War II era.

According to much individual testimony of that time, gay men and women often did marry but never lost the sense that *something was wrong,* a very common phrase. Of these, some divorced and later formed a permanent bond with a partner of the same gender. Others continued the approved form of marriage for too many reasons to list and either had secret lovers or cruised the night streets much as Durant did over seven hundred years ago. Despite our greater knowledge of sexuality and improved, but hardly complete, tolerance, some continue to fall into this pattern today, a potential cause of profound anguish for both spouses.

Bibliography

Historical fiction, like most human endeavors, may contain factual errors, but the writers of the best works are passionate about accuracy. Their books serve an important function within the broader study of history by bringing our ancestors alive to a wide audience of fiction readers and making historical events feel immediate. If we see ourselves in those characters and understand how their times resonate with ours, we might be more inclined to avoid some of the errors they wish they had.

To the scholars who inspire me, I am grateful and, in thanks, always mention a few books that might intrigue other readers as well. This time, I offer the following with the understanding that far more are available to tempt the reader:

The Shrine of Our Lady of Walsingham, by J. C. Dickinson, Cambridge University Press, 1956.

Miracles and Pilgrims: Popular Beliefs in Medieval England, by Ronald C. Finucane, St. Martin's Press, 1995.

Sexuality in Medieval Europe: Doing Unto Others, by Ruth Mazo Karras, Routledge, 2005.

A Great and Terrible King: Edward I and the Forging of Britain, by Marc Morris, Windmill, 2008.

Pilgrim Souvenirs and Secular Badges, by Brian Spencer, Boydell, 2010.

Pilgrimages: the Great Adventure of the Middle Ages, by John Ure, Carroll & Graf, 2006.

Pilgrimage in Medieval England, by Diana Webb, Hambledon and London, 2000.

To receive a free catalog of Poisoned Pen Press titles, please contact us in one of the following ways:

Phone: 1-800-421-3976
Facsimile: 1-480-949-1707
Email: info@poisonedpenpress.com
Website: www.poisonedpenpress.com

Poisoned Pen Press
6962 E. First Ave. Ste 103
Scottsdale, AZ 85251